BELLA ANDRE

It Must Be Your Love

MIRA®

MIRA®

Recycling programs for this product may not exist in your area.

ISBN-13: 978-0-7783-1731-9

It Must Be Your Love

MIRA Books/February 2015

First published by Bella Andre

For questions and comments about the quality of this book, please contact us at CustomerService@Harlequin.com.

www.MIRABooks.com

Printed in U.S.A.

Dear Reader,

After writing more than twenty books, I've learned that every story has its own rhythm. Some are fast and hot, some are slower and sweeter…and others, like this book, are all of the above!

I have always loved writing about the Sullivan women (Sophie "Nice" Sullivan in *I Only Have Eyes For You* and Lori "Naughty" Sullivan in *Always On My Mind*) because they have such a passion for life. That's why it was a total thrill to finally give Mia Sullivan her happy-ever-after with Ford, her sizzling-hot rock star hero.

I also had a total blast checking in with the first eight San Francisco Sullivans at Marcus and Nicola's wedding (yay, it's about time!)…and I *can't wait* for you to find out the identity of the woman who is going to completely steal Ian Sullivan's heart in *Just to Be With You*. Trust me when I say that you are going to love her.

I should also note that if this is your first time reading about the Sullivans, you can easily read each book as a stand-alone—and there is a Sullivan family tree available on my website (bellaandre.com) so that you can easily see how the books connect together.

Thank you, again, for being the most amazing readers in the world! Your emails, Tweets, and Facebook and Goodreads messages always make my day.

Happy reading,

Bella Andre

It Must Be Your Love

One

The music was still ringing in his ears as Ford Vincent headed through the winding halls at the back of the stadium he'd just played in Tempe, Arizona. Nearly seventy-five thousand people had been in the audience tonight and he'd given everything he had to them. And now, like every night on the road, dozens of women were waiting for him just outside the back door yelling, *"I love you, Ford!"* and *"I'll do anything to be with you tonight!"*

Despite his security staff doing their best to keep things from getting out of control, at least five women pressed up against any part of his body they could reach as soon as he stepped out of the building. It would be easiest to keep his head down and push through the crowd, but disrespecting his fans had never sat well with Ford. Even if they often crossed over his personal boundaries.

This was what he'd always wanted, he reminded

himself as he started signing autographs. For people to love him. For people to appreciate him. And he'd succeeded beyond his wildest dreams.

So then why did it all feel so hollow?

Ford was nearly through the crowd when a fresh wave of women saw him from around the corner of the parking lot. He signaled to his security staff to clear the way for him and at long last got onto his tour bus.

Natasha Lawrence was sitting in the dining booth with her computer open. Looking up, she said, "Pretty rowdy bunch out there tonight, aren't they? Go take your shower and then I've got a couple of things I'd like to show you."

She was one of the most respected documentary filmmakers in the business, and after the past couple of months working with her, Ford not only appreciated her skill and talent, but also her utter faithfulness to her husband and family. After what he'd seen and experienced during more than a decade of touring, he'd come to believe that kind of devotion was very, very rare. The only man he'd ever seen her light up for was her husband. After years of being a sex symbol, he relished being around a woman who wasn't even the slightest bit inclined to whip off her bra and throw it at him.

A minute later, he let out a breath of relief as he stood under the hot spray. His postshow shower was his only real must-have when he came offstage. Other rockers needed women, drugs, booze and their entourage. He could have had any one of those women tonight by doing nothing more than snapping his fingers in her direction. But the morning-after aches and pains, the fogged-up mind and the ass-kissing "friends" had stopped being fun long before he hit thirty. Not to mention that waking up next to a stranger got old *really* quick.

Especially when he always, inevitably, compared those women to the only one he'd ever truly enjoyed waking up with…

He rinsed the shampoo and soap from his hair and body, then let the warm water run over him for a few more seconds before turning off the shower. After shaking the water out of his hair, he opened the door and reached for a towel hanging from a metal rack in the small tiled space. After quickly drying off, he yanked on a pair of jeans and a T-shirt.

"We got some great footage tonight," Natasha told him as he slid into the booth and she clicked Play on one of the windows on her computer screen. "Really colorful crowd, and—" she added with a grin "—the music didn't suck, either."

"Arizona is always good," he agreed.

But despite the enthusiasm of the crowd and his great band backing him up, Ford knew it hadn't been his best show. The magic used to be there all the time the moment he stepped onto a stage, but now he had to work harder and harder every night to light those sparks. Some nights, like tonight, he left the stage feeling as if he hadn't quite earned the encores.

Natasha slid a couple bottles of water over to him just as the bus started moving, and he downed one in a long swig to replace the sweat he'd lost tearing across the stage with his guitar and microphone during the three-hour show. She would be filming his next stadium show in Albuquerque, New Mexico, the following night, and given that it usually took Ford a couple of hours to come down from a performance, it made sense for them to get in some work on the film, even if it meant midnight meetings like this one.

"As you know, I've been collecting video clips from the earlier stages of your career—mostly taken by news cameras and people's personal devices." She shut down the video window with tonight's show playing and opened a new one that had obviously been filmed with a far less high-end camera. "While the quality of some of these clips isn't spectacular, a few of them are powerful enough that I can easily make quick cuts in and out of them without the overall quality of the film being affected."

Initially, Ford hadn't been interested in participating in a film about himself. Not just because he still sometimes felt like a kid playing in the sandbox of the rock-and-roll playground with Jagger and Bowie having earned their places on the swings, but also because he had no interest whatsoever in strangers digging into his past. It had only been when Natasha had made it clear that she was only interested in his music, and the powerful way it affected people around the world, that he consented to allow her to begin filming his current tour. Of course, he also had final approval over anything that went into the film. So far, he'd been nothing but impressed with what Natasha had shown him—not only clips from his shows and interviews with his band members and recording engineers, but also interesting discussions with music therapists who used his music to help heal their patients.

"This recording is from five years ago. You were playing a small club in Seattle as a preview for your first major label release, so there were plenty of cameras filming the gig. I found some better-quality clips, but I thought this was one of the most interesting, and I'd like to know what you think of it."

Five years ago?

Seattle?

Ford's grip tightened on the new water bottle he'd been about to open as she clicked Play.

Holy hell, there she was.

The cameraman had zoomed in on Ford walking out onstage to play his first song before panning back from the stage to an audience that was going crazy. His fans danced, sang along and hollered out praise, but one woman stood out from among them all.

In her little silver dress, with blond hair falling over her shoulders and an expression of pure sensual pleasure on her face, she let his music wash over her. The cameraman clearly couldn't pull his lens away from her.

Ford hadn't been able to drag his gaze away from

her, either. When the camera zoomed out to frame both Ford and the crowd, the moment when he and Mia Sullivan looked into each other's eyes for the first time was caught on film.

And it was utterly electric.

Everything came back to him in such a rush—the amazement that a woman could be *that* beautiful, the shock that someone could allow a stranger to see so much honest emotion in her eyes. Every inch of her silky hair, soft skin and luscious curves was pure sensuality—and Ford nearly reached for the computer screen. The belated realization that Natasha was watching him carefully held him back.

"You were amazing that night, Ford."

Natasha was right. That night in Seattle had been one of the best shows he'd ever played. Because for the first time ever, he'd played for more than just himself and a crowd of strangers.

He'd played for *Mia*.

Natasha paused playback, and before he could get his brain to work to tell her to stop, she opened another small window to the right of her screen. "I also wanted you to check out this backstage clip."

Every muscle in Ford's body was tense now as she clicked Play again and he guessed correctly at what he was about to see: Mia being brought backstage. From that first glimpse of her in the audience, Ford had been desperate to meet her, to touch her… to claim her as *his*.

If the sparks between them had been hot when

he'd been onstage and she'd been in the audience, flames nearly shot from the screen as they approached each other in the windowless backstage room where he had been about to do his postshow meet and greet with the press.

As Ford took Mia's hand in his, Natasha pushed Pause. "Do you remember her?"

Though they'd had only one week together, Ford hadn't been able to stop himself from periodically checking online to see if Mia was in a serious relationship. Again and again, over the years, he continued to torture himself like this, even though every time he saw a picture of her with some other guy, his heart would stop, just as it had tonight. To try to recover, he'd drink more, party harder, spend even more hours in the studio and on the road to try to forget her.

But he never could.

Because Mia Sullivan was unforgettable.

"Since this documentary is about my music and not my private life, I don't see why it matters."

Unlike most people, who only wanted to know how high to go when he said *Jump*, Natasha didn't back off at his clear message to do just that. And even though he hadn't yet confirmed that he remembered Mia, Natasha asked, "Have you kept in touch with her?"

"No." The one short word from his lips was little more than an irritated growl.

Unable to remain sitting in the booth anymore, he

got to his feet. Ford had never played the rock star card with Natasha before, but seeing Mia onscreen so unexpectedly made every inch of him, inside and out, feel raw.

"Why the hell do you want to know this?"

"I've spent the past couple of months practically living in your back pocket, Ford. You're great with your crew and fans, and I meant it when I said my intention with this film is to capture your music. Where it comes from. How it affects people. But there's no way I could do any of that—or do it well—without learning, and showing, what's made you who you are and why you write these songs. And I'm afraid that somewhere along the way, I've started to like you," she said with a small smile. "Quite a bit more than I thought I'd ever like a rock star who has the entire world at his feet."

Natasha looked back at the footage that had captured two of the most important moments of his life. "I've never seen this woman before. I've never heard you talk about her. But as soon as I saw these clips, my gut told me that she was vitally important. I've learned the hard way over the years to always listen to my gut—even," she added with a slightly apologetic look, "when I know it's going to piss off the subject of my film-in-progress."

She slid off her reading glasses and looked at him in the way he'd always thought a sister or a mother who cared about him might have if he'd been lucky enough to have either of those people in his life. "I promise you, when I'm asking you about this woman, this isn't about my film anymore. This is me talking to you as your friend."

The shade was up on the long window behind the built-in table, and as they traveled at a steady sixty-five miles an hour on the freeway at midnight, all Ford could see was a blur of taillights, lit-up billboards and gas station signs. He'd spent his entire adult life with the blacktop burning up beneath the tires of his van, then bigger and bigger buses as his fame and income grew. He often rented hotel suites in Los Angeles and New York City for occasional days off the road here or there, but he never thought of them as home. He'd always told himself he didn't want or need that, the road was his home and that was just the way he'd always wanted it.

But he wasn't stupid enough or young enough anymore to pretend that the day when he'd be too old to run around on a stage every night wasn't coming. Especially considering how much a three-hour show took out of him now. What would it be like in five years at this relentless pace? In ten? Where would he go then? And with whom would he go?

He couldn't see himself back in Boston, where he'd grown up—or in New York City, Los Angeles or London, cities where he conducted the bulk of his non-touring business. No matter how hard he tried to stop it, his brain always circled back to Seattle, where he'd spent one incredible week with the most beautiful girl in the world.

"How long has it been since you've seen her?"

Over the years, Ford had worked with many musicians who were recovering alcoholics. He understood that even if an addict was sober for years, one sip was all it would take for their addiction to come raging back even stronger than it had been before, as if the years of abstinence had never happened. Now he knew exactly what that felt like, because he couldn't stop staring at the computer screen, where Mia's beauty and vitality drew him even more now than it had then.

"Five years."

"Have you ever tried to get back in touch with her?"

Again, his answer was a curt, "No."

He'd done everything *but* that. He'd worked like hell to try to forget, to try to bury what he'd felt for her. He'd moved from one woman to another, one city to another, one stage to another. But, God, just thinking about having Mia back in his arms sent long-simmering yearnings and cravings rushing through him.

"Why haven't you?"

How could he explain how good it had been with Mia…and then how badly it had ended? Especially since, even if he could put words to it, he knew he shouldn't tell Natasha anything more. Not when he'd already told—and shown—her too much. Because if she decided to break her promise to him and go public with any of this, his grave was already dug. Deep.

Interestingly, just as writing a song felt like discovering the mystery of what he truly believed, one lyric at a time, he was surprised to find that so did this very unexpected conversation.

Finally, he admitted, "We were young."

But that wasn't the whole truth. Not even close. He'd made every mistake in the book with Mia. Pride. Ego. Blame. They'd all been huge forces in his decision to leave her, and then his staying away.

"*I* was young. Stupid. Just like you said, I thought the whole world should be waiting at my feet. Including her."

"We were all young and stupid once," Natasha pointed out, "but if you ask me, the fact that you're still in love with her trumps all of that."

She waited then, as if to give him a chance to try to deny that he was still in love with Mia. But he couldn't.

Not when he now realized that every word of the denial would be a bald-faced lie.

"The way you looked at her from that stage in Seattle five years ago…I wish I had been filming you just now so you could see that you looked at her image on my computer screen in exactly the same way. And, Ford, what if she's still just as much in love with you, too?" Her voice gentled as she added, "I know people think you have everything. Fame. Success. Packed stadiums and hit songs. And I've personally seen that you really enjoy what you do." She looked around at the luxurious interior of the tour bus. "But I have to wonder—if the two of you *could* make things work this time around, what would you be willing to give up to have her back?"

The word *everything* busted into his brain at the exact moment the old backstage video clicked back on. Watching it, he remembered that Mia had just told him her name when several scantily clad groupies had pushed between the two of them. Even as he'd given the women their autographs, he'd been counting down the seconds until he could be with Mia again.

Now, as he stood in his tricked-out tour bus, Ford realized he'd never stopped counting those seconds for the entire five years since he'd last seen her.

Once upon a time, he'd believed that his music, his guitar and his songs were everything he needed. But tonight, as his tour bus roared down yet another highway to yet another stadium, Ford finally realized that his songs and audiences could never even come close to filling the hole inside of him.

Only one thing—only one person—had ever been able to do that.

Only Mia.

Two

Mia Sullivan knew nothing about the man she was about to meet…except that he must be rich.

Really stinking rich.

Mia had been contacted the previous day by a lawyer representing a client who was in the market for a home in Seattle. The budget? Ten million dollars, give or take a few million, if necessary.

The location? On the water, of course.

The time frame? Immediately.

The client? Anonymous until today's showing.

As the owner of Sullivan Realty with a half-dozen agents working under her, Mia already had a full slate of showings and meetings set up for Friday morning. Plus, she'd found the anonymous-buyer aspect more than a little suspect. What possible reason could a potential client have for keeping his or her identity a secret from her? Especially when she'd previously sold property to some of the wealthiest men in the world, not to mention being cousin to movie star Smith Sullivan and pro-baseball player Ryan Sullivan. Quickly running through various possibilities in her head, Mia figured it was possible that the buyer might be a wealthy and dangerous convict who had done his time and now wanted to restart his life with a big estate on the water in the Pacific Northwest.

Of course, she'd love the commission on a ten-million-dollar sale, but at this point she didn't absolutely need it. Besides, Mia Sullivan had four older brothers and loving parents who had taught her well about looking out for herself, and she was nobody's fool.

Well, that is, apart from that one week five years ago when she'd been a complete and utter fool, all for love...

Shoving that ugly thought back into the dark depths where it belonged, she'd point-blank asked, "Has your client done time for a horrible crime?"

It had sounded as though the lawyer was barely restraining his laughter as he'd said, "No. I can promise you that he is most definitely not a felon."

Then she'd known it was a man, at least. "I'm afraid it's going to be extremely difficult to help choose the perfect house for a client who insists on remaining anonymous." At the lawyer's continued silence, she'd added, "I'd have to know his age and the size of his family or staff, at the very least."

"I truly do apologize for not being able to divulge

any further details about my client, but I can promise that he is of sound mind and does not intend to do you any harm."

"If that's intended to be reassuring—"

"I have also couriered over a check for twenty thousand dollars as a down payment on your fee. Whether you are able to find a home that my client wishes to purchase or not, the money is yours."

As if it had been choreographed, Mia's assistant, Orlando, brought in an envelope just as the lawyer finished speaking.

Mia had slid out the cashier's check for twenty grand, and this time when her mouth opened, no further protests had come out. So despite the red flags waving inside her head, warning that something was definitely off with this whole situation, the fact was that no Realtor on the planet would ignore this client. Anonymous or not, he was clearly serious about buying a waterfront home in Seattle, so she'd decided to shift her original Friday clients to Orlando and book new showings at three of the best waterfront listings in Seattle.

In any case, Mia thought as she headed up the front walk of the first house, it was far more likely that the client was going to end up being a twenty-two-year-old nerd who had struck it rich with a high-tech start-up and didn't have any social skills to speak of, rather than a crazy, dangerous convict sprung from prison on a technicality.

As she unlocked the front door to the amazing

waterfront estate, she gave silent thanks that it was a perfect day. The clouds were white and fluffy in a brilliantly blue sky, and the water of Lake Washington was so calm it looked like glass. Mia really enjoyed living in her high-rise condo looking out over downtown Seattle, but she could certainly see the allure of a place like this. No doubt about it, she thought with a grin as she walked into the spectacular house, if she had ten million dollars lying around collecting dust, she would definitely buy a place like this for herself.

Quickly and efficiently, she made her way through each room on the ground floor, turning on lights, adjusting vases of flowers and shifting furniture slightly to make the house look truly perfect.

Not, however, that this home needed much help in that department. Because while she believed all three houses on today's agenda would suit even the pickiest buyer, she was particularly partial to this one because of one very unique feature.

The tower.

What girl didn't love the thought of a gorgeous, strapping prince climbing up stone and vines to give his true love a kiss in the tower? And what boy wouldn't have loved to stealthily track invaders from high above as a warrior would have so many centuries ago? Plus, on a more practical note, the tower had great light, beautiful stone walls and an incredible view.

The house was currently owned by a really nice

couple who were, unfortunately, splitting up. Mia had attended a few of their parties over the years and had always been amazed by how similar they were—everything from their blond good looks to their classic fashion sense. She'd been extremely surprised when they had called to let her know they were getting a divorce and wanted her to list their home. As far as she had seen, they had never argued or been angry at each other. They never hid behind brittle smiles and fake endearments, as so many couples often did. Then again, the more she'd thought about it, she couldn't ever remember them touching, either. Their divorce, it seemed, was now proceeding with as little passion as their marriage.

Mia stopped halfway up the spiral staircase that led to the tower room and gazed out a small window that overlooked the extensive grounds.

How, she wondered, *do people ever figure out the balance between love and lust? Friendship and passion?*

Gazing out at the blue lake and the yacht moored just outside the window, she barely saw them as she mulled over the questions that had been popping into her head again and again now that so many of her family members had found *the one*. First, her eight cousins in San Francisco had all fallen in love. Four were already married and another four were engaged, with Marcus and Nicola's wedding coming up on Sunday at his winery in Napa Valley. And then, this past summer, her brother Rafe had fallen head over heels in love with their old friend Brooke.

Of course, Mia was thrilled for her brother and cousins. But after seeing each of the happy couples together, she'd seriously begun to doubt that she'd find what they all had with each other. Especially when, given her past big relationship mistake, she clearly had no idea what real love was.

The sounds of a seagull squawking just a few yards outside the window yanked her from her musings. Her anonymous buyer would be arriving in fifteen minutes, and she wanted to be completely ready for him. Taking the final stairs two at a time, she reached the thick wooden door to the tower room thirty seconds later.

She was slightly surprised to find the door open. But when she stepped inside she was *far* more surprised to realize that the room wasn't empty...and that the anonymous buyer was the very last man on earth she ever wanted to see again.

Just that quickly, five years fell away, and she was reliving the moment when she'd seen him for the very first time.

Five years ago, in downtown Seattle...

Mia Sullivan was having the best day of her life. She'd sold her first seven-figure property and had had a great Friday night dinner with her family at her parents' house, where her mother, father and four brothers had surprised her with a huge arrange-ment of flowers and champagne to toast her achieve-ment. After heading home to change into something less professional and more slinky, she was out con-tinuing the celebration at a well-known Seattle club with some of her colleagues who had also closed good deals that week.

She'd been too amped up at dinner with her fam-ily to take more than a few sips of the champagne they'd popped on her behalf and now her mojito had never tasted better. Bursting with energy, Mia was ready and raring for the band to start playing so that she could hit the dance floor. She felt especially sexy tonight in her shimmering silver dress with thin spaghetti straps and a deep plunge in the back. Mia wasn't particularly tall, but with the hem of her dress barely skimming her thighs and her five-inch silver heels, she felt as though she could go toe-to-toe with any of the supermodels-in-training in the audience.

The cute guy she was flirting with had just gone to get her another drink when the house music and the lights went down, and dozens of girls in the crowd started squealing. Mia didn't follow the music scene very closely but, evidently, this show tonight was the hottest ticket in town. Mia was more into navy SEAL types with their muscles and strength, rather than rockers with their tattoos and leather. Still, the way the other women in the room were acting had her more than a little curious about the singer.

How great could Ford Vincent possibly be?

Just then, a deep male voice cut through the noise of the crowd and the squeals grew louder—then, miraculously, fell away entirely as his voice resonated down into all of their souls.

Mia forgot all about the guy she'd been flirting with as she moved through the crowd to get closer to the stage. She had nearly made it to the front when the spotlight lit up the stage.

Oh, my God, the singer was gorgeous. *But not in the typical rock star way. Yes, he had on leather pants and his dark hair was long enough to brush the tops of his shoulders, but he was beautifully built, with a broad chest, muscular arms and thighs, and a surprising ruggedness, as if he regularly spent time lifting something heavier than an electric guitar.*

But a few seconds later, Mia realized it didn't matter what he looked like...because she was utterly lost in the music, her eyes closing as she let it move her body.

When an elbow poked her in the side, Mia opened her eyes to see who was knocking into her. The girl next to her said, "He's singing straight to you!"

A moment later, Mia turned toward the stage and found herself looking right into the singer's heated gaze. She'd never been afraid of her own innate sensuality, but...oh...the way just one look from this man instantly melted her insides sent a rare, and very surprising, red flag of caution up inside her chest.

She'd always been the one in control of her relationships, was used to being the one who was wanted

*and needed more than she'd ever wanted or needed
anyone. Relationships, and sex, had all been just
for fun. In twenty-three years, her heart had never,
ever been at risk—and she'd been okay with that.
She figured she had plenty of time to find the one.*

*Snared in the heat and intensity of Ford's gaze,
Mia couldn't do anything but stand in the audience
of crazed fans and stare back at him. It wasn't until
the crowd lost its mind at the end of the song and
the bassist said something to Ford that pulled his
attention away, that she was dragged out of what
had been as close to a hypnotic state as she'd ever
been in.*

*Her body felt strange, her mouth dry, her hands
and feet tingling...and her heart was pounding way
too hard. Trying to regain her bearings, she turned
away from the stage and scanned the crowd for her
friends. She needed another drink to wet her throat
and then, even though it wasn't all that late, maybe
she'd head back home.*

*But instead of finding any of her colleagues in the
crowd that seemed to have quadrupled during the
amazing first song, all she could see were dozens
of gorgeous girls who would clearly do anything to
score a night in the singer's bed.*

"You're one hell of an audience, aren't you?"

*Ford's question, spoken in that low voice that ran
shivers of need through Mia's entire body, had the
crowd shouting and screaming back that they loved*

*him, that he was their hero, that he could have them
any way he wanted them.*

"I was already going to make it good for you," he
said in a voice laced with sexual undertones, "but
now you've got me wanting to make it really good."

She swore she could feel his gaze burning a hole
through her as he spoke, and something told her his
words weren't just meant for the audience...but as
a challenge for her because he'd seen that she was
about to leave.

Mia had never been afraid of anything in her life.
Plus, she couldn't stop asking herself if one look—
if just the sound of his voice—could affect her so
deeply, what would one touch do? One kiss?

She shivered at the delicious thought of those
hands that worked over his electric guitar with such
reverence doing the same over her naked skin. She
was here to celebrate, after all, and what could one
hot night with a rocker hurt?

When she finally turned to face the stage, Ford
raised his eyebrow as if in question. She let her lips
lift into an answering smile. A smile that said, "If
you want a night with me, rock star, you're going to
have to earn it."

And that night, when he finally got her into his
bed, did he ever...

Three

Beautiful.

As he looked at her standing there surprised—and then, a moment later, utterly furious—Mia Sullivan was still the most beautiful woman Ford had ever seen.

She'd also been approximately ten feet away the first time he'd ever set eyes on her in the middle of the crowded dance floor, wearing a little silver dress, the tips of her blond hair just sweeping over the swell of her breasts. That night in Seattle, the way she'd looked as she closed her eyes to move to the song he'd written—so sensual that he'd almost forgotten the lyrics—had made it impossible to look away. And when she'd opened her eyes and looked at him, he'd felt the impact of it like a bass drum reverberating all the way into his soul.

That night, he'd desperately wanted to know how soft her skin would feel beneath his calloused fingertips, how sweet her mouth would taste against his and how good it would be to hold her. Five years later, he could still remember how he could never get enough of touching her, caressing every one of her sweet curves and sinful hollows over and over until both of them were driven mad with desire.

That night in the club, her tiny little dress had shown off her incredible legs, but somehow, in the pale yellow wrap dress she had on now, her legs looked even sexier. Her hair was a little longer now, but her eyes were just as bright a blue and her full red mouth was slightly damp, as if she'd licked her lips just before walking through the doorway.

But it wasn't just her beauty that stunned him… it was the music that came into the room with her. She'd inspired his greatest songs five years ago— for one week straight he'd either been making love to her or notating the endless riffs and lyrics that were streaming into his head. The longer they'd been apart, the less freely the music had come.

"What the hell are you doing here?"

Damn, he thought as her eyes sparked with heat and fury, she was spectacular. "You're even prettier than I remember."

He thought he glimpsed pleasure flash in her eyes at his honest compliment before her rage returned.

"And you're an even bigger jackass than I remember." Her voice was steady, but not at all cool, as she continued, "Now that you've had your fun, I want you to get the hell out of this house so I can lock it up and get on with my day."

Ford wanted to drag her into his arms. He'd never forgotten, not for one single second of the past five years, how perfectly they'd fit together. But, for now, he had no doubt whatsoever that touching Mia— or worse, grabbing her—was completely forbidden.

Seeing just how angry she was, Ford knew he needed to tread carefully. It wouldn't be enough just to say he was sorry for having been an immature jerk five years ago and for not realizing it sooner— no matter how true that was. Mia clearly wouldn't believe a word of it. Not yet, anyway.

So instead of making the mistake of trying, and failing, to woo her back into his arms with soft words, Ford planned to take a very different approach. Namely, by playing off the intense sparks of attraction that were just as strong between them now as they'd been years before.

"I thought," he said while leaning against the stone wall as if he were perfectly at ease, "that showing me this house *is* your day."

"For your information," she said as she advanced toward him, her gorgeous chest rising and falling beneath the soft fabric of her pretty dress, her eyes flashing, her skin flushed with emotion, "if I'd had even the slightest inkling that you were going to be my anonymous client, I would have said no so fast your lawyer's head would still be spinning."

"Really?" Ford made sure the one word out of his

mouth was right in the gray area between a question and a taunt, even though he'd set himself up as her anonymous client to make absolutely certain they *would* come face-to-face again. "You wouldn't have wanted the chance to see me again after all these years?"

At that, one of her eyebrows rose. "I get that you're a raging egomaniac, but even you can't possibly be serious." She laughed then, but it was a bitter sound. "Why on earth would you think I would *ever* want to see you again?"

Because you never stopped loving me, the way I now know I never stopped loving you, was the answer he hoped like hell was still in her heart, even if it was buried way down deep. But since he knew he had years of anger to make up for first, he said, "From this distance, you could do a lot of damage to me with the heel of your shoe." As her expression told him she was actually considering it, he added, "And just think of the other ways you could mess me up if you got even closer."

"Tempting," she muttered as she looked down at her spiked heels. "So incredibly tempting. But I couldn't stand to have all your weeping fans on my conscience if I ruined your pretty face."

As if she realized she was rising to the bait by reacting to him, she suddenly took a deep, steadying breath that had her flushed skin cooling and her fists unclenching. Another man might have thought this was a step in the right direction, but Ford knew otherwise. Mia Sullivan was meant to be fire and sparks.

Cool meant that he was losing her.

He'd lost her once. No matter what he had to do, he wouldn't lose her again.

Now she was the one leaning lightly against the door frame, crossing her gorgeous legs at the ankles, her mouth curving up slightly at the corners in a mocking smile. "Are you really in the market for a home in Seattle? Or were you just feeling a little bored on the road and ready to have a laugh today at my expense?"

Yes, he couldn't deny that having his lawyer call her about seeing houses in Seattle had been pure, unavoidable impulse. But before Mia had arrived this morning, he'd spent some time wandering around the property before heading up to the tower, where he had been pleased to find an unlocked door. He should have been more surprised that the thought of living in Seattle full-time was a good one. Especially since, in all his adult life, he'd never spent long enough anywhere to have grass of his own to cut or a kitchen to keep clean. Instead of those things he had a tour bus that he swapped out every year for the newest, flashiest model. But there was something strangely enticing about those grounding household chores.

The idea of giving up *everything* for Mia had come at him from out of the blue. But being near her again confirmed that his feelings had always been there, humming away inside him for five long years in the same way that some melodies toyed with him for weeks, months, even years, before the day they finally became a real song.

"I do want a house in Seattle," he confirmed, just barely keeping the words *because of you* from falling out of his mouth. It was too much, too soon, but he had to tell her, "And I needed to see you again."

"Congratulations," she said in that same icy tone. "You got what you wanted. You saw me. For the very last time."

Though she was still only a few feet away, as she turned from him Ford felt as if she was almost as good as gone. Which meant he had nothing to lose by saying, "I never thought I'd see you like this." When she didn't turn back, he upped the ante with, "So frightened of seeing me again that you're walking away in less than five minutes."

The ice that she'd encased herself in cracked more and more as each word came out of his mouth until he watched it shatter and fall completely away from the force of her renewed fury. She spun to face him.

"I'm not frightened of anything." She tossed her head, her long, dirty-blond hair flowing down over her shoulders and breasts. "Certainly not of *you*."

This time he was the one raising an eyebrow. Still forcefully shoving down the urge to move across the circular room to drag her against him, he shrugged. "Could have fooled me."

Even as her fists clenched tighter, she moved closer to him. Her scent—a sweet hint of flowers wrapped in sinfully hot spice—wound through him. Lord, he loved her passion. The problem was that he'd been too young, too idiotic, to know how to appreciate it…or to know the true worth of one woman's love versus ruling the world from a concert stage.

"Fear isn't why I don't want to take you on as a client. It's because you're fickle and self-centered, and I don't have time for people like you who say you want a home in Seattle, but are really just wasting my time because you're bored with all your money and playthings and staff scraping and bowing at your every command."

"Seattle has always been my favorite city," he told her in an easy voice. He shrugged again. "But I understand if you don't think you can take me on as a client because you're not over me."

"Not over you?" Her glare was sharp enough that he could almost feel it slicing through his clothes to pierce his skin. "If you're done with this really fun trip down memory lane, we've got three houses to see today." She gestured toward the room with a flick of her hand. "This is the tower. It's unique and one of my favorite things about this house. The stones were imported from a thirteenth-century castle in the north of England."

Each word was clipped and scrupulously professional, but he still had to work like hell not to smile—at least not until she'd turned her back on him to head for the stairs.

Ford Vincent had been onstage in front of millions of people, had crushed music industry sales records with his last release and had some of the most famous people in the world on speed dial…but he hadn't felt this alive in years.

Four

In that first moment that Mia set eyes on Ford, looking gorgeous and strong as he stood in the tower, her heart had leaped as if he were the fairy-tale prince finally coming to wake her from her emotional slumber with his kiss of true love.

By moment two, thank God, she'd remembered the truth of who he really was.

Even so, she couldn't deny that seeing him again had been a punch in the gut. It had been a punch in her heart...and her libido, too.

The week she'd met Ford five years ago had begun as the best of her life, and had ended as the worst... all because her every fantasy of love had been kindled, then left to burn out and smoke, her eyes watering long after he'd gone.

Ford walked just a little too close behind her as they made their way down the staircase. Close enough that she could smell his clean, masculine scent, the same one that had driven her wild on those nights when they'd lain skin to skin, their hearts racing from their fierce, wild lovemaking. She had never been able to get close enough to him at the time. She'd thought it was just a physical manifestation of how badly she wanted him.

Only after he'd gone had she understood that there had been an actual distance between them, because for every part of her heart that she'd given him, he'd returned little of his own.

Unfortunately, Mia could feel his warmth again now in the small stairwell, and her skin automatically heated up as if he'd touched her. A bolt of pure, instinctive need shot through her at the thought of his hands on her skin again. He was in dark pants and a T-shirt that was worn enough for her to see that he was even more muscular than he'd been five years ago, as if he'd grown into his body. With a half-dozen tattoos snaking up his arms and even along the base of his neck and broad shoulders, it made her mouth water just to look at his incredible masculine beauty.

No matter how much she hated him, the truth was that no one had ever made her feel so good, so alive…or, she harshly reminded herself, so devastated.

Until Ford, Mia had always been the heartbreaker. Not because she relished hurting men, but simply because she had never returned any of her boyfriends' feelings with the same intensity. But after Ford had broken her heart, as much as she hated the thought of being the forlorn woman, that was nearly what she'd become after he'd left. She'd almost given up everything for him, had almost lost her own identity in the name of *love*.

Frankly, she still wasn't sure whom she'd hated more: him for being a bastard, or herself for being so weak. And so stupid.

Although, she reminded herself as they headed back through to the main part of the house, she really shouldn't be too hard on herself for the past. After all, she'd been only twenty-three the first time she saw Ford onstage in that club downtown, young and full of dreams. The fact was, *any* woman would have been hard-pressed not to feel special when his eyes had locked with hers in the crowd and he'd sung directly to her. It was only natural that someone as young and idealistic as she had been would have believed the fantasy that she'd be Yoko to his Lennon, that she could be the only woman who mattered when he could have had anyone…and that it would be okay to let her own passions and dreams dissolve into his just because she loved him.

Well, Mia thought as she stopped in the kitchen and slowly turned to face him, she was a hell of a lot smarter this time around. No matter how great a guy he was, she would never again lose sight of her own dreams, her own identity or her career. And she definitely wasn't going to fall for Ford's charm, or his good looks, or her memories of how good making love with him had been, or—

Damn it, enough already. He was a client. And she was here to sell him a house. Nothing more.

Reaching into her leather bag with a steady hand, she pulled out a color flyer and handed it to him. "Okay, Rutherford, here are the details on the house."

He gripped her hand along with the flyer. "You know how I feel about people calling me that."

He didn't hide the emotion in his eyes, and she got lost in the dark brown depths for a moment too long. "You're right," she replied as she yanked her hand out of his. "Anyone who's read *Rolling Stone* knows you don't like your given name."

It was a perfect reminder that she'd never been any more important to him than any other groupie he'd slept with, since the reason he hated his full name was just one of the many things he hadn't cared enough about her to explain.

She'd spat the *Rolling Stone* comment out in an offhand, albeit bitter, way, but was surprised when he seemed to be warring with himself. Was he finally going to confide in her? Five years too late, but still...

His too-beautiful mouth tightened down right before he said, "That name doesn't fit me. It never has and it never will."

She waited for him to say something more, to explain why Rutherford didn't fit but Ford did, until she realized she was being a fool again.

Nothing. He'd shared precisely the same *nothing* he'd given her before.

Disappointment came before she could pretend it hadn't. How many times did she have to learn this lesson?

Ford took everything…and then gave just enough to keep her hooked.

Still, she shouldn't have been so petty as to use his formal first name when she knew he hated it, even if she didn't know why. It wasn't just mean of her, it was sinking to his level. And if there was one thing she absolutely needed to do, it was rise above.

Not fall any deeper.

Mia forced her pride far enough to the side to be able to say, "I apologize. That was unprofessional."

He looked momentarily surprised by her apology, before moving toward her. "Mia—"

She cut him off as she took a step away from him. "This home has four bedrooms, five and a half baths, an Olympic-size pool, a custom-built wine cellar that was featured in *Wine Spectator* magazine, and, of course, you've already found the tower."

"Alana told me it was where she would go when she wanted to be alone to think."

"You know Alana?" Mia's mind immediately swam with visions of just how intimately he knew the owner of the home they were standing in.

"She's my business manager's sister," he said, and then clearly reading her mind, added, "And she's never been anything but a friend."

Pushing aside the relief, she snapped, "I don't need a list of everyone you slept with before or after me." Realizing too late that she was doing a terrible job of remaining cool and unruffled, she said, "Look, Ford, I think you'll agree that the best way to do this is to keep things strictly professional."

"No, Mia," he said in as steady a voice as she'd used on him, "I can't agree with that."

Heat—and senseless desperate desire—shot through her before she could stop it. "If you want me to be your Realtor," she informed him, "you're going to have to agree."

His eyes were dark and as mysterious now as they'd always been. "I won't promise anything about the future, Mia, but for today, I'll try."

It wasn't much of a concession to the rules she was setting up between them, nor anything close to a promise. She shouldn't have accepted his comment; she should simply have turned and left. Instead, she found it impossible to walk away from him. Telling herself she was just doing her job, she asked, "Have you spent much time in this house apart from the tower?"

"No."

"Then why don't we start with the ground floor?" Reminding herself to treat him just as she would any other client, as they moved from the kitchen into the large formal living room, she began to ask the questions she would normally already know the answers to if her client hadn't insisted on remaining anonymous until the first showing. "Will this be a primary residence or a vacation home?"

They were standing side by side in the elegant room that looked out on the exceptional water views when he answered, "Primary."

She barely stopped herself from whirling to face him in surprise, and quickly had to clarify, "But since you're on the road all the time, I'm assuming you'll probably use it about as much as you would a vacation home."

"No," he said with a firm shake of his head. "I'm not going to tour anymore."

This time she couldn't hold back her surprise. "Wait a minute. *You* aren't going to tour anymore?" When he shook his head again, she had to ask, "Why would you do that?"

"Because I've finally figured out some things are more important than being on the road." His gaze intensified as he turned from the water to look her in the eyes. "*Much* more important. So as soon as this tour ends next week, I'm done."

Keeping her voice scrupulously professional even as she reeled at the thought of Ford giving up the touring that was clearly his life's blood, she asked, "And how many people will be in full-time residence?"

"Just me, at first. Though I'm hoping it won't remain like that for too long."

Odds were, she suddenly decided, this whole home-buying thing had come up because he had a gorgeous—and annoyingly insipid—girlfriend who was dying to play house with him and redecorate down to the last inch of trim along the floorboards of the laundry room. Even though the house and the furnishings that came with it were already perfect as they were.

But what kind of woman would claim to care about Ford and then ask him to give up everything that mattered to him for her?

Telling herself it was none of her business, and that it shouldn't matter to her what he did with the rest of his life, Mia pointedly didn't ask any more questions about his personal life as they walked through the rest of the ground-floor rooms. Instead, she pointed out the many features of the beautifully built house. And all the while, she did her very best to ignore the way Ford always seemed to stand a little too close to her, or worse, brush up against her as he went to take a closer look at something.

Finally, they reached the master suite, and Ford's mouth curved up as he walked over to the large bed. Running a hand over the plush cover, he said, "Nice bedroom, isn't it?"

Professional. She needed to remain professional even when he was purposely trying to push every single one of her buttons. Mia was self-aware enough to know that with her passionate temperament, she had quite a few.

"Yes," she agreed, "the architect did a fabulous job of giving Alana and her husband a great view of the lake while keeping the room extremely private, both from the rest of the house and the grounds outside."

Of course, Ford had to get on the bed, cross his hands beneath his head on the pillow and settle in as if he'd already bought the place. "You're right. The view is just as good even when you're lying down." He turned his dark gaze from the stunning water view back to her. "Any chance you know how well the room is soundproofed?"

She'd expected him to hit her with something blatantly sexual in the bedroom, so despite the fact that her body instantly responded to the implication of loud, crazy sex, she was able to sound unruffled as she replied, "You'll probably need to do some extra soundproofing for playing your electric guitar if you don't want the sound to get out through the rest of the house." Or whatever else it was he was actually going to do in here with his beautiful, brainless girlfriend, whom Mia couldn't help but hate. She pointed toward the bathroom. "There is a large his-and-hers bathroom and two big walk-in closets. If you'd like to take a look at those, we can go check out the second floor next."

Though Ford slid his long legs over the edge of the bed, walked over to poke his head into the bathroom and the closets, and said, "Looks good," she couldn't escape the feeling that he was barely holding himself in check…or that his testing-out-the-bed escapade wasn't even close to the full extent of how far he was going to try to push her today.

Extremely glad to get out of the master suite, she took him up the stairs to the second floor, and when they reached the landing, she said, "In addition to the master suite on the ground floor, there are three other bedrooms upstairs."

"Only three, huh?" He went into one of the smaller bedrooms and picked up a soccer trophy that the home stager had put out on a boy's desk. "Well, I guess the kids could share rooms."

"Kids? Sharing rooms?" She shook her head, wondering how on earth he could possibly have kids she didn't know about. Because no matter how much she'd wanted to keep her head buried in the sand whenever his name came up on TV, on the radio or in a magazine over the years, it had simply been impossible. He was too famous. "Whose kids are going to live here?"

"Hopefully, mine, one day. You had five in your family, right?" Still reeling from the brand-new information that he was planning on having a big family, she couldn't manage anything more than a nod. And when he asked, "Didn't you say one of your uncles had six?" she immediately corrected him with, "Eight."

"Wow, eight kids." He grinned at the thought of it. "Must have been a pretty fun house for them, growing up with all those kids in it."

"It was," she agreed, before she realized just how strange a direction their conversation had taken.

"Your uncle and his wife must have really been

into each other, given all those kids they couldn't help but make."

"My uncle died when I was little, but from what my mother and father say about Uncle Jack and Aunt Mary, they were crazy in love with each other."

"Crazy in love," he said in a low voice that sent warmth rolling through her, head to toe. "I know just how that feels."

Wait…what was she doing telling him all this personal stuff? And why on earth would she ever have been stupid enough to bring up love in his presence, when he was the last person who could possibly understand what real love was?

"Let's head out to the grounds." It would be good to get out of the house. Because even as big as it was, standing in the same room with Ford had been way too close.

Directly off the back patio was an incredible rose garden. Between the tower, the roses and the water view, this property felt close to heaven. Even when she was doing a showing, she couldn't resist stopping to smell the roses. But the last thing she expected was for Ford to do the very same thing.

"I've only seen this October Moon rose in a handful of places outside of Seattle." He inhaled their sweet scent, then said, "It's your favorite, isn't it?"

During their week together, they hadn't often emerged from his luxurious hotel suite—particularly the king bed—but on one of their few spontaneous outings, he'd asked her to take him to her favorite place in Seattle. She'd taken him to the Rose Garden at Woodland Park Zoo and together they'd smelled every rose in the garden. By the time they'd returned to his hotel, ravenous for each other again after less than two hours out of each other's arms, she'd learned that when Ford had stepped away in the garden to make a quick phone call, it hadn't been to discuss business. He'd ordered buckets of roses to be delivered to his hotel room while they were out.

Long into the night, he'd brushed the soft blooms over her skin until she was begging for more than just the sensation of the petals touching her.

With the potent memories washing over her, she couldn't lie, couldn't do anything but nod. All these years, Mia had forced herself to bury all the good memories of being with Ford. But with the scent of her favorite rose perfuming the air, it was nearly impossible to push away the heady visions of the two of them laughing and loving together. He'd thrown her off balance by appearing unannounced as her anonymous client. But it was the sweetness of these memories that was really throwing her off.

Badly wanting to shift things away from their past and back toward the house, she asked, as they headed toward the pool patio, "So how do you like this house so far?"

"How do *you* like it?"

Telling herself it wasn't that strange a question to parry back at her—clients often wanted to know if she thought a house was a good investment before getting attached to it—she said, "It's well designed, well built and in an exceptional location. And even though the tower is unique, it manages to add to the property rather than being something that would turn off future prospective buyers."

"But can you see a family living here?"

Mia had never done anything but her very best for a client, so she made herself push away her personal feelings for Ford and take in the house from the standpoint of a woman with a husband and kids.

"Yes," she told him as they walked around the pool. "I can see how much fun it would be for kids to run and play on the grass, and to use the tower as a secret playhouse. And even though it's a big property, I think it's just the right size for a parent to make sure no one's getting hurt or being too nuts with their brothers and sisters."

"Good. I wouldn't want a place where people felt like they had to worry about breaking things, or where I'd need a staff to run it."

Finally, despite herself, she felt as if she was getting to know something about the real Ford. Too late, yes, but still interesting. "Honestly, while the house is great, what you're really paying for is the location. I actually know a lot of local families who live in similar houses and I definitely don't think it's too fancy for a handful of messy kids to feel perfectly comfortable tracking mud into the kitchen." Thinking about how often she and her brothers had done that, much to the consternation of her parents, she grinned. "When we were kids, the amount of mud on the floor was directly equivalent to the amount of fun we had playing outside."

Before she could remember why they shouldn't be smiling at each other, Ford was heading across the bricks to a slight grassy rise on the side of the house that looked out over the water and that was completely surrounded on the other three sides by tall, leafy shrubs.

"This spot reminds me of that day we found that small park with the great view," he said. "Do you remember?"

How could she ever forget? Blue skies had turned to drizzle by the time they'd laid out a blanket in Kerry Park behind the thick shrubbery that hid them from the rest of the neighborhood, but Ford had kept her warm with his body over hers. She'd believed his was the love she'd been waiting for, and that no other man could thrill her the way he did.

Unfortunately, while she'd been wrong about the love…she'd been dead right about the thrill. No other man had ever come anywhere close to making her feel so wild or so good.

She shook the memories away as she kept her gaze focused on the water at the edge of the property. "The view here really is beautiful."

"You were a thousand times more beautiful that day than this view could ever be," he said, each of his softly spoken words scoring a direct hit right in her heart, which she'd momentarily forgotten to guard. "You still are, Mia."

"No." She backed away from him, from his sweet yet loaded words and the way they made her feel things that she could never allow herself to feel for him again. "We already agreed that you can't talk to me like that."

"The hardest thing I've ever done is not touch you during the past hour." He dropped his gaze to her lips. "No, that's not true," he said almost to himself as his eyes darkened further with desire. "It's been a hell of a lot harder not kissing you."

Five years ago she hadn't known any better than to let him sweep her off her feet so that she forgot everything but him. But now, even though she *did* know better, she still badly wanted his forbidden kiss.

"You think I don't know your game? Showing up as an anonymous client to catch me off guard, brushing up against me when you go through a doorway, toying with me with your hot glances and sexy words? We both know it's what you *do*, Ford. You're a master at making women want you. You don't need to try to reel me back in to prove that."

"There's only one woman I want to want me, Mia."

Determined not to let anything he said or did affect her from here on out, she rolled her eyes. Honestly, at this point, it was ridiculous to think that she could look for a house for him in any kind of professional way. "I'm sure I'm supposed to be flattered that you thought one look at you standing in the tower like the conquering hero come home would make me drop to my knees and unzip you with my teeth." She laughed out loud to let him know what she thought of that vision, praying he believed she was actually disgusted at the thought of being with him again. Her heart and mind were, of course— it was just her body that was busy trying to betray the rest of her. "Scrubbing the kitchen floor with a toothbrush sounds a thousand times better than that."

"So," he said with deceptive ease, "just to be clear, you're saying you're not interested in me anymore?"

"Not the slightest bit."

"And you haven't felt any sparks jumping between us the way they always did?"

"Nope." She shrugged as if the answer to his question were totally obvious. "Nothing."

"Funny, I was thinking just the opposite was true."

"Then you were thinking wrong."

"How's this, then? You let me kiss you, and if you're right and there's nothing between us after all, I'll stop pushing you where you don't want to go. But if there is—"

"Do you really think I'm going to fall for some stupid dare where you're going to declare afterward, no matter what happens, that there are *sparks* between us?"

"You're the one who's saying I leave you cold."

He hadn't taken his eyes from hers, and in the span of a handful of words, they'd grown darker, more intense. "One kiss, Mia. Surely you can walk away from that."

What had she done to deserve his return into her life? She'd packed up every beautiful moment, every sweet and sinful memory of being with Ford, and had buried them all in the deepest, darkest part of her heart. She'd worked so hard to put the past to rest. She'd been over him.

He couldn't just come back like this, couldn't make her want him like this, couldn't send her emotions into turmoil with nothing but a dark look and a few tossed-off words in his deep, mesmerizing voice. Heck, she had a date tonight with a really great guy who could very well end up being *the one*.

But now, after less than an hour alone with Ford, she was grappling with all of her old demons.

She needed to take a step away from him, and then another and another until she was far enough that she couldn't see him anymore, couldn't smell him, couldn't reach out to find out if his skin was still as hot to the touch as it had once been.

Pride be damned, she was going to have to let him win this round by running from him…if only to make sure he didn't win back the one thing that really mattered.

Her heart.

Or worse, her soul.

But her feet still weren't listening, because instead

of taking her farther from him, they were moving her closer, then closer still, until he was right there within kissing distance.

"One kiss," she found herself agreeing though she knew better. "And when you realize that it, and you, mean absolutely nothing to me—" She shouldn't need to pause, shouldn't feel even the slightest hesitation in stating what she *knew* needed to happen. "—you'll promise never to come near me again."

He didn't so much as blink before agreeing with a husky, "You have my word."

And then he cupped her face in his hands and lowered his head to hers…

Five

Ford had never been much of a planner; he'd always chosen to follow his passion, instead. But, until now, there had never been this much on the line before. One kiss to decide if Mia would remain in his life… or if he'd have to give her up forever.

Only, even if he'd had the foresight to plan the kiss carefully by playing off all her sensual trigger points, Ford wouldn't have been able to follow through on that plan. Because the instant she agreed to the kiss, the desperation to touch her again ripped through every other thought, every other sense, every other need.

Just being near her tore his control to shreds.

The entire world thought Ford Vincent was the ultimate ladies' man, and that there wasn't a woman alive who had the power to bring him to his knees. But the world was wrong. Dead wrong.

Mia was the only woman who had ever truly

marked him. Not just his body, but his heart…and even down deeper than that. He'd never felt passion like this for anyone else.

He felt her breath hitch in her chest as his thumbs brushed gently over her cheekbones, his fingertips lightly caressing her jaw and the very tips of her earlobes. Earlobes he knew to be extremely sensitive. All he'd had to do when they were together before was score one of her lobes with the edge of his teeth and she would start begging him to take her.

She'd had on a fresh coat of lipstick when she first walked into the tower, and though it was mostly gone now, a faint stain of red pigment remained. Her eyes were still open, but her lashes were fluttering in her fight to keep them from closing.

The breath from her lips was warm, and so damned seductive against his as he tried to prolong the moment. But Ford just didn't have it in him to draw out the anticipation any longer, not when he was dying to taste her again.

Finally, with her name on his lips, he closed the final distance between them.

There was no way he could have held back his groan of pleasure at how good the simple touch of Mia's lips was against his own. He felt almost drunk from the press of her curves, though she was trying to remain stiff and unyielding against him.

Shifting his hands up into her hair, Ford slicked his tongue in a slow path along her lower lip. For all his memories of how good kissing her had been, memories had never tasted this good, nor made his heart nearly leap out of his chest.

Her hands had come up to press against his chest, as if to push him away. But as his tongue made a second trip over her upper lip, ducking into the bow in the middle before tracking a damp path to the sensitive corner, he could feel her warring with herself. He knew full well her intention upon rising to his challenge was to remain cold and unmoved by his kiss. And she believed she could pull it off.

But when her fingers began to clench on his shirt all it would have taken was one slight shift to push him away and end the kiss before it really even got a chance to begin. Instead, she grabbed the cotton and dragged him even closer.

Thank God.

Mia had mentally braced herself for pleasure. She had physically prepared herself for heat.

But it wasn't until Ford actually touched her skin with calloused fingertips, then waited for her to have no choice but to respond to his sinfully sweet caresses before finally dropping his mouth to hers, that she remembered just how enormous his powers of seduction were.

Worse still, as if the mere press of his lips over hers wasn't already enough to start melting her from the core outward, he'd dragged his tongue over her lips. And that was when her memories became even clearer.

Because Ford had never simply seduced her. He had demanded her passion, instead. Right from that first moment when he'd been onstage and she'd been in the audience, he'd forced her to face what was already between them. It hadn't mattered that they were two complete strangers, because with nothing more than a look, and a song, she'd been his. Just as he was making her his again with this kiss, even as she tried to remind herself that she should be keeping him from touching any part of her, body or soul.

But as his tongue stroked against hers once, then twice, then three gorgeous times, sending shivers through her, head to toe, and her hands involuntarily clutched the fabric of his shirt even harder, their kiss deepened the way it always had. From nothing to *everything* in the span of one heartbeat, one breath.

And now that his heat, his strength, were beneath her hands and pressed hard against the length of her body, Mia couldn't help but give in to the need that she hadn't wanted to admit had been bubbling away inside of her for the past five years.

As the years fell away and her memories were replaced with shockingly potent and dizzying real-life pleasure, Mia also couldn't possibly deny that this kiss trumped every one of their previous kisses. Not just because they'd both obviously been waiting five long and painful years for another one, but because everything was different now.

She'd been a girl then, caught up in dreams and fairy tales, and though she still looked much the same on the outside, their breakup had changed something inside her forever. Ford had barely been more than a boy himself when he'd broken her heart. Now he was not only a man, but also a superstar who had the entire world at his feet. Mia had always believed she was a strong woman, but even so, she'd wanted Ford so badly at twenty-three that she'd nearly given up her entire life for him.

If he'd nearly been able to take everything from her then, what would he take now if she were stupid enough to let him?

"Jesus," he said in wonder against her lips, "even in my wildest memories, I never remembered anything this hot."

Though his shirt was still in her hands and her body was urging her to yank him closer, she suddenly realized that if she didn't put her walls back up, and make every last effort at resistance, then Ford might have the power to actually break her this time, rather than just bruise her.

Gathering up every possible ounce of determination she possessed, she pushed him away, hard enough that her fingers had no choice but to break free of their hold on him. Her move was so sudden that one of his hands remained tangled in her hair and, momentarily, left her scalp stinging as they finally came apart.

She couldn't do this—she had known better than to step up to his careless dare. No one but Ford had

ever made her want like this, so effortlessly, so
deeply, so passionately…so foolishly.

All these years she'd told herself that she would
never be stupid enough to be susceptible to him
again. But now she knew with 100 percent certainty
that it wouldn't matter how many years passed.

She'd still be held in his thrall.

Both of them were breathing hard, and the way
his chest rose against the thin fabric of his short-
sleeved cotton shirt outlined his well-developed
muscles against the fabric in a horribly distracting
way. Denying their physical connection would just
prove her to be an even bigger fool, so she didn't
bother to try.

"You're right," she agreed. "It was hot." She made
sure to pause a beat so that he wouldn't miss her next
words. "But you still mean nothing to me."

"We both know that's a lie." He looked arrogant
and beautiful as he told her, flat out, "You've never
been able to forget me any more than I've been able
to forget you."

"Stop it." She backed up. But, before she could get
any farther from him and the words she knew he intended to use in exactly the same way he'd used his
kiss—not to seduce, but to *demand*—her path was
blocked by a thick shrub. "Don't you dare look at me
like that, like that kiss was special, like it mattered
to you. Not when we both know it didn't."

For the first time since she'd seen him standing
in the tower, anger flared in his eyes. "How the hell

can you say that to me after that kiss? How can you act like you aren't special to me, or that you don't matter—when no one has ever mattered as much as you do? If I thought you'd listen to reason, if I thought you'd listen to my apologies, I would have started with those, but you're so damned stubborn that I *had* to lead with the kiss just to get you to admit you felt anything at all."

Hating the way her lips still tingled, how good the taste of him was even now and, worse, how desperately she suddenly wanted to hear his apologies, she relinquished any final attempt at composure.

"You didn't attempt to contact me for five years!" She was flat-out yelling now, but didn't care anymore what he thought of her. "And then when you did, you tricked me with a call from a lawyer so I wouldn't know it was you lying in wait for me in the tower. You are just as much of an egocentric jerk as you always were because, clearly, it's still all about what *you* want, and no one else's life—or wishes—matter. So don't you dare stand here and try to convince me I'm special, or that you're finally ready to give me some apologies that are going to make everything all better. We were good in bed together. That's all there is, or ever was, between us. But do you know what the worst part of it is? I was almost stupid enough let you buy your way back into my life."

She reached into her jacket pocket, pulled out the check she hadn't yet taken to the bank and ripped it in half. The two pieces of paper fluttered to the ground as she said, "Five years ago, you were the one who told me goodbye. Now I'm saying it to you." Head held high, she turned and walked away.

Six

In reality, the last thing Ford had time for right now was a house-hunting trip in Seattle. His touring crew and management team were in Los Angeles preparing for his Sunday-night show at the Staples Center. He'd had half a dozen major interviews scheduled for today, but when his lawyer had confirmed that Mia was available, he'd had his PR team reschedule everything. Despite his fame, he'd never been a particularly high-maintenance client, so they'd been happy to take care of it because they figured something important must have come up. Tonight and Saturday were going to be pretty rough without any breathing room between the extra interviews they'd had to cram in.

As he boarded his private plane to head down to Southern California, his brain, his body—hell, every last part of him—was wrapped up in Mia. Yes, she'd been angry with him for showing up unexpectedly.

And there was no question at all that she was still furious about the way things had ended between them.

But even bigger than her anger had been the intensity and the heat of the sparks between them. Whether they were talking or kissing—sweet Lord, that kiss had completely blown his mind—their connection was undeniable. He'd prayed that the kiss would melt the walls of ice around her heart enough for her to listen to him. Instead, it was the thing that had finally made her snap…and tell him to get out of her life forever.

And, damn it, she'd been right. He *had* acted like an egotistical ass by setting up the anonymous showing. Somehow he needed to figure out how to convince her to spend more time with him so that he could make her see that he had changed…and so that he could actually get things right this time.

But how was he going to pull that off when she was so determined to keep her distance? And how could he do it without acting like a self-obsessed jerk who thought he ruled the world the way he had today?

His phone rang and if it had been anyone but his personal assistant, he would have let it go. Carol Vale had worked for a hugely famous British musician for several years before she'd decided she wanted to be back in the US to be closer to her kids. She wasn't impressed by money or fame…and she was a freakin' genius with details.

"How was the house?"

The house? He'd walked through every room and over most of the grounds, but all he could really remember about it was Mia being there. How beautiful she'd looked standing in the tower with light streaming in over her hair. The gorgeous flush of her skin when she watched him lie down on the bed in the master suite. The surprise on her face when he'd talked about wanting kids someday.

Then again, she hadn't been the only one surprised by that comment. They hadn't just been empty words… He'd actually been able to visualize kids running around the house. Kids who were an exact combination of him and Mia.

Finally, he replied, "It's a killer place."

Efficient as ever, Carol went over his interview and sound-check schedule. But before she signed off, she said, "One other thing—you wanted to attend Nico's wedding this weekend, is that correct?"

He'd always thought Nico—or Nicola, as the well-known pop star preferred that her friends call her—was a great girl. He had to turn down most wedding invitations for one reason or another, but the two of them had become friends over the years of criss-crossing tours, and the handful of weeks when they'd even toured together a few years back.

"Right," he confirmed, "but I thought we couldn't get the schedule to work out?"

"While I still need to do a little more juggling," Carol said, "it's looking like you could at least make the ceremony. Just as long as you remember that you're going to have a show that night, so you probably shouldn't enjoy too much of Sullivan Winery's finest while you're in Napa."

Wait a minute. "The wedding is at Sullivan Winery?"

"Nico is marrying the owner. I thought you knew that."

He'd been so busy trying to figure out a way to sneak back into Mia's life that he'd been blind to the opportunity that had been staring him in the face.

Namely, that Mia was a cousin of the guy who owned Sullivan Winery!

Just like that, the music that had started playing in his head when he saw Mia again was suddenly like an entire orchestra trying to be heard.

"Thanks for making the arrangements, Carol. I'll call Nicola to let her know I'll be there." But even as he placed the call, he was grabbing one of the guitars he kept onboard his plane.

Finally, inspiration had come…and, yet again, it was all because of Mia.

Her date was six-two with blond hair. His muscles were big and his smile was sexy as he greeted Mia that evening outside the wine bar located two blocks down from her office. He gave her a kiss on the cheek.

"You look gorgeous," he said, his words echoing what she could see in his eyes. It was almost exactly what Ford had said to her that morning. Only when Ford said it, every cell in her body had leaped to life, as if no other words had ever meant so much. Whereas the compliment from her date was having no impact on her cells whatsoever. They simply stayed right where they were as if lying in wait for her real date to arrive.

Mia gave herself a little mental shake as she made herself focus on the man standing in front of her, rather than the one who had driven her crazy all morning.

Her date was incredibly handsome. Given the cut of his suit and the watch on his wrist he was obviously successful at the financial firm where he worked. Mia should have been all over him.

Instead of her pulse racing, or her skin heating up, every instinct in her was trying to get her to move away from him. As if she were already taken.

No! What was she thinking? Worse, what was she feeling way down deep in her heart?

She most definitely was *not* taken. On the contrary, she was perfectly free to do exactly what she pleased with whomever she wanted. And wouldn't it serve Ford right if he found out that after she'd left him today she'd shared an intimate evening with another man? Oh, yes, that would be the perfect way to end her horrible day, the only way to truly make sure that she'd blanked out Ford and everything he'd made her feel.

But when she looked up into her date's eyes, for a moment she couldn't remember his name. The blank spot in her brain widened for a few moments before she recovered.

"James," she finally said in too-obvious relief.

He looked bemused by her strange greeting, before smiling down at her again and speaking her name back at her in the same tone. "Mia."

She laughed then, glad the moment she'd felt absolutely nothing at all for him had finally passed.

When he held out his arm, she put her hand in the crook of his elbow and let him take her inside to an empty booth in a somewhat private corner of the busy wine bar. This was one of her usual stomping grounds with the girls and a safe place for a first date. The bartenders and cocktail waitresses knew her so well that one signal from her was enough for them to come and extricate her from anyone with whom she didn't feel safe.

If only, she thought with a small sigh, she could have had some help extricating herself from Ford this morning.

Ugh. Why was she still thinking about him?

Until this morning, she'd been looking forward to this date with James. They'd met last weekend jogging around Green Lake Park, and she'd been inspired to run just a little faster than usual to keep up with his excellent form. She'd planned to get to know that "form" of his a little better tonight. A lot better, even, if it felt right. But here she was about to plead a headache just so she could get out of there…and do what? Brood over Ford? About the way he'd tricked her into seeing him again? Or worse, about all the stupidly traitorous feelings that had risen inside her that morning as though five years had never passed?

No, damn it, there had to be something between her and James, at least a little of that spark she'd felt last weekend when they were jogging together. Because if there wasn't—if it turned out that it was all gone due to one arrogant and infuriating rock star's unwelcome reappearance in her life—then she was going to have yet one more reason to be mad at Ford.

And how could she manage to remain emotionless about Ford, and make sure he meant less than nothing to her from here until eternity, if she was constantly getting angry with him?

"So," she said to James with a bright smile that she hoped didn't look as forced as it felt, "have you been on any good runs this week?"

"None as good as ours together last Sunday." His eyes darkened slightly as he reached for her hand and rubbed his thumb over her palm. "I've been thinking about you all week, Mia. Tonight couldn't come soon enough."

It was exactly the right thing to say, exactly the right way to touch her. Or rather, it should have been. She should have been drooling all over him, should have been thanking her lucky stars that they'd both been out on the running path last weekend.

Instead, she was wondering why the cocktail waitress couldn't get over to their table quicker so that she could have a drink to hold instead of James's hand.

"I thought about you, too," she made herself say, and it was true—she really *had* thought about James during the week. She'd told her friends about him, had even texted them a sneaky picture she'd taken of him running before he'd noticed she was behind him.

It had only been since the moment she'd set eyes on Ford in the tower that all thoughts of other men, including James, had fled like racehorses in the Kentucky Derby.

Forcing herself to lean in a little closer, rather than away, she said, "I want to know everything about you."

"How about we start with the basics and then later," he said with a charming pause, "I'll give you more if you still want it."

Seriously, could this guy be any better? But when the cocktail waitress stepped up to their table with a "What can I get you?" Mia took the opportunity to slide her hand out of his and put a few precious inches of space between them in a booth that suddenly seemed much too small. Next time she'd have to remember to have a first date in a bowling alley, or somewhere similarly less intimate.

They gave their orders, and Mia prayed that the drink would arrive quickly so that she could begin to dull all the cray-cray thoughts about Ford that wouldn't leave her alone.

"I already know you're gorgeous and sweet," she said to James, though she hated feeling as if she was leading him on. "What else can you tell me?"

bibliotheca SelfCheck System
Lafayette Library & Learning Center
Contra Costa County Library
3491 Mt. Diablo Blvd.
Lafayette, Ca. 94549
925-385-2280

Customer ID: **************

Items that you checked out

Title: It must be your love /
ID: 31901057135479
Due: Tuesday, September 25, 2018
Messages:
Item checked out.

Total items: 1
Account balance: $0.00
9/4/2018 6:42 PM
Ready for pickup: 0

Renew online or by phone
ccclib.org
1-800-984-4636

Have a nice day!

"I'm thirty-five. Never been married. I'm a VP at Anderson Financial."

Mia worked to make all of the appropriate responses. "I always thought it would be fun to play with other people's money," she said after taking a much-needed drink—or three—of her dirty martini. "Are those all the basics you're going to give me tonight?"

His smile should have set her blood on fire. "How about one more for our first round, and then it's your turn." When she nodded with what she hoped looked like anticipation, he said, "I've also got a major thing for intelligent women who run their own businesses."

James was looking at her with an interest that she could see went above and beyond just wanting to do her. Unlike Ford, who had been deep into his one-track I-want-you-and-won't-stop-until-I-have-you caveman act this morning. When he'd kissed her, she'd stupidly felt her heart stir at least as much as her body had...even though she'd known he was simply playing with her like a cat carelessly playing with a ball of yarn. It would be fun until he got bored with the game.

Mia had never been a particularly big drinker, but tonight she could have tossed back another couple by now. "I grew up in Seattle. I love selling houses. And don't freak out when I tell you this next bit, okay?" His eyebrows rose as she said, "I have four older brothers."

"How's this for not freaking out?" he said, and

then the next thing she knew, he was lowering his mouth to hers.

Panic rose in her chest, but she forced herself to push it down and let his lips touch hers. His kiss was warm and soft. She leaned in closer and let him take it deeper, his tongue stroking over hers.

And that was when Mia finally had to admit complete and utter defeat. There was no use in continuing with this farce of a date. Because if she wasn't feeling James's kiss, then she was well and truly done for.

Splaying her hands on his chest, instead of gripping his shirt to pull him closer the way she had with Ford, she firmly pushed him back.

"You're great, James," she said in a gentle voice, "and I can't believe I'm about to say this, but—"

"We were just getting warmed up, Mia. Let me kiss you again."

God, this date with James should have been so hot. But nothing about being with him felt right. Not his arms around her. Not his mouth on hers. Not even the way he looked at her—as if he was hoping she would let him inside her head and heart. Instead, the last thing she wanted was for him to know all of her deepest secrets.

It took no effort whatsoever for her to say, "I'm sorry, but I can't," and slide completely out of his arms. So different from the way it had nearly killed her to walk away from Ford this morning after only one kiss.

Especially when one kiss from Ford had never, ever been enough…

To make matters worse, one of Ford's hits started playing right then. No matter how hard she tried, how was she ever going to get away from her memories of him?

"It's someone else, isn't it?"

With the sounds of flirting and laughter all around them James's question pulled her back.

She tried to shake her head, tried to deny it, but before she could pull that off, James said, "If you ever get over him, give me a call."

She could see the regret in James's eyes before he put a twenty on the table, slipped his jacket on and headed for the door. A half-dozen single girls in the bar watched him go, and when they looked back and saw Mia sitting alone in the booth, she could read the clear question in their eyes. *How could you have screwed that up?*

Mia pulled out her phone and texted her two best friends: EMERGENCY DRINKS NEEDED @ K WINE BAR.

Seven

Colbie Michaels and Brooke Jansen walked into the cocktail bar just seconds apart, and when they found Mia sitting in the back booth, they both immediately said, "What's wrong?"

Mia barely stopped herself from dropping her head into her hands as they slid in on either side of her. "I got a call yesterday from a lawyer about an anonymous client who wanted to buy a ten-million-dollar house on the waterfront." She could see from her friends' expressions that they thought it was as strange as she had, but they didn't interrupt. "Right away I knew something had to be up. I mean, what reasons could a superrich guy have for needing to remain anonymous with his Realtor? But against my better judgment, I decided to set up a few showings for today."

She picked up the new drink she'd ordered after James left and downed it in one gulp. But she knew

it wouldn't do a darn thing to help her forget Ford…
or the fact that she could still feel his lips on hers.

"When I got to the first house this morning, Ford
Vincent was waiting for me."

"Oh. My. God." Brooke's eyes were huge. "You're
working with Ford Vincent?"

"He is *so* sexy," Colbie said, fanning herself.
"Back before I met Noah, I actually used to fantasize that—"

"We slept together five years ago."

The way both Brooke's and Colbie's mouths fell
open would have been comical if Mia had been anywhere close to laughing.

"You *slept* with *Ford Vincent*?" Colbie asked in
a shocked whisper.

"Oh. My. God," was all Brooke could manage
again. Until she had to ask, "How was it?"

Mia put her drink to her lips before realizing with
dismay that she'd already emptied it. Slamming the
glass down on the table so hard the stem got a hair-
line crack, she admitted, "Amazing."

Oh, hell, now that she'd started the story, she
might as well tell them *everything*.

"Sleeping with Ford is the best sex you can possibly imagine. Being with him was so good it should
have taken me hours to recover from each round,
but before I could he'd start in on me all over again,
and the next thing I knew a week had passed and
I'd barely done anything but Ford the whole time."

"I knew it would be like that with him," Colbie

said, but her elation at so accurately predicting Ford's sexual prowess from a distance was short-lived as she realized something. "Why the heck didn't you tell me?"

Mia felt terrible about it. Clearly, sleeping with one of the biggest rock stars in the world was a whopper of an omission between best friends. Colbie and Mia had been inseparable since they'd been in kindergarten. Colbie had told Mia about every guy she'd ever been with before she had fallen in love with Noah Bryant earlier that year. And Mia had told Colbie about every guy she'd been with, too…except for the one who had mattered most.

But before Mia could begin to explain why she'd kept it to herself, Brooke asked, "And why did you *stop* sleeping with him?"

Thank God the cocktail waitress automatically brought over their regular drink orders just then. Needing to get another fortifying sip under her belt before answering, Mia put her new drink down more carefully. "At first, I didn't tell you because it all happened so fast. We met at one of his shows, and it seemed like he was the guy I'd been waiting for my whole life. You should have heard the poetry he spouted between our sex sessions, the way he swore I was everything he wanted, too. He had a week off between gigs, so I called in to the office to book some last-second vacation time I'd accrued so that I could spend every single second of it with him. I should have called you, Colbie, because then you would have had a chance to call me on my crazy." Mia shook her head. "Which is exactly why I think I didn't say anything to you or anyone in my family—because I didn't want anyone to pop the fantasy bubble I was living in. God, I was *so* stupid!"

Colbie put her hand over hers and squeezed it gently. "What happened at the end of the week?"

"He asked me to come with him, out on the road. I'd known him one week, and he wanted me to give up everything in my life to follow him on buses and planes all over the world. And the thing is, even though I loved my work, loved my family and you guys, and the life I had in Seattle, I was so tempted— more tempted than I should have been. But I guess I paused just a little too long, and when I didn't immediately jump up and down screaming *YES* as if I were the luckiest girl in the world to be wanted by him, Ford shut down. Completely. He said if I really loved him, I wouldn't have to think about it. He said he couldn't believe that he'd let me fool him into believing I actually loved him. Just that fast, he was gone."

"Couldn't he see that he was asking you to change your whole life for him—while he got to do exactly what he wanted?" Brooke protested.

"No, he obviously didn't see that. And when I looked back on that week, I realized that while I'd shared everything with him, he really hadn't shared anything more than his body with me. Apart from how he felt about his music I didn't know anything about him. Nothing about his family or his past or his fears or dreams. But do you want to know the worst thing? Even though I should have felt like I'd dodged a bullet, I can't even begin to explain how much I missed him. So badly that I decided I'd made a huge mistake by not immediately dropping everything for him. I decided I could figure out a way to have a career on the road, maybe not real estate, but something I could do while always on the move, and that I would just call you guys and my family all the time to make sure we didn't lose touch. I decided to surprise him at a show in Miami."

She closed her eyes at the wave of pain that hit her as she relived that horrible night. "The guys on his crew who had brought me backstage that first night in Seattle didn't want to let me through to the back in Miami. I tried to tell myself it was because I had hurt him by needing some extra time to make my decision, but—" Her voice started to break, but damn it, she wasn't going to cry over him again.

"You don't have to relive any more of it," Brooke said, squeezing her hand.

But Mia knew it was better if she did. She needed to remind herself and to tell the people who loved her most exactly why she needed to stay away from Ford Vincent. "I don't think I'll ever get the picture of that girl on his lap out of my head. She was half-naked, and he had his hands on—" Oh, God, maybe the full replay wasn't such a good idea, after all. "For a few seconds I was frozen in the doorway and the girl was busy making all her fake porn-star moans, but he looked straight at me." The breath she tried to take shook her lungs. "I picked up some drumsticks that had been left on a table by the door and threw them at him. And then I got the hell out of there."

"The bastard didn't even go running after you?" Brooke asked.

"No." And that was how she'd known for sure that everything he'd said to her during their one week together had been a lie. Every sweet and sexy word that she'd been stupid enough to believe.

"I hate his guts," Colbie snarled. "I'm more sorry than you know that I ever had one single fantasy about that piece of dirt, and I'm pledging to you now that I'll never listen to one of his songs again."

"Considering they're constantly on the radio and TV and playing in every single bar—" Mia pointed to the speaker on the ceiling, where they could hear Ford singing yet another one of his huge hits "—that's going to be pretty hard to do. But I love you for offering."

"Well," Brooke said, "we might be stuck listening to them from time to time when we can't avoid it, but we won't enjoy any of them. Excuse me for a second." She walked over to the bartender and said something to him. A few seconds later, Ford's song stopped and the acoustic version of Nico's "One Moment" began to play instead.

Mia appreciated her friends' solidarity, even though she knew how hard it would be for any of them to avoid Ford's presence, not just on the radio, but in the media, too, which had always had a love affair with him.

"Did he ever contact you again?" Colbie asked.

"Nope." Not only had he not come running after her in Miami, but he hadn't called, emailed or written so much as a text begging her to forgive him. "And I certainly never tried to contact him."

"So he waits five years and then makes sure you'll show up at the house by dangling a huge potential sale in your face while not disclosing who he really is." Colbie's snarl curled her lips even tighter. "What a jerk. I double hate him now."

This was why Mia had texted her best friends tonight. They always knew how to make her smile, even when she was feeling at her very lowest. But her smile didn't last long, because there was one more thing she needed to confess.

"I let him kiss me. This morning. In the house I was showing him."

Her friends both looked at her as though she'd lost her mind before Brooke all but yelled, "You let him *kiss* you today?"

A dozen heads swiveled around to see what the fuss was all about, and Mia could feel her face turning even redder. "The kiss was supposed to prove how completely over him I was. You might double hate him now," she said to her friends, "but I'm the two-time idiot."

"The way he set you up this morning has made it *way* more than double hate now," Colbie declared.

But instead of agreeing, Brooke said, "He's obviously still hooked on you."

Mia shook her head in denial. "Nothing is obvious with Ford. On the surface, he's every girl's sexy rock-god dream, but underneath—" She scowled into her drink, then took a long sip before finishing her sentence. "He never let me find out what was underneath. Every time we got close, he'd pull back. For a moment today I actually thought maybe things had changed, but he wouldn't even tell me why he hates being called Rutherford so much. And if he won't tell me something little like that, I seriously doubt he's going to spill anything else in his dark soul."

Brooke held up her phone. "We could do a Google search on him to find out."

For every one of the thousand times Mia had wanted to look up Ford's past on the internet, all she'd had to do was remind herself how pathetic it was to long for tidbits of his life from journalists and Twitter feeds.

"No." She took Brooke's phone from her hand and dropped it back into her soon-to-be sister-in-law's purse. "Imagine how it would have felt for you to have to research Rafe's past on Google. My brother cares so much about you that he dug deep and told you everything about his past and how much it had messed him up, even though it was really hard for him to do that."

Brooke put her hand on Mia's arm. "You're right. And I'm sorry if I sounded like I was defending Ford when I said he's still hooked on you. It's just that—" Brooke shook her head. "No, never mind."

"I've always hoped I could take the truth from my best friends as well as I can dish it out to them," Mia said softly. "What were you going to say?"

Her friend sighed, as though she knew there was no getting away with a *never mind* this time. "We all know what Ford Vincent looks like, and I can imagine what poetry falling from his lips would sound like, especially if the sex really was as great as you said. Honestly, I don't know how easy it would be for anyone to get over someone like him."

Mia's stomach twisted tight at Brooke's words. She could always lie to herself. But to her friends? It was another one of the big reasons she'd never mentioned her week with Ford. Because she wouldn't have been able to lie about what it had done to her.

"He's the only man I've ever loved. And no matter how many times I look back and remind myself that I was young and foolish and still in a place where I believed that fantasies were possible, and that it was perfectly normal for me to lose myself entirely in him and his oversize life…" She sighed. "What I felt for him was still real, despite all of that other nonsense."

"You know," Colbie said slowly, "maybe there's another reason why he was able to get past your defenses this morning. From everything you've just told us, it sounds like you never got a chance to give him a piece of your mind, not five years ago and not today, either, because he made sure to take you by surprise. I, for one, would sure like to hear you rip him to shreds."

Though Mia had already said what was supposed to be her final goodbye to Ford, she couldn't help but feel that Colbie was onto something.

Brooke gave Mia a pointed look. "The only problem is, do you think you could give him a tongue-lashing without yours ending up in his mouth again?"

It was the same question Mia was already asking herself. Because she hadn't yet figured out the honest answer to it, she said, "What has my brother done to you, Brooke? I never thought you'd talk about tongues lashing in any way."

Her friend was flushing but grinning a wicked little grin as she said, "Don't you mean, what have *I* done to *him*?"

Halfway through her friend's sentence, Mia's hands were over her ears. "I'm going to pretend I didn't hear you say that. Although it's totally my fault since I keep forgetting how weird it is to think about my brother's sex life. Especially when it's with one of my best friends." She made a show of scrunching her eyes up and shaking her head hard a couple of times as if to toss the vision away. Far, far away from her brain.

"Does that mean that it's *not* weird for you to think about my sex life with Noah, since he's not related to you?" Colbie teased.

"Are you kidding?" Mia replied, glad to feel as though she was back in the normal world for a few seconds. "If you knew how many times I've thought about your fiancé naked…"

The three of them laughed, but all the while Brooke's unanswered question hung in the air between them. Mia had never been a woman who wavered. She had neither the time nor the inclination to waffle back and forth on important decisions. She wouldn't start now.

"We've got Marcus and Nicola's wedding in Napa this weekend," she said to Brooke, who would be attending with Rafe. "That should give me a little time and space from Ford's sudden appearance this morning. I'll call him on Monday morning and finally get it all off my chest." Having a plan made her feel better, back in control of her life, the way she should be. "I'll even let him make whatever apologies he feels he needs to make and then I'll forgive—and forget—him completely." She met her friends' gazes, one after the other, before adding, "And I promise there will be absolutely no instances of my tongue going into his mouth during any of it."

"Here's to only putting our tongues into the mouths of the men who deserve us!" Colbie said as she raised her glass in a toast.

"To Mia, for being one of the most strong and amazing women I've ever known," Brooke added as she raised her glass.

Mia lifted her glass to press it against those of Colbie and Brooke. "And to both of you for being the very best friends a girl could ever have."

Eight

Saturday flew by with back-to-back estate showings for a big-money CEO who was planning to move from New York to Seattle. It wasn't until Mia boarded the plane to head to Napa Valley late that afternoon that she finally had a chance to take a full breath.

She'd always had plenty of energy—her poor mother had had to chase her all over Seattle when she was a little girl just to try to wear her out by bedtime. But today she'd had to work twice as hard to keep a smile on her face. Despite the girls totally coming to her aid the night before at the wine bar, Mia still hadn't been able to get Ford all the way out of her head as she'd tossed and turned for most of the night. Even worse, one of the properties she'd taken the CEO to was the tower house that Ford had liked so much. When the CEO said that he thought the tower was a "terrible addition" to the otherwise "decent" house, Mia had been dismayed by the relief that flooded through her, feeling almost as if Ford should be the only person to have the house. Where, she'd wondered again and again since the previous morning, was her legendary self-control?

Normally she would be more than happy to accept a glass of champagne from the first-class flight attendant and strike up a chat with whatever sexy, single businessman was sitting beside her on the plane. Today, however, she not only turned down the bubbly, but also paid more attention to the spreadsheet she was going over on her computer than the hot guy who'd slid into the seat next to her. The problem was that if she let herself get too relaxed with a glass of wine, she was afraid memories of the superhot, toe-melting kiss Ford had given her would overcome her...and leave her aching for him at thirty thousand feet.

Unfortunately, just the thought of trying *not* to think about Ford's kiss was enough to distract her from her computer screen. When the guy sitting next to her thought she was trying to make eye contact with him, he immediately asked, "So, is your trip to Napa for business or pleasure?"

She couldn't even muster up so much as a flirty smile as she simply said, "My cousin is getting married," then pointedly shifted her attention back to her computer.

What the hell was happening to her? First, she'd booted James out of the wine bar last night, and now she seemed to have lost not only the ability to flirt, but the will to do it, as well. Ford had already stolen her heart all those years ago. Was she going to give up the joy of flirting and her enjoyment in meeting new people, too?

Mia slammed her laptop closed and shifted so far in her seat that she was practically sitting on the guy's lap. "What I meant to say is that I'm Mia and this is a pleasure trip." She waved over the flight attendant for one of those glasses of champagne. "What about you? Business…" She purposely lowered her voice before saying, "Or pleasure?"

Instantly forgiven for the way she'd blown him off a minute ago, she learned his name was Scott, that he was a thirty-four-year-old sales rep for an Italian shoe company and that he'd noticed her in the airport's waiting area before the flight and couldn't believe his luck at being seated beside her. The conversation was engaging, everything he said to her was flattering and any way she looked at it, he was pretty much the perfect guy.

But as they got off the plane and she walked toward the limo waiting for her outside the small Napa Valley airport, she couldn't bring herself to care one single bit about whether she ever saw Scott again.

The limo took Mia straight to her cousin's house in Napa. Marcus Sullivan owned Sullivan Winery, a very successful vineyard and wine business in the heart of wine country. He and Nicola lived there together when his bride-to-be wasn't on the road touring the world to support her music career. Mia was amazed by the way Marcus had shifted his life around in such a huge way so that he could be with Nicola as much as possible. He ran a huge, very lucrative business, and she knew he could easily have stayed in Napa three hundred and sixty-five days a year to focus on his winery. Instead, he chose to travel the world with Nicola so he could spend his time with the woman he loved.

What, Mia wondered, had made Marcus decide to do that? Had Nicola given him an ultimatum as Ford had given her? Had she demanded that he choose her over everything else in his life or else she'd leave him, love be damned?

No, Mia thought with a shake of her head as she headed up the crushed-gravel walkway to Marcus's front door, *I can't imagine Nicola ever doing something like that.* Because when you were really in love the way Marcus and Nicola were, you just wouldn't hurt the person you loved like that. Instead, what Mia had always thought from watching her own parents' marriage was that real love meant you tried to support your partner in any way that you could, and they would do anything they could to support you in the same way.

That was the kind of man Mia was waiting for. One who put her first at the same time that she put him first, too. A true lasting partnership. Not a quick flash of heat that was doused at the first sign of a problem.

Speaking of great men, when she looked up she saw her brother Ian standing in front of her. She dropped her dress bag onto the gravel and ran into his arms.

"You made it!"

Her oldest brother was living in London running his investment business, and since his past few trips home had been canceled at the last minute, she'd begun to miss him terribly. Of course she loved her other brothers, Adam, Rafe and Dylan, but she'd always had a special relationship with Ian.

His arms were strong and steady around her as his hug lifted her off the ground. "I've missed you, little girl."

He was the only one who could get away with calling her that. Well, there was the way her father called her pumpkin. But that was it for nicknames that she would tolerate, and only because her father and brother were two of her all-time favorite people on the planet.

"I've missed you, too," she said. "So much. Please tell me you're going to move back to Seattle soon."

Normally, when she said that, he would shake his head as though there was no chance of his coming back to America. But this time he simply smiled and said, "I've got a few things to wrap up in London first."

Joy shot through her as she immediately forgot

her grumpy mood. But as she gave a happy shout while hugging him tight, absolutely thrilled at the thought of having her big brother nearby again, he said, "Don't say anything to Mom and Dad about it yet. I'd hate for them to be disappointed if my plans change."

She pulled back to poke him in the chest. "Well, you'd better not disappoint me, either."

He kissed her on the forehead, and then frowned as he finally got a look at the dark smudges beneath her eyes. "I hate not being close enough to watch over you. You're tired. What's going on?"

As close as she and Ian were, she couldn't possibly tell him about Ford. Not if she wanted to keep her big brother out of jail, because he'd surely do terrible things to the rock star if he found out Ford had hurt her in any way.

Fortunately, right then a toddler shot out of the front door, with her mother laughing as she chased her. Mia bent down and scooped up Emma. "Hey, cutie, where are you headed in such a hurry?"

Emma giggled at suddenly being weightless, then put her hands on either side of Mia's cheeks and gave her a wet smooch. *Oh,* Mia thought as she snuggled the pretty little girl close, *it's going to be so wonderful to spend the weekend with my family.* Especially when she'd arrived so off-kilter and now already felt a thousand times better.

Chloe's face lit up when she saw Mia. "You're here!" When they hugged, Chloe's new baby bump pressed between them. "We were waiting to start the party until you arrived."

Chloe had married Mia's cousin Chase a couple of years ago, after the two of them had met at this very winery when Chloe had been on the run from her dangerous ex-husband. Chase had been there every step of the way to love her exactly the way she needed to be loved, and Chloe had fallen just as hard for him. Chase was a famous photographer, Chloe was a world-class quilter and on top of that they were fantastic parents.

"Doesn't look like Miss Emma was waiting," Mia teased as she wound one of Emma's curls around her little finger.

Ian also couldn't resist stroking her soft hair. For as stern and intimidating as her nearly-a-billionaire brother could seem to strangers, Mia knew what a softie he was for little kids. Given that he'd been such a huge and influential part of his four younger siblings' lives, she didn't think it should be such a surprise to people. Being rich and powerful didn't mean you had to be a total jerk.

Well, except in Ford's case, where that was *exactly* what it meant.

When the toddler began to wriggle in Mia's arms to get back down on the ground and resume her mad dash, Chloe quickly suggested, "Emma, do you want to be the one to officially bring Aunt Mia inside so that we can start our girls' party for Aunt Nicola?"

The little girl's big eyes lit up. Standing on her

own two feet again, she reached up with her little hand to take Mia's. "Inside." Her grin showed off her four perfect teeth. "Party!"

And as Mia let little Emma pull her down the path and through the front door on determined steps of her adorably chubby toddler's legs, she knew everything was going to be okay after all.

Because with her family all around her, how could anything possibly go wrong this weekend?

Nine

Where most brides-to-be would likely want a really flashy bachelorette party, despite the fact that Nicola was one of the world's biggest pop stars and money and location were no object, Marcus's fiancée had no interest whatsoever in flashy or crazy. On the contrary, both Nicola and Marcus seemed to be of like mind in that *mellow* was what was on the menu tonight.

Mia laughed when she found out that Marcus was having his "bachelor party" barbecue on the opposite side of the house. She couldn't think of another couple who had set up their bachelorette and bachelor parties at the same place—all of the women on one side of the house and all the men on the other. But given the way Nicola disappeared twice in the first thirty minutes, Mia suspected the setup was all about the fact that the bride and groom couldn't stand to be apart from one another. Especially not on the eve of one of the most important days of their lives, when they were about to make vows of forever to each other.

Mia was sitting next to her cousin Sophie, who had another little Sullivan on her lap. Jackie wasn't quite at the walking or talking stage, but she'd clearly already had quite a big day, because all she wanted to do was cuddle when Mia asked to hold her. Jackie's twin brother was at the boys' barbecue with his father, Jake.

"I can take her back if she's getting too heavy for you," Sophie offered when Jackie's eyes immediately fluttered closed.

But Mia loved the soft weight of the baby on her lap. She wasn't yet ready for children herself, which was why having so many cousins with kids was so much fun. "You get her all the time. Don't you dare take her from me tonight," Mia said as she drew Jackie closer to breathe in her fresh baby smell.

Off mommy duty for a few minutes, Sophie relaxed deeper into the plush outdoor couch they were sitting on together and picked up her glass of wine. The view out over the vines as the sun fell in the sky was pretty darn mind-blowing. It didn't hurt that a full bottle of Marcus's finest cabernet was within reach.

"We had such a great time up at the lake with all of you this past summer," Sophie said. "Jake wants to head up to Seattle to show the kids the Space Needle. And since he refuses to accept that they might still be a little young to remember anything about the trip," Sophie said with a laugh, "I expect we'll be knocking on your door any day now."

When Mia had first heard that her soft-spoken librarian cousin Sophie had hooked up with tattooed Irish pub owner Jake McCann—and had gotten pregnant from a one-night stand, no less—she'd been pretty shocked. Especially since Sophie's nickname was Nice, and nice girls didn't usually seduce tattooed bad boys. But though they seemed very different, obviously they were an absolutely perfect fit.

Just as with Nicola and Marcus, Mia had learned from watching her cousins fall in love over the years that love didn't always make sense on paper. But it didn't have to. It only had to make sense to the two people falling for each other.

"Definitely sign me up as your tour guide for the visit. Although," Mia clarified, "I'm afraid my guide duties won't include diaper duty."

"You get used to changing them after a while."

Mia scrunched up her nose. "Right…you just keep telling yourself that, and maybe one day you'll actually believe it."

Her cousin Gabe's wife, Megan, sat down on a couch facing them. "Believe what?"

"That changing these little beauties—" she pointed at Jackie's bottom "—isn't totally gross."

"I honestly don't remember. It's been such a long time since the diaper days with Summer. Funny," Megan said as she looked down at her about-to-pop-any-second-now stomach, "I thought I was done with all of that after she was finally potty trained. But I never bet on meeting Gabe."

Seriously, Mia thought, as she sat with the girls in the glow of the setting Napa Valley sun, there was so much freaking love in the Sullivan family. All of her San Francisco cousins, and her brother Rafe, were either married or engaged. It was fabulous. She was super happy for all of them. And, maybe, just a teensy bit jealous about how perfectly all of their lives were working out.

Especially when hers was such a mess.

Mia was watching Chloe out on the grass holding Emma's hand while her daughter jumped on a mini-trampoline, when Valentina appeared around the corner. Her fiancé, Smith, was holding her hand, and before he let her go, he pulled her back into him for a lingering kiss. One that had everyone watching from the outdoor couches sighing at how sweet they were together. When Smith finally let Valentina head over to join the rest of the girls, he took over trampoline duty with Emma.

Mia's cousin Smith was one of the world's biggest movie stars, but he'd never played the star with his family, and Mia often forgot that just the sight of him sent most other women into cardiac arrest. He and Valentina had met when Valentina's sister, Tatiana, starred in the movie *Gravity* with him. From what Mia had heard, Valentina had tried her hardest to resist him but, in the end, she hadn't had a chance of keeping her heart safe. Considering the kinds of crazy things Smith had to deal with in Hollywood, it was great that Valentina was such a steady, solid person who wasn't at all interested in the spotlight.

Valentina had her cell phone to her ear as she walked past the pool onto the patio where everyone was sitting. After a really quick conversation, Mia heard her say, "Sounds great, T—see you soon." Valentina slipped her phone back into the pocket of her elegant dress. "My sister will be here soon. She says her interview ran a little long, but she's just about to leave the hotel."

Mia loved Tatiana Landon. Only in her early twenties, she was an actress on the rise, especially after her star turn with Smith. But, somehow, instead of turning into a vapid shell under the harsh spotlights of Hollywood, she remained totally sweet and unaffected.

Valentina looked great in a yellow linen dress that skimmed her curves and floated around her calves. "It's great to see you again, Mia," she said before pressing a kiss to sleeping Jackie's cheek. "I call dibs on the baby for her next nap," Valentina informed everyone as she grabbed a glass of wine from a circulating waiter and sat down beside Gabe's wife. "As long as that's all right with you, Soph."

"Of course it is," Sophie said with a smile. "What parent wouldn't want their kid to have more than a half dozen of the coolest aunts in the world who can't wait to spend time with her? And speaking of cool, here comes the woman we're all celebrating."

Nicola appeared from within the house and came out to the patio. In perfect pop-star fashion, her hair was streaked with light pink and blue, but Mia was amazed at how elegant it looked on her.

"Can I squeeze in?" She shimmied her hips into the space on the couch between Mia and Sophie. Her cheeks were flushed and her eyes were bright enough that Mia easily guessed she'd just been off on another little meet-up with Marcus.

There were more women laughing together over by the fountain, including Mia's mother; Nicola's mother; Brooke; Sophie's twin, Lori; Ryan's fiancée, Vicki; and Zach's fiancée, Heather. Mia knew she'd get a chance to spend time with all of them later, but for right now, this group of women she was sitting with was just the perfect size so that they could all easily talk together.

Nicola was stroking a gentle fingertip back and forth across the bottom of one of baby Jackie's feet as she gave each woman sitting with her a big smile. "I'm so happy that you're all here." Her blue eyes grew damp as she said, "I love having all my favorite women in one place. What do you say we get together like this every weekend?"

"There are certainly enough Sullivan weddings coming up," Mia said, "that I think we could probably pull it off."

"There's so much love everywhere in this family," Nicola agreed as everyone laughed, "that when I want to write a good breakup song, I end up having to harass my band and dancers to mine whatever messy things are going on in their lives."

"You could always just call me," Mia blurted before she realized what she was saying. She'd said it in a joking voice, but of course every pair of eyes landed on her.

"Do tell," Sophie encouraged.

Mia forced a grin she didn't completely feel. "You know the story—if he's bad news, I've got to have him."

Fortunately, instead of digging for more info, Sophie nodded her head. "Boy, do I know what you're talking about." She looked at Mia. "Jake had to be one of the biggest players on the planet when I finally decided to seduce him. Talk about bad news."

"Fortunately," Mia said, "he was smart enough to appreciate that you were the best thing that ever happened to him."

Megan raised her wineglass in a toast. "To our men appreciating us."

As Mia shifted Jackie's weight slightly in her left arm so that she could lift her glass and clink it with everyone else's, she noticed that every one of the women she was sitting with had the same happy smile. Wanting to drown the stupid sense of jealousy that they'd all found love when she was as far from it as she could possibly be, Mia took a long drink from her glass.

"I've never seen Marcus like this, Nicola," Sophie said. "He's always been so calm and steady, but today he was practically bouncing off the walls, he's so excited about finally getting to marry you."

Nicola's skin hadn't yet lost the flush from her latest secret assignation with Marcus, and now that they were talking about him, the pretty rose color flooded even more deeply into her cheeks. "I'm crazy excited, too. Sometimes—" She stopped and shook her head as if she didn't quite know how to put everything she was feeling into words. "Sometimes I wonder how I got so lucky. I mean, if I hadn't met him that night at the club, and then if Lori hadn't been choreographing my video and invited him to watch rehearsals the next day, I would have missed out on the best thing in my life."

"If not at the club that night, you and Marcus would have met another place, another way," Valentina said softly, which surprised Mia, because she would have said Valentina was more practical than dreamy. "Smith and I always talk about how the two of us circled each other in the film and TV business for years without ever actually meeting, until my sister was offered the part in *Gravity*. But I think the reason we didn't meet until last year is because the timing wasn't right, and neither of us would have been ready for the other."

"Or you all could have just followed my example and thrown yourself naked at the guy you'd been wanting your entire life so that you ended up knocked up with twins," Sophie said with a grin.

The group's laughter was accompanied by more

wine and snacks being passed around. As each fell naturally into conversation with the person next to her, Nicola shifted to turn to talk to Mia.

"It's really great to see you. I wish Marcus and I had had more time in Seattle after the last show to spend some time with you."

"And what a show it was," Mia said. "You were amazing. And you have to know how cute Marcus was out in the audience with me. He's so proud of you."

"Poor guy has heard these songs a thousand times already, at least."

"And he'd gladly sign up for another thousand," Mia said with utter certainty. "But can I ask you a question?"

"Sure," the other woman said. "Anything. Especially if you'll pass the baby over to me first."

"Nope, I'm not done getting my cuddles in yet. Besides, Valentina already called dibs on the next lap session."

"But I'm the one getting married," Nicola protested. "That should push me up to the top of the dibs list."

"Nice try," Mia said as she snuggled Jackie a little closer, "but you're still going to have to get in line for baby love."

Nothing could make a person feel better about the world than a soft, warm bundle on her lap breathing evenly in sleep. Unlike her friends, Mia had loved to babysit the little ones when she was a teenager.

Sure, sometimes they were fussy, but they were also so darned cute. Kids were yet another thing she and Ford hadn't talked about during their week together. Yes, she'd fallen in love with him, but clearly there hadn't been any real foundation to it. Not like yesterday, when he'd talked about kids running through the house she'd shown him.

Darn it, why was she thinking of him again?

"So what's up?" Nicola asked, bringing Mia back to the question *she'd* been wanting to ask.

"How do you and Marcus make things work so well? Not just that," she added before Nicola could respond, "but you make it look so easy. And I know it can't possibly be, with your busy touring and recording schedule and the demands of this vineyard."

"No," Nicola agreed with a small smile, "it definitely isn't easy. I don't know how much you know about our relationship, but we were a mess at first. A total mess, actually. I was so adamant that he couldn't handle the circus of my life that I literally kicked him out of it, even when it was the very last thing I really wanted, because I was already head over heels in love with him. But you know Marcus." Nicola's face softened even further with a look of pure love. "When he made up his mind that he could most definitely deal with the circus, he was suddenly showing up at all of my shows all over the country. How was I supposed to resist focus and determination like that? Especially when it proved how much he was willing to change his own life for me.

I'm not going to lie and say that figuring out how to make our two schedules work together is always a perfectly smooth ride, but I'll take a few bumps in the road over being without him, anytime." With that, she popped a grape into her mouth, and then asked Mia a question of her own. "Does this question have anything to do with this *bad news* man of yours, whom I'm going to assume is superhot, too?"

"Not just bad news. Old news," Mia said with a careless wave of her free hand. But obviously feeling her tense at the blatant lie, Jackie made a face in her sleep and shifted in Mia's arms. "Sorry, baby girl," she whispered before turning her gaze back up to Nicola. "I did meet a cute guy on the flight out here, though."

Nicola raised an eyebrow; clearly not about to fall for the diversion Mia was trying to throw at her. "If it takes me all weekend, I'll get you to spill the details on your secret hot guy. Although, speaking of hot guys, I just got some great news about a guest, who told me he can come to the wedding tomorrow, after all. I'll give you a hint—he's one of the most amazing rockers on the planet."

Even as Mia tried to be rational and think about the odds against *his* name coming out of Nicola's mouth, she couldn't stop a heavy feeling from coming over her. Her mouth felt dry, and it took every ounce of self-control to keep from fidgeting so that she didn't wake up the baby in her arms.

"Ford Vincent!" Nicola was so excited that she

didn't notice the way all the blood drained out of Mia's face. "I'm such a huge fan that I always get a little giddy every time I listen to him sing, and he's also really nice."

Ford might make other big stars like Nicola giddy, but Mia was anything but giddy right now.

More like sick to her stomach.

Of course Ford and Nicola would know each other. They were in the same business, for God's sake. Now that she thought about it, hadn't the two of them played some shows together before Nicola had met Marcus?

"Ford is coming here?" Mia's voice sounded hollow to her own ears. "To the winery? For your wedding?"

One dumb question after another kept falling from her lips, but she couldn't stop any of them. Not when she felt as though she was barely keeping it together. If not for the baby on her lap, she might have jumped up off the couch to go running like little Emma through the vineyard.

Nicola was giving Mia a strange look when Sophie's ears finally picked up on Ford's name. "Wait a minute," she said, echoing Mia's questions for everyone to hear, "are you telling us that Ford Vincent is coming here for the wedding? How did I not know that?"

"He couldn't come at first because of a scheduling conflict," Nicola explained. "He called my cell yesterday afternoon out of the blue and asked if the invitation was still open."

"Yesterday afternoon. Of course that's when he would have called," Mia said, almost to herself. There was no way that call could have been a co-incidence. He hadn't come after her in Miami five years ago but, all of a sudden, now he wouldn't take *get the hell out of my life* seriously. It was obvious that, with him, everything *always* had to be on his terms, and if he wasn't the one to say goodbye, then those words didn't count.

Again, Nicola frowned in Mia's direction, but So-phie's twin, Lori, had walked over to the group by then. Nicknamed Naughty to Sophie's Nice, Lori was wearing a cowboy hat and the cutest red cowboy boots with her short, strapless red dress. The women in the group were beautiful, but of them all, Lori was the most striking. Whether she was dancing onstage or getting dirty with the pigs on the farm she shared with her husband, Grayson, people simply couldn't take their eyes off her.

"You're not going to believe who's coming to the wedding," Sophie told her twin. "Ford Vincent!"

Mia was shocked when Lori gasped. Actually *gasped*. "Don't mess with me, Soph." She turned to Nicola with big eyes. "Is this for real? Is he *really* going to be here?"

Nicola was nodding and about to say something more about it when Mia simply couldn't take it any-more. "I'm just not getting what the big deal is about him. So he has some pretty good songs, but all of you have totally great men already."

"You're joking, right?" Lori said. "I love my husband to pieces, but I'm not *dead*."

"It's true," Megan murmured. "Ford is pretty darn gorgeous."

Mia watched with shock as one after the other, including the levelheaded Valentina, agreed that Ford was a special exclusion to their usual rule of not noticing other men. Of course, her tension passed through to the baby in her arms, because right then Jackie abruptly woke up, looked into eyes that weren't her mother's, and her face scrunched up into a pre-wail.

"Uh-oh," Sophie said, quickly standing and lifting her little girl onto her hip, "looks like someone's hungry. Which means her brother is probably about to give the boys trouble, too. I'll be back soon."

With no bundle of joy on her lap, Mia felt stripped naked in front of her family, with all of her stupid emotions out in the open. Which was the very last place she wanted them.

Lori turned to Brooke as she walked up to the group. "You're a Ford Vincent fan, aren't you?"

Brooke immediately made an angry face. "No. I *hate* him."

Everyone's eyes got huge, and Mia realized she needed to do some major damage control—and fast. "What Brooke means is that she hates how hot he is when she's only supposed to be thinking about my brother now."

Brooke gave her a confused look before it suddenly dawned on her that she'd very nearly given something away to the group.

"He's coming to the wedding this weekend," Mia told Brooke.

She tried really hard to keep the bitterness out of her voice, but when Brooke grabbed her arm and said, "Could you help me with my dress inside? There's something weird going on with the zipper," Mia knew she hadn't succeeded.

No doubt everyone was wondering what was wrong with the two of them, but both Mia and Brooke continued to act as if nothing was amiss until they were back inside the house and behind the locked door of Marcus's home office.

"How can he even *think* of intruding on Nicola's wedding like this? I don't care if he was invited. He should know better than to ruin this weekend for you." Brooke, who was one of the sweetest, gentlest souls Mia had ever known, looked like a general preparing to go to war. "I simply cannot wait to tear that man to pieces and then sic all of your brothers and cousins on him."

"No, please don't do that. If anyone finds out what happened between us, it will become a whole huge thing. And I'll never forgive myself if I let him ruin Marcus and Nicola's wedding."

But Brooke was right. Showing up at the open

house was one thing, but coming to a family wedding was another entirely.

"I've had enough of his little surprises. As soon as Ford gets here, he and I are going to have a rational, adult discussion about things in private. And by the time we're done, I'll make damn sure he understands that everything that was once between us will be firmly, and totally, in the past."

Ten

Though Ford was desperate to make up for lost time with Mia, he didn't want to ruin Nicola's big day, which was why he planned to slip in just before the ceremony started. Not that he thought he was *all that* anymore, but he'd been in enough similar situations to know that people tended to go a little crazy around musicians, even at the most inappropriate times.

He wasn't much for suits, but Nicola deserved his taking the time to scrub up and throw on a tie. He knew Mia would think he'd deliberately changed his schedule this weekend so that he could continue to be in her face, but while that was an awesome cosmic bonus, he truly had been hoping he could shift his packed schedule by just a few hours so that he could witness his friend make her vows.

In Ford's experience, real love was pretty damned rare. And when two incredibly busy and successful people like Nicola and Marcus were actually able to

make it work, he thought that deserved to be cele-
brated in a major way.

Billy, his bodyguard, was already waiting for him
in the passenger seat of the black Tesla they'd rented
for the day. When Ford slid in behind the wheel, Billy
said, "I love you," into his phone, then slid it back
into his pocket.

"Nice suit and tie, sir."

Ford grinned at the sarcastic compliment. "Hoping to impress a lady today and figured it was time
to pull out the big guns. How's Susan doing?"

Billy rarely had to use any force as a bodyguard
simply because he was so big and looked so scary
that people didn't dare try anything with Ford. But
being asked a question about his wife softened his
features until he was almost approachable. "She's
pretty ready to have the kid, now that we're only
four weeks out."

Ford had already picked out a great baby gift for
Susan and Billy. The highest safety-rated vehicle
on the road would be waiting for them in the hospital parking lot right after she gave birth to their
mini-me.

A few minutes later, Ford pulled into the back entrance to Sullivan Winery. Nicola had prepped the
valet for his arrival so they were waved right through.
A guy in a blue suit was speaking into a headset as
he walked up to their car. "Welcome, Mr. Vincent.
Ms. Harding wanted me to let you know that the

ceremony will begin in five minutes. Please head in via that side door."

Giving both valets a healthy tip, Ford put on a dark hat and kept his head down just in case any of the guests were still milling around outside as he and Billy made their way across the gravel lot. Nicola and Marcus would be saying their vows in a huge converted barn, painted red and renovated with enormous windows that looked out over the rolling acres of vines.

It was one heck of a spot to get married, Ford thought, as he made a mental note about the winery for the future he hoped to have with Mia.

As he opened the side door, the first notes of the "Wedding March" rang out from an old organ that had been installed in a loft in the barn. The front half of the barn had been set up to resemble an old country church, with built-in wooden pews and an aisle down the middle.

Even though the pews were full, it took Ford less than five seconds to find Mia. She was in the first row with what he guessed had to be other family members. She was wearing a dark pink silk dress that looked as though it had been made just for her, as elegant as it was sexy. She wore it the way she wore everything—including nothing at all—with innate confidence and a sensuality that made it impossible for Ford to look away.

She was standing and looking down the aisle waiting for Nicola to appear, which meant that Ford could quietly squeeze in behind her. Fortunately, everyone else's gaze was trained on the door, as well.

Though it was nearly impossible to pull his gaze from Mia, Ford made himself take a few seconds to look around. Ford had seen grooms looking green and worried at the altar but, apart from the slight impatience on this groom's face to have his woman in his arms, Marcus Sullivan looked like the happiest dude on the planet.

Years ago, Ford wouldn't have believed love was real. But now he was starting to realize that love was more powerful than anything else. More important than career, or money, or pride.

There were five guys standing to one side of Marcus, and they all resembled him enough that Ford quickly realized they had to be either brothers or cousins. He recognized Smith Sullivan, of course, not only from his movies, but also because the two of them had been in and out of a few of the same Hollywood parties over the years. They'd never actually sat down and talked, but Smith had always struck Ford as a good guy, and surprisingly normal considering his enormous fame and success.

Five women stood beside each other on the other side of the officiant, and that was when he had to do a double take. The officiant was the best damn looking woman on the far side of sixty that he'd ever set eyes on. And if she wasn't closely related to Marcus and his groomsmen, Ford would eat his shoes.

He'd known Mia's family was close, but it looked as though all the other branches of the family were, too.

Had Marcus actually chosen his own mother to marry him and Nicola?

Jesus, Ford couldn't imagine his own mother so much as even considering doing that for him. Her society circle would never get over something so unconventional. Nor could he imagine a world in which he'd want her to. When he finally got married, frankly, he wasn't even sure his parents would attend, not if they had another more socially important event to attend. Besides, they'd probably be terrified that he'd show up to his own wedding in leather, with his tattoos on display.

What, he wondered, would it be like to be part of a family like the Sullivans?

An emotion he couldn't immediately define rose up and momentarily choked him. As a songwriter, his brain automatically searched for the right word.

It wasn't jealousy, exactly. More like…yearning. Not just for the woman he still loved to love him back, but for a family that actually cared about him in the way the Sullivans cared about each other.

Mia was standing close enough to him that he could have so easily given in to that desperate yearning by slipping his arm around her waist and pulling her into him. As it was, her exotic scent was driving him halfway to crazy. But, damn it, he'd promised himself he wouldn't do anything to ruin Nicola's wedding—and the fuss Mia was bound to put up if he dared touch her like that would surely do that. But, just then, it was a hell of a job to hold himself in check.

Soon, however, he knew his control was bound to break…

A collective gasp rang out in the barn as Nicola appeared on her father's arm.

"Oh, my gosh, she looks so beautiful," Mia whispered to herself.

And as his friend moved slowly down the rose-petal-strewn aisle with her father, Ford agreed wholeheartedly. Nicola was naturally a very pretty woman, but today she was positively glowing in finely sewn white lace with a crown of small white and yellow flowers over her pink-and-blue-streaked blond hair.

The gray-haired man at Ford's back shifted to see better, which shoved Ford's hips into Mia's gorgeous backside.

Caught, he thought with a grin as he felt her body heat up in front of his, before going stiff.

Lord, he'd never forgotten what it was like to have her in his arms, the inferno of passion and sweetness that nothing else he'd ever experienced had come close to touching. Not winning a half-dozen Grammys in one night or playing for a crowd of two hundred thousand people in Japan.

Fortunately, no one but Mia seemed to have noticed Ford yet, and he instinctively pulled his hat down further as he turned toward the front of the barn. That was when he saw Marcus break away from the group up front. With long strides, he met Nicola and her father in the middle of the aisle.

After shaking Marcus's hand, her father pressed a kiss to his daughter's forehead. Nicola's eyes were clearly wet as she hugged her father, but after Marcus took her hands in his and pulled her into him for a passionate kiss, she couldn't stop smiling.

Even though the bride and groom had just broken wedding protocol, their guests went wild with applause, not to mention the loud whistles from the groomsmen. Even Mia, despite her obvious shock that Ford was behind her, couldn't help but clap her hands and laugh as the bride and groom finally pulled apart and pretty much ran together up to the front of the barn to make things official.

With the crowd still laughing as they sat down, Ford turned to whisper to Mia, "You're beautiful."

With her eyes still on the bride and groom, she leaned toward him and whispered back, "And you're a sneaky dirtbag."

Only through sheer force of will did Ford keep himself from laughing out loud. Because just sitting next to Mia Sullivan made him feel happier than anything else ever could.

Eleven

"Dear friends and family, we're so glad you could be here with us today to celebrate the love between Marcus and Nicola."

As Mary Sullivan addressed the wedding guests, Mia worked to fight back the tears that were already starting to come. The problem was that just watching Nicola walk down the aisle had been enough to get her choked up, and when Marcus had been too impatient to stop himself from running down the aisle to steal his bride away from her father...well, could there be any more beautiful example of just how much he loved her?

Mia had never been a crier, not when she'd learned as a little girl that if she wanted her brothers to include her in their adventures, she'd better suck it up when she fell off stuff and got hurt. But she'd decided long ago that at family weddings she was allowed to break her no-crying rule. They were always highly

emotional experiences for her, and by the time the
bride made her appearance and the vows were spoken, Mia was inevitably lost in emotion.

Today, it wasn't the crying she objected to. It was
letting any part of her guard down around Ford. Because being in a heightened emotional state was a
terrible place to be with him sitting next to her.

She should be stone cold around him. Or she
should remember to be angry so that she kept her
walls up. Both of those reactions would have made
sense.

Anything made sense right now but feeling as
if it was too *much*, too *good*, too *right* to be sitting
this close to him.

No. She needed to stop focusing on Ford. Today
was about Marcus and Nicola. If she couldn't help
but cry, c'est la vie. The important thing was that
her tears wouldn't have a single thing to do with the
man who'd had the nerve to sneak into the barn and
squeeze in next to her in the already-crowded pew.
Heck, by now, she felt as if she was practically sitting on his lap…and she refused to admit to herself
just how downright sexy that thought was.

Focus, Mia!

With laser precision, she trained her gaze on her
cousin, knowing Marcus had never looked happier.
She was so happy for him, especially considering
how much of his own life he'd put on hold when her
uncle Jack had passed away and Marcus had taken
over the reins of the family to help raise his seven

younger brothers and sisters. Every single person in the barn could see the way he looked at his bride, as if she was absolutely everything to him.

It was an expression she regularly saw on the faces of her cousins and her brother when they looked at the women they'd fallen for. But, she found herself thinking, for the very first time she'd recently seen that look in a more personal way. But where?

Suddenly it hit her: it was *exactly* how Ford had looked when he first saw her walk into the tower on Friday morning!

Oh, God…she couldn't be right about this. She had to be spinning out from a combination of things: one drink too many on Friday night with the girls, and not enough sleep, and a stressful workweek, and all the emotion here in the barn.

And yet, before she could stop herself, pure shock at the thought that it might be true had her turning to look directly at Ford for the first time since he'd slid in beside her.

Do you really feel that way about me?

As if he'd been able to read her mind, his dark eyes immediately held hers. The heat—and emotion—in them held her completely still while she could have sworn he answered back.

Always.

Somehow, Mia managed to drag her gaze away. She forced herself to keep breathing slowly and evenly until she got her heart rate back to normal. That had always been her problem with Ford: when she was this near to him, her brain went haywire, straight into crazy-town, where rock stars who regularly hopped into multiple beds in a single night actually wanted to be with one woman for the rest of their lives.

Sure, she knew her cousins Smith and Ryan were such big stars that they could have bed-hopped forever if they'd wanted to, rather than both being happily engaged to awesome women. Still, the worlds of movies and professional sports never seemed to be quite at the *sinning* level of rock stars. In point of fact, off the top of her head, she could think of half a dozen rock-and-roll tell-alls that had been written by groupies detailing just how rampant nonexclusive sex was in the music business.

And no wonder sex fairly poured off the rock star sitting next to her, given how devastatingly sexy he was in his dark suit and tie, with the scruff he often wore on his chin freshly shaved, and a hat pulled down low over his slightly-too-long dark hair.

What woman wouldn't throw herself at him? Once the wedding guests realized he was here, Mia wouldn't be surprised if otherwise sane women started throwing their bras at him.

As if he knew she was cataloging each separate element of his sexiness factor, out of the corner of her eye she could see him grin. Clearly, he thought he was winning this round between them.

But Mia had already vowed not to let him win one more thing where she was concerned. Filled with renewed determination, she used every last ounce of focus to tune back in to what her aunt Mary was saying.

Instead of speaking to the wedding guests, Mary extended one of her hands to Nicola. "As soon as I spoke with you that first night when you met my son, I knew that you were going to change his life in the most wonderful ways." Mary then took Marcus's hand, and the three of them held on to each other as she said, "Oh, honey, I—" When she became too choked up to continue, Mary laughed softly through her tears and said, "I think it's time for you and Nicola to say your vows."

Neither Marcus nor Nicola had even spoken yet, but Mia was already wiping away the tears spilling down her cheeks. She could feel Ford's eyes on her, but she didn't have a prayer of holding her emotions in check for another second, even if she knew he was planning to prey on her weakness afterward.

Marcus and Nicola turned to face each other, both hands linked. There had to be more than three hundred wedding guests looking on, but Mia got the sense that her cousin and his bride were aware of only each other. Marcus lifted Nicola's hands to his lips for a kiss before she began to speak.

"The night we met," Nicola began in her melodic voice, one that easily carried throughout the barn due to all her years onstage, "your mother told me that you are one of the best men she's ever known. And then she said I would be safe with you." Nicola looked back at Mary. "Thank you for doing such a beautiful job raising the man I'm going to spend the rest of my life loving with all my heart and my soul." Mary smiled through the tears that she was wiping away one after the other.

Nicola turned her gaze back to Marcus and said, in a voice that trembled with love and wonder, "All the greatest love songs in the world could never come close to expressing just how much I love you. And every day I promise to try to love you even more than I already do."

Marcus threaded his hands into Nicola's loose waves and dragged her in for a kiss that nearly set the old wood barn on fire. And thank God he did, because at least that gave Mia a few seconds to try to corral her freely flowing tears. She wasn't the only one losing it, given all the sniffles and sighs coming from the people all around her.

Just then, Ford reached out to gently wipe away one of her tears. His hand lingered on her cheek a few beats too long, long enough for her to feel that the current between them was still superstrong, no matter how much she wished it were otherwise.

Right then, she wouldn't have been able to bring herself to move his hand away, but for the first time, he didn't push his luck. And when he took his hand from her skin, she felt the loss deep within.

Looking back up at the bride and groom, Mia saw they were standing so close that Nicola's wedding dress had tangled all around Marcus's legs. "The moment I set eyes on you," Marcus said, his deep, resonant voice filling the barn, "I knew you were the one. And every moment since, I've fallen more in love with your intelligence, your talent, and most of all, your amazingly beautiful heart. I never truly understood what *forever* meant until I met you."

This time Nicola was the one lifting her hands to his face, to bring him closer for another kiss. Mia had been to at least a dozen weddings in the past few years—weddings that were fun and happy events, but where everyone was so careful to follow the rules. Only at her cousins' weddings were those rule books tossed out the window. Love was the only thing that mattered, and the *I do's* would happen in their own good time.

As Marcus and Nicola turned back to his mother so that she could finalize their vows and proclaim them husband and wife, Marcus grinned and said, "And thanks again, Mom, for saying exactly the right thing to Nicola on that night when she was wondering if she should be leaving the club with me."

The guests swung back again from laughter to tears as, in a voice that rang with pride and love, Mary Sullivan finally declared, "I now pronounce you husband and wife. And," she said with a wide smile, "you may now kiss the bride. *Again*."

All of the wedding guests erupted into applause as Marcus and Nicola kissed yet again. As soon as the bride and groom had begun to make their way back

down the aisle, with their groomsmen and brides-
maids following, Mia grabbed a fistful of Ford's
black suit and yanked him close enough to whisper,
"We need to talk. Now."

Twelve

Ford gladly let Mia pull him out through the barn's side door and across a brick patio into a small outbuilding. The storeroom was dark and smelled like leather and old planks of wood, but there was a skylight in the peak of the roof that let in the sunlight.

Light that streamed over Mia's glossy hair like a halo.

"You blindsided me at the tower house on Friday, but now that I've had some time to think, I've decided it's long past time that I give you a piece of my mind." She narrowed her eyes. "And don't even think about leaving until I'm done."

"There's nowhere I'd rather be," he said honestly. "And no one I'd rather be with."

He saw the effect his words had on her before she took a step away from him, one hand over her heart as if that would be enough to keep what he felt for her from getting in.

"That right there is one of the big problems I have with you. You're so good with words. Too good. I was twenty-three years old when we first met. The tattoos and leather pants would have gotten me more than halfway there, but how could I not fall for every word that fell out of your mouth, whether you were singing them or saying them? For a long time I beat myself up for being so stupid, so naive—but then I realized something." She looked resigned as she said, "I don't think there would have been very many women who *wouldn't* have fallen for you just the way I did."

"*You* had me more than halfway there with your slinky silver dress and gorgeous eyes," he told her, "but you weren't the only one who fell for more than just looks, Mia. You're not only beautiful. You're intelligent, too. Spirited. Driven. There are a million beautiful women out there, but there's never been anyone like you."

Mia made a sound of disbelief. "You're a walking musical encyclopedia, so I know you know that Joni Mitchell song where she sings about *pretty lies*. Like I just said, you're a master of them, Ford. But they only work if the woman you're with still wants to believe in roses and kisses from pretty men like you." She shook her head. "I'm way past that now."

"Nothing I've ever said to you was a lie. Not then. Not now." But she'd already made it clear that more pretty words weren't going to help his cause, so he ripped past them to say, "And neither is the fact that neither of us has ever had this deep or strong a connection with anyone else."

"Trust the rock star to turn *hot sex* into a *deep connection*."

"The hottest sex I've ever had," he agreed, "but now who's lying, Mia? You know damn well what we had was more than that."

"Only you would be so certain that I've never connected with another man."

"If that guy existed, you'd have married him."

She shot back, "I didn't marry you."

"You didn't marry me because I was an idiot. And if I thought there was a chance in hell that you'd say yes to marrying me now, I'd drag you out to have Marcus's mother marry us in the middle of this vineyard with your whole family here to be a part of it."

He watched Mia's beautiful, full lips open slightly in shock. "Stop it! Stop saying things like that to me."

On Friday, he hadn't come close to saying everything he needed to. Today, he'd risk it all, including his pride.

"You're right. Setting myself up as your anonymous buyer was the wrong thing to do. It was pulling my same old bullshit. But I wanted to come to Nicola's wedding long before I knew you were related to Marcus." She looked surprised at his admissions, and when she didn't immediately shut him down again, he hoped she was finally ready to believe that what he was saying was true. "I'm a changed man, Mia. And hopefully I've learned enough this time around to admit when I'm wrong, when I've screwed up…and to try not to repeat the same mistakes I made five years ago."

But these frank admissions weren't enough, because she shook her head and took a step back from him. "I can't do this again, Ford. I just can't."

"Tell me why. Tell me why you can't believe that I love you. Tell me why you won't believe that I never stopped loving you. Tell me why you won't listen when I tell you that I'm sorry for what I did five years ago, so damned sorry that I've replayed what an idiot I was in my head at least a thousand times."

Ford hadn't just fallen for Mia because she was beautiful and she made him laugh. He'd fallen in love with her strength.

Strength that she now used to make sure she didn't let him in.

"Miami was—" She took a breath so deep it shook her chest. "It was horrible. Walking in on you backstage with that stranger touching you was like being stuck in a nightmare I couldn't wake up from."

"Mia." He started to reach for her to soothe away the remnants of that nightmare, but she quickly put up a hand to stop him.

"You said you wanted to know why, and I can't get my brain to work right when you're touching me."

Filing that accidental admission away for later, Ford said, "I do want to know why. I can't stand to see you standing here in pain and know that I did that to you."

"Don't give yourself too much credit, rock star. Like I said, I was young and stupid and willing to believe in fantasies that could never be real."

"I hadn't touched anyone else in that week after I left Seattle. And that girl in Miami, I swear she didn't mean anything to me."

"Wow, a whole week without a groupie in your bed," she said in a sarcastic tone. "Do you think that makes what you did any better? Do you think that makes you less of a jerk?"

"No, I don't. Not anymore. Back then, I was an immature kid who dug his heels in and backed himself into a corner and tried to tell himself he was right about what he'd done for way, way too long." Ford let out a harsh breath. "But now I know that I never should have left you with the ultimatum that if you weren't all in, it meant you were out."

"So you *do* know what you did."

"*Now* I do," he told her, "but back then, when you didn't jump at the chance to go on tour with me, I was sure it meant you didn't love me the way I loved you."

"You asked me to give up everything in my life, and barely gave me fifteen minutes to say yes and pack and get on the bus." Her eyes flashed with hurt. "You acted like your life was the only one that was important. That my family, my career, my own dreams were just a footnote to the Ford Vincent show, and I was supposed to feel lucky to be a part of it."

"Everything I thought I wanted was coming to me fast and easy and on a silver platter. Fame. Money. Recognition. And then, out of the blue, there you were. I'm not telling you this to make excuses. There are none for what I did or for how long I tried to convince myself that I was right. But I need you to know that I would never ask you to make a decision like that again."

"Okay," she said slowly, the very first time that she'd actually seemed to take in one of his apologies. "But it wasn't just seeing the naked girl on your lap that hurt me. It was more than the way you belittled my career and life in Seattle. *You* hurt me, Ford."

"How?"

But he knew how, didn't he? Because when she'd given him an opening to change in the tower house on Friday morning, he hadn't taken it. And when she sighed this time, he sensed that she'd let down most of her walls. She didn't seem to be particularly angry with him anymore, and the sarcasm was gone now, too.

But disappointment remained.

Unfortunately, he knew from personal experience with his parents that disappointment wasn't a step up from angry. It was a wound that went so much deeper.

"So many of my cousins have fallen in love this year," she told him. "My brother Rafe, too. I've only watched from the sidelines, but something I've seen over and over again with each of them is that they trust each other. With everything, especially the parts of themselves that they've never been brave enough to share with anyone else. I know you and I were young, and I'm not saying you weren't in a crazy position with your career and personal life all zooming up in the same moment, but even though you said you loved me, you never shared any more of yourself with me than you did with your fans every night from the stage."

He knew it hadn't been any easier for her to say all of this to him than it was for him to hear it. "If you'll give me another chance, Mia, I promise I won't screw up this time."

"I—" Her eyes were big and clearly conflicted, but then he watched them fill with a sad determination. "I'm sorry, Ford. I think it's great that we've finally cleared the past. And I want you to know that I forgive you for everything that happened five years ago, even for the way you blindsided me at the tower house on Friday, and then again today during the ceremony. But it's time for me to move on with my life." She paused and looked him directly in the eye. "Without you."

Thirteen

Mia was halfway to the door when Ford reached out and slid an arm around her waist to stop her. The blood was pumping in his veins at the thought of opening himself up to her. It would be easier to continue to keep his feelings about his family hidden.

Easy…and empty.

Five years ago, she'd given him everything—not just her body, but her heart and soul, too. But he'd been scared shitless to do the same. He needed to find a way to fight that fear now.

Or he'd lose her.

"The reason I hate the name Rutherford is because my parents gave it to me."

He felt her shock at his sudden statement, and the way he'd just made his feelings about his parents perfectly clear to her in one simple sentence. That shock was what held her where she was in his arms a few seconds longer, her back to his front.

"Rutherford is the son they'd planned to have. Blue blood. Privileged. Top of the class in French. English literature. Polo. Lacrosse. Rutherford was supposed to attend an Ivy League school, graduate with top honors, then proceed to acquire a law degree."

He'd never said this much to anyone else about his parents. Journalists had probed like crazy over the years, but he'd never given them so much as a sound bite. But there was a big difference between telling his story to *Rolling Stone* and finally sharing it with the woman he loved. So even though each word felt like gravel in his throat, and every instinct in him said he should stop and protect himself the way he always had, Ford knew he only had this one chance to prove to Mia that he could change for her…and that he could now give her what he'd been unable to give her before.

"I remember everything you said to me about how close you are to your family, and I just saw what love means to the Sullivans. It means *everything*. And that's obviously what Marcus and Nicola are going to give each other. Absolutely everything, nothing held back, not out of pride or any other reason." His hand shook where it lay across Mia's stomach. He needed her now to hold on to and was glad that she hadn't yet tried to move away from him. "Rutherford never had a chance in hell of finding love. Not with his parents, and not with anyone else. I wasn't even ten when I figured out that all that kid was ever going to have was money and status and ice-cold emptiness. That's when I became Ford…and I vowed to never, ever let myself turn back into the machine my parents had tried to create with nannies and tutors and endless lists of what was and was not appropriate."

Finally, Mia turned to face him, and he wasn't sure she realized she was still in his arms as she asked, "Do you honestly believe they're not impressed with you? You're one of the biggest rock stars in the world, and it didn't happen because you're part of some industry machine. It's because of how *good* you are at what you do."

She was so beautiful and so earnest in her belief that any parent would be proud of him, that he was sorely tempted to kiss her. But now that it looked as though he'd finally made some headway, he knew better than to blow it with an unwanted kiss.

"My career is inconsequential at best, a total embarrassment at worst. The sons of my parents' contemporaries are stockbrokers and gallery owners and run charities."

"But you give away a fortune every year, probably to those very charities."

He raised an eyebrow at her admission that she knew something about his life.

"I'd have to be deaf and blind not to hear and read the news, but I just don't see how your parents could miss the fact that they have a truly remarkable son." She rolled her eyes as she belatedly realized what she'd said. "I mean that from a career achievement point of view, of course. Because even when I hated you, I couldn't quite bring myself to hate your songs."

Compliments were a dime a dozen for Ford. But hearing Mia call him remarkable meant more than a million accolades from his fans ever could.

"My parents dislike every single song I've ever written and performed," he said with perfect certainty. "Rock music breaks every rule I was bred to follow. Hell, even bringing an oboe into a string quartet is pushing it for them."

Her mouth tipped up a teeny bit in each corner as she said, "And you love breaking those rules, don't you?"

He smiled back at her. "I first picked up an electric guitar to hurt them the way they'd hurt me. And the honest truth is that the first time I turned that amp up to eleven and hit the A chord so that it shook the walls all the way down to the formal dining room, where they were having a dinner party, is still one of my favorite memories. I had no idea music would save my life by finally giving me something to love. But even though it saved me for so many years, I realized too late that it isn't enough."

"You have millions of fans. Everyone around the world loves your songs. How can that not be enough?"

"Because music can't tell me when I'm being a self-obsessed jerk. Music can't light up my day with nothing more than a smile. Music can't love me back. And—" he paused to gently caress her cheek "—music will never be *you*."

Back when they were lovers, Ford had been amazed by the way Mia could let herself be strong in one moment, then soft and pliable the next. Today, with her emotions running high from the wedding, he sensed that he could easily push her into not just another kiss, but so much more. Ford desperately wanted to feel her bare skin against his, needed so badly to hear those beautiful, breathless sounds she made when she came apart in his arms.

But he needed a future with her more than he needed a few fleeting moments of pleasure that would surely end with all of her walls back up.

"I want us to start over fresh, Mia." He reached out to tip her chin up with his finger so that she had to look him in the eye. "No ultimatums this time. I know you're going to need time for me to convince you that I can be the man you need me to be."

"You're serious, aren't you?" She looked truly shocked by her realization that he meant every word he'd said to her since Friday morning. "You actually *didn't* set up the showing at the tower house to mess with me for a laugh, did you?"

"I've never been more serious about anyone or anything in my life, Mia. I want you back."

"Why do you keep pushing when I've already said no so many times?"

"Because what I see in your eyes, and what I feel

in your touch, have both told me something else entirely."

She turned her cheek into his palm for a brief, beautiful moment, before she drew herself away from him. "I heard what you said about giving me time to think about things, but I know you. You're like a dog until you get your bone. And I can only imagine what you'll do to make your case once we're both out there at the reception. So since I *really* don't want anyone in my family to know that we were once a very, very brief item—because then I'll be bombarded with a trillion questions I don't want to answer—how about we make a deal?"

"What do you have in mind?"

"Now that I know you're truly serious about buying a home in Seattle, I'll agree to be your Realtor again. As a bonus, it means we'll have a bona fide reason to know each other outside of this wedding, because I really don't want to have to lie to my family about not knowing you at all when I'm pretty sure they'd all see right through that."

"Won't they wonder why today is the first time you've mentioned that we're working together?"

"I'll tell them we had a client confidentiality agreement, which, considering you came to me as an anonymous client, I'd say we did. And that I just cleared it with you that it's okay for me to talk publicly about our business arrangement." She poked him in the chest. "But if you don't stop looking at me like that in public, they're going to figure out that there's more than business between us."

He'd just told her he wouldn't push too hard, that he wouldn't give her ultimatums. God, though, it was hard not to reach for her again, not to kiss her to prove to her exactly how good they were together.

"How am I looking at you?"

"Like I'm Little Red to your Big Bad Wolf."

"Well," he said slowly, "I do want to eat you."

She was half laughing as she shook her head at his completely distasteful joke. "Do we have a deal or not?"

If he hadn't noticed the wicked gleam in her eyes growing brighter and hotter during the past few minutes they'd been verbally sparring, he would simply have agreed with her initial suggestion. But he knew neither of them would be satisfied with that.

"One kiss, Mia." He let his words—and the heat that came with them—sink in before he added, "One kiss and I'll be your dirty little secret. Although, once you agree to marry me, you're going to have to tell a few people."

"See, I knew you'd do this. That you'd tell me you weren't going to push in one breath, then immediately start talking about my marrying you in the next."

"You're right. I'm sorry."

She looked utterly taken aback. "You are?"

"I am," he said. "Now, about that kiss to seal the deal."

Her laughter was utterly unexpected and amazingly beautiful. All he wanted to do for the rest of his life was find new ways to make her happy.

"You and your obsession with getting a kiss out of me. You're really pushing your luck, rock star." But even as she said it, he could read the anticipation in her eyes. "Fine. You can have one kiss, but—" she lifted a finger to make sure he heeded her condition "—no tongues."

He wanted her so badly that it took his brain longer than it should have to make sense of what she'd just said. "Did you just say *no tongues*?"

"I promised myself that we'd have this little air-clearing chat today without my tongue ending up in your mouth."

Jesus, just flirting like this with Mia was crazy hot. Especially because her voice was growing huskier with every word she spoke even as she informed him that he'd need to keep the kiss to a simple peck on the lips.

"What about my tongue ending up in *your* mouth?"

"Nope," she confirmed as her lips yet again fought the battle against smiling. "But if you're not up to a tongueless kiss—"

"I'm definitely up for the challenge," he interjected. "Give me any challenge at all, Mia, and I'm going to rise to meet it."

Her eyes darkened further as she clearly began to understand that he meant it. And as she grabbed his tie and yanked him against her so that she could control their kiss this time, the chorus of Leonard Cohen's famous song "Hallelujah" began playing in his head.

Mia had tried to lie to herself for five years about how much Ford had meant to her. But it was pretty much impossible to keep up the ruse when he was right here with her, his mouth only a breath away, his eyes dark with desire as he waited for her to press her lips against his.

She was still reeling, not only from having him so close to her during the beautiful wedding ceremony, but also from what they'd shared with each other today. Finally, they'd addressed the past. The wounds weren't anywhere near completely healed yet, of course, but now that she'd said her piece, she knew that healing could truly begin in earnest.

But as important as dealing with their past in an open and honest way was, it was what he'd told her about his name and his parents that had truly been a shock. And even more than what he'd shared with her were his reasons for sharing that had sent her way off-kilter.

He wanted to start over fresh.

But could they really?

Would she ever really be able to believe that they wouldn't eventually end up exactly where they had the first time around?

And, more to the point, regardless of what the

answers were, how could she possibly do anything right now but close the distance between them for one more kiss?

His mouth was so warm and soft against hers that a sigh of pleasure escaped her before she could stop it. There was absolutely no reason that Ford's lips simply brushing back and forth against hers in a mesmerizing pattern of heat should be so arousing. But with every sinfully sweet brush of his mouth over hers, she fell deeper and deeper into the sensual spell that only he had ever been able to weave around her. And when his mouth moved from hers to create a path of heat across her cheek and then her jaw, she didn't even consider fighting the instinct to tilt back so that he could press more kisses down her neck, then into the hollow of her throat.

One of her hands was still clenched on his tie, holding him tightly against her, but her other hand had slipped into his dark hair of its own volition. Arching into the sweet pressure of his mouth on her skin, she heard Ford's low groan of pleasure as if from a distance as he cupped her hips in his hands and dragged her even closer.

The scratch of his teeth over her bare shoulder sent shudders through her. *"Ford."*

"I'm not breaking your promise," he murmured against her skin before pressing his lips over the slight ache he'd just created, then roaming with lips and teeth—but no tongue—across her collarbone to her other shoulder, where he took another nip.

She'd been so sure that abiding by her promise to keep tongues out of the kiss would also keep it from sending her senses into overdrive. But, oh, how wrong she'd been.

Because of all the kisses the two of them had ever shared, this one was quickly becoming the absolute hottest.

Fourteen

"Hi, I'm Tatiana. We met briefly last night at the party." Tatiana Landon seemed a little nervous as she said, "You're Ian, right?"

Ian Sullivan looked down into a face so beautiful it actually made his chest ache just to look at her. Ian had met Tatiana's older sister, Valentina, at his cousin Gabe's wedding in Lake Tahoe. Valentina and his cousin Smith had just become engaged over the holidays and Ian had been surprised that his movie star cousin had managed to find true love in the middle of his Hollywood world filled with paparazzi and on-line gossip columns. Last night, Ian had finally met Tatiana when she'd arrived late to Nicola's bachelorette party. They'd been quickly introduced before the girls had pulled her over to their side of the barbecue. He'd shaken plenty of hands last night, but the feel of hers had stuck with him for some reason he hadn't wanted to dissect.

Did she really think there was a chance in hell that he wouldn't know who she was when the Oscar buzz around her performance with Smith Sullivan in *Gravity* was so big that even a guy like him—who very rarely made it out of a conference room and into a movie theater—could miss it? Or was this just some cute little act the starlet put on with strangers?

Not for the first time, Ian thought how different Tatiana and her sister, Valentina, were. Smith's fiancée was long and lean, with an exotic air about her. Valentina's younger sister, on the other hand, was small and curvy, with an air of innocence that had a guy wanting nothing more than to see what it would take to get her to sin. Even the dress Tatiana was wearing was understated, as if she was trying to make sure she didn't draw any attention away from the bride. Of course, as a movie star, she obviously craved the spotlight, so he figured she must have another reason to dress so conservatively. No doubt it was another of her actress tricks to try to convince people that she didn't have a huge ego so that they'd be even *more* likely to give her whatever she wanted. He'd learned plenty of those tricks the hard way, living with his ex-wife.

Ian made sure none of his speculations were evident as he said, "It's nice to see you again today, Tatiana."

"It was such a beautiful wedding, wasn't it?"

The dreaminess in her eyes told him that she believed wholeheartedly in love and forever. Ian had also believed in it once, until his own marriage had gone straight down the tubes. He was happy for his cousins, for his brother Rafe, and he hoped his other siblings all found great people to fall in love with, too. But for himself, Ian couldn't imagine a world in which he'd willingly marry again.

"Marcus and Nicola are both good people."

Tatiana's eyebrows went up. "I take it you're not a big fan of love?"

Well, this wasn't what he'd expected from the beautiful star. Not even close. He figured she'd be so busy positioning herself in the best possible light that she wouldn't notice anything about anyone else.

Intrigued despite himself, he said, "I have no doubt that the two of them are in love."

"So if it's not love that bothers you, it must be marriage?"

Ian couldn't think of the last time anyone had been this in his face about love and marriage. His business associates and male friends never talked about relationships. And with the women he casually saw, he deliberately kept pleasure to a no-strings-attached policy.

Rather than directly answering her intrusive question, he asked her one to which he could already guess the answer. "How old were you the first time you dressed up in a wedding gown?"

Her answering smile was so bright, and pretty, that he could have sworn the sun had been behind a cloud until now—even though rationally he knew that the Northern California sky was as blue and cloud-free as ever.

"I was probably four or five. My mom had the most amazing wedding dress with lace and satin and sparkles. Even though I could have ruined it, she always let me play in it." Her smile widened. "Plus, she had satin-covered shoes, a tiara and long white gloves with ribbons that ran from the inside of the wrist to the elbow. Well, her elbow, but my shoulder." Tatiana gave a happy little sigh, as though the memory was precious to her. "It was awesome wearing her wedding dress, like being in a fairy tale, except for the fact that my dog never turned into a prince when I kissed him."

As he listened to her tell him about her childhood, it was nearly impossible to remember that she was a movie star with the entire world falling at her feet. Still, she'd asked him point-blank for his thoughts about love and marriage, and he hadn't yet finished making his own point.

"How often do you think those fairy tales come true?"

She tilted her head and thought about it for a few moments. "I hope," she said in a soft voice, "that they come true all the time."

Very few people had ever made Ian speechless, but Tatiana Landon had just done it inside of five minutes. Ian could break down his life into a handful of moments when everything had turned on a dime. The day his father had told their family he'd lost his job. The day Ian found out that everything his ex-wife had told him had been big lies.

And, strangely, right now, as he stood in the middle of his cousin's vineyard with a young, stunningly beautiful movie star.

Fortunately, he'd had a chance to see *Gravity* and hadn't even come close to forgetting the way Tatiana's love scene with his cousin Smith had steamed up the screen. Sure, they were both great actors, but despite the fact that there clearly wasn't anything between Smith and Tatiana in real life, it still meant that Ian couldn't quite believe that Tatiana was as innocent as she seemed.

No virgin could drip with the kind of sensuality that he—and millions of viewers around the world— had witnessed in that movie.

She gave him another smile, one that was just a little bit crooked, an imperfection that only managed to make her more beautiful. "Actually, I didn't come to quiz you on your feelings about love and marriage. I was wondering if you'd seen Mia. The photographer needs all the Sullivan girls together soon and since I'm not a Sullivan I volunteered to find her."

Since he'd actually been looking for Mia, too— even from the far end of the pew he'd thought something hadn't seemed quite right about his sister during the ceremony—he said, "I'll help you look for her."

The two of them headed toward a grove of oak trees where the bartenders were doing a steady busi-

ness serving up Marcus's wine. A light breeze over
the vineyard blew Tatiana's scent to him. It was
fresh, sweet and so mouthwateringly tantalizing
that he had to work to push back his arousal at simply being near her.

"Mia said you flew in from London for the wedding. When do you need to go back?"

"First thing tomorrow morning."

"I only have today away from the set in Boston,
too. But next time I'm in London, it will be nice to
know there's family there. Well, almost family, since
as soon as Valentina and Smith say their own *I do's*,
you and I will be…" She scrunched up her gorgeous
face and turned to him to ask, "What exactly will
we be since I'm Valentina's sister and you're Smith's
cousin?"

It was hard to think of this gorgeous woman next
to him as family. Just as hard as it was to remember
that she was even younger than his sister. Both really,
really good reasons for Ian not to have any business
mentally stripping her dress off her.

But, Lord, even those extremely rational reasons
couldn't stop him from wondering just how soft her
skin would be…and if she would taste as good as
she smelled.

"We'll be cousins by marriage."

They'd made it to the grove of oak trees by then,
but neither of them could spot Mia. Ian looked out
over the rolling, vine-covered hills. "She's been to
enough of these weddings to know pictures are about

to be taken," he mused aloud. "Where could she have gone?"

Tatiana touched his arm to get his attention. Their eyes met as undeniable electricity rushed between them. With the sun shining down over her, he could see her pulse beneath the skin on her neck. He couldn't remember the last time he'd wanted a woman this much. Not even the woman he'd so foolishly married.

As she pulled back her hand from his arm, the heat from her touch remained as she asked, "Do you think she could be with Ford Vincent?"

"Ford Vincent is here?"

"He slipped in the side door right before the ceremony started and sat next to Mia. Didn't Marcus mention he was coming?" When Ian shook his head, Tatiana said, "Nicola seemed pretty thrilled that Ford was able to rearrange his schedule to make it. I kind of figured he might come in incognito like that—with a hat on—since people can get weird about musicians."

"Don't people get weird about actors, too?"

"They do, but even the other engaged and married girls were freaking out last night about Ford coming today. He's *really* popular. Even more than Smith is, I think."

Worry for his sister was the only thing that could possibly have made Ian forget his attraction to Tatiana. Because, damn it, Ian could only imagine what moves the *really popular* rock star was trying to pull on Mia. He knew his sister wasn't exactly innocent, but though Ian had taught her enough martial arts as a teenager to make sure she could fend for herself, he couldn't risk leaving her alone with some guy who thought he was God's gift to women...and likely acted accordingly.

Where, Ian asked himself, would he go if he were a rock star intent on getting some from a pretty girl he'd just met at a wedding? Especially if he wanted to get her alone before the rest of the guests discovered that he'd arrived and started making a fuss over him?

Ian scanned the grounds with narrowed eyes. It didn't take him long to realize that the outbuilding beside the barn would be the perfect place for an impromptu post-wedding tryst.

"Over there."

His long legs ate up the distance between the oak grove and the barn, but though Tatiana was at least a foot shorter and was wearing heels, she kept up with him. "Why do you think they're in that small building?"

"I'm a guy. I know how to think like scum."

She reached for his arm again as if she were trying to slow him down. "Wait. What if she *is* in there with Ford? Maybe we shouldn't just barge in on them like that. I mean, if I were trying to steal a little private time with someone, I know I'd be upset if my sister interrupted us."

It didn't even occur to Ian that Tatiana could have a point, or that Mia could have made the *choice* to fool around with the rock star today. He yanked open the door to the storeroom so hard that it slammed back against the wall...to find exactly what he'd feared.

The bastard didn't just have his hands all over Mia, but his mouth was on her, too. Ian immediately saw red as any appreciation he might have had for the guy's music disappeared.

"Get your filthy mouth off my sister."

Fifteen

Clearly, neither Mia nor the scumbag who was holding her had heard the door open or Tatiana's gasp of shock at finding them wrapped around each other like that. The horrible picture of the guy pawing and drooling all over his little sister was seared into Ian's brain. He didn't think he'd ever be able to forget it.

"Ian? Tatiana?" Mia's skin was flushed, and her eyes remained slightly unfocused. Until, suddenly, she seemed to realize just how bad things looked.

He was halfway to lunging across the storeroom to wrap his hands around Ford's throat, when Mia pulled out of the guy's arms and grabbed Ian. With surprising strength, she dragged Ian outside, away from both the storeroom and the guy whose face he wanted to rearrange with his fists.

"I can't believe you just did that!"

She looked furious and embarrassed, but Ian was so lost in his haze of fury that he couldn't stop himself from shooting back, "I can't believe you were in there with that scumbag!" He worked to pull away from her grip. "You and I are going to have a long talk about just what the hell you were doing. After I tear him to pieces."

"No!" She yanked harder on his suit jacket, until they both heard a seam begin to tear. "I can handle him myself."

"*That* was handling him?" He cursed, one harsh word that landed between them like a stone. "Did you *want* him to kiss you?"

She paused just a little too long before sighing and saying, "You know what, I actually think I did."

"Damn it, Mia, it's my job to protect you. You've got to let me—"

"If you do one more thing to embarrass me like that again, I'll never forgive you."

His sister had always been full of fire, but he'd never seen her quite this worked up.

"You know I'd never do anything to hurt you," he tried to explain in a calm, reasonable voice, "but I can't let anyone else hurt you, either. And I've known guys like him. They're too rich, too famous, to think they need to play by anyone else's rules. You've got to understand that."

Now that they were standing behind a large hedge of roses, she'd relaxed her grip on his jacket. "I do understand. And you've been the best big brother ever, but what happened between me and Ford isn't something I want anyone to know about until I've figured out exactly how *I* feel about him. This re-action you're having is exactly why I didn't tell you about him five years ago."

Ian's blood pressure shot all the way back up as he asked, "You didn't just meet him here today? What the hell, Mia? How could you keep a secret like this from me?"

"Because if you're acting like this when I'm a twenty-eight-year-old woman who runs her own very successful business, how do you think you would have reacted five years ago if I'd come to you and said, 'Guess what, big brother, I'm dating a rock star. Can I have your blessing?' Would you have actually given it to me?"

He had to admit, "I would have hunted him down."

"Exactly. And the thing is, you've always let me make my own mistakes in business, but never with love." She put her hand on his arm more softly now. "I know you don't ever want me to get hurt, but what if falling in love sometimes means risking enough to royally screw up a few times along the way?"

Intellectually, Ian knew his sister was an adult. But there was a big difference between respecting her business acumen…and accepting that she could lose her heart to some douchebag without his being able to protect her.

"So you've been together with him for five years without any of us knowing?"

"No. It was just one week. I didn't see him again until a couple of days ago."

"What does he want now that he's back?" She'd never been able to lie to him, and he knew how difficult it must have been for her to keep her relationship with Ford a secret for so long. "Apart from the obvious," he added in frustration.

"A fresh start."

Ian wanted answers to a dozen other questions, but there was really only one that mattered. "Are you in love with him?"

His sister sighed again, and there was so much pain in the sound and in the expression on her face that Ian put his arms around her.

"Once upon a time I thought I was, and then I was sure that I wasn't." She laughed against his chest, but there was no humor in it, only frustration. She pulled back to look up at him. "Have you ever wanted to punch and kiss someone at the same time?"

He grimaced. "Please don't remind me of that kiss again if you want me to keep my fists from changing the entire shape of his face."

"Does that mean you've agreed to stay on your side of the ring today?"

This time he was the one sighing. "For today," he agreed against his better judgment. "But no promises come twelve-oh-one."

She laid her cheek against his chest and snuggled against him the way she always had from the time she was a baby. When their mother hadn't been able to get her to stop crying as a little girl, all Claudia Sullivan had to do was hand Mia over to Ian and she'd immediately settle.

They'd always been so close that he hated to think she'd kept something from him because she thought he couldn't handle it. Then again, he'd never really talked with her about his marriage, had he? Both of them had kept secrets from each other, and even now that she'd told him hers, he was still keeping his.

Forcing down his frustration at not being able to deal with Ford the way he wanted to, Ian gently brushed her hair back from her forehead. "Looks like they're ready for pictures with you now."

Mia stepped back and smoothed a hand over her dress. "Do I look okay?"

"You're absolutely beautiful, as always, little girl."

"And you're devastatingly handsome, as always, big brother." As the two of them headed toward the area where the wedding photos were being taken, she said, "I wonder what Tatiana is thinking after what she saw?"

Damn it, he'd left her behind with Ford. But when he turned to look back at the storeroom, he didn't see either of them nearby.

"Why were you and Tatiana together, anyway?" Mia wanted to know.

"She was looking for you."

He thought he'd been careful to speak about Tatiana with absolutely no inflection, but when Mia shot him a sidelong glance heavy with curiosity, he knew he'd blown it.

"She's beautiful, isn't she? And so nice I keep forgetting to be awed by what a great actress she is. Hey," she said when he didn't immediately respond, "wouldn't it be amazing if Valentina married Smith and then you and Tatiana—"

"She's not my type."

Mia actually laughed at that one. "Are you kidding? She's *everyone's* type. Heck, I'm not the least bit into women, and I can barely keep from drooling over her every time we're together." She patted his hand as if he shouldn't blame himself for already being a lost cause. "I want to see you happy, too, you know."

With that, she pressed a kiss to his cheek and left him to go be in the pictures.

"Any chance you can fill me in on what just happened there?" Ford asked.

Tatiana had a feeling she looked just as shell-shocked as Ford. Not because she'd been particularly stunned to see him and Mia kissing, but because *she* had wanted to pull Ian Sullivan into some other private room on the property and kiss *him* just like that.

She'd never felt that kind of electric attraction to anyone before. His eyes were such a deep brown she'd gotten lost in them, even as she'd felt as though he was looking all the way down into her soul. Men had always taken a distant second place to acting. She rarely dated, and when she did she often wished she was alone with a script or spending time with her sister. But for the first time in her life, she understood the kind of desire that could drive people to do crazy things...like wanting to head back out into the throngs of wedding guests to find Ian again so that she could give him a kiss that would, hopefully, blow both of their minds.

"Mia's brother was looking for her."

"No wonder he looked like he wanted to kill me. I'm surprised he hasn't come back to tear my heart out through my throat."

Tatiana felt she should be honest with him. "Actually, based on the way he was acting when he found out you two might be together, I'm kind of surprised, too."

"I knew I was going to have to deal with her brothers soon, anyway. But it's a small price to pay if she'll have me."

Wow, he was going to willingly offer himself up to Ian, Adam, Dylan and Rafe, who were all tall and full of muscles and had grown up wrestling with each other? Tatiana sighed at how sweet it was that Mia obviously meant that much to him.

"I'm Ford, by the way," he said as he reached out to shake her hand. "I've seen your last couple of films. Great work."

She smiled at him. "I like your work, too."

There wasn't even a speck of attraction between them. Only the immediate bond that she sometimes felt with other people who were also in the public eye. Life for people with their kinds of careers was great in lots of ways, of course, but it could be difficult, too, when simple things like going out to get a cup of coffee could be a trial. Sometimes Tatiana felt like a hermit holed up in her house because it was easier to order in than put on makeup and an outfit and do her hair just to go out to pick up some milk.

"I don't think he's got anything against you personally," she said, wanting Ford to understand. "It's more that he wants to protect his sister against *all* men."

"Smart guy." He took off his hat and left it on a rough wood shelf. "Care to join me in what could very well be my last drink if Ian Sullivan gets a hold of me?"

Laughing, she took the arm he held out to her as they stepped into the very bright sunlight. "I've seen you onstage. You're pretty fast. I think you could outrun him if you really needed to."

"How about you distract him so I can get a head start? Maybe drag him into a dark corner and kiss him senseless before he realizes I've gotten away?"

The deep flush that took over her cheeks instantly gave away just how much she liked that idea.

"Ah," he said in a gentle voice, "so that's the way the wind blows."

"No," she said, shaking her head. "Ian and I just met last night. And we've only spent fifteen minutes together today."

"Sometimes," he said very seriously, "fifteen minutes is all it takes for your entire life to change."

But before he could say anything more, a large group of wedding guests finally realized they had a rock star in their midst, and he was completely surrounded by fans.

Sixteen

For the next half hour, the photographers took dozens of shots, first of the girls and then the whole family together. Mia had hated knowing how upset Ian had been about what he'd seen, but though his nickname for her was *little girl*, he had to know that she wasn't one anymore, right?

Of course, it didn't help that just a few minutes after Mia had made it to the group for pictures, Ford finally emerged from beneath his dark hat. The wedding guests' excitement began as murmured exclamations of surprise, but soon escalated to the point that Mia was starting to feel as if she was in the audience at one of his shows.

Nicola, thankfully, didn't seem the least bit bothered by the commotion, and when she jokingly rolled her eyes and said, "Musicians always have to be the center of attention, don't they?" everyone laughed. Everyone except Ian, who looked as though he was barely restraining himself from tearing across the grounds to pummel Ford.

Mia shot Ian a pointed look between photos. *You promised.*

Today only, was the reminder he sent back in just as pointed a manner.

Through it all, Mia was pretty darn pleased with how well she pulled off her relaxed smile. Only Ian and Brooke knew just how hard she was working to manage it.

As the second photographer declared the family photo session complete, Brooke pulled her aside. "How are you doing?"

"Well," Mia said in a low voice that she made sure wouldn't carry to anyone else, especially her other brothers, "I'm glad I gave Ford a piece of my mind."

In the way that only a true friend could, Brooke raised her eyebrows as she scanned Mia's slightly messy hair, obviously well-kissed lips and flushed skin. "It certainly looks like you gave him *something.*"

"I didn't break my promise!" Mia insisted. "There were no tongues in either direction."

"Well, that's good, I guess," Brooke said in a rather doubtful voice.

"It was good," Mia had to admit. So good that she could still feel the imprint of his lips all across her skin. "At least until Ian walked in on us."

Brooke's eyebrows shot up twice as high as they'd been before. "How is Ford still alive?"

Mia looked over to where he was signing autographs, and a rush of heat moved through her when he lifted his gaze to meet hers. "He might not be for long," she murmured, even as she found it impossible to look away.

Just then Rafe walked up to them and slid his arm around his fiancée. "Something's up with Ian. He looks like he's going to burst a vein soon. And when did Ford Vincent get here?"

Mia didn't even have to send her friend a save-me look before Brooke pressed a very distracting kiss to Rafe's lips. "I think we're supposed to sit down now for the meal and toasts." Before Rafe could say anything more about Ian, Brooke began a rather one-sided conversation about how beautiful the wedding had been and how pretty the vineyard was and how she was absolutely starved. Anything and everything she could think of to keep Rafe off the scent.

Yet again Mia thought as she squared her shoulders to prepare herself to make it through the rest of today's wedding in one piece, she owed Brooke big-time.

Although when she found her name card at one of the family tables up at the front of the reception area, Mia decided she might very well have to kill Nicola and Marcus, even though it was their special day…

Because, as luck would have it, they'd seated her right next to Ford.

When Ford realized where he was seated for the meal, he hoped Nicola's new husband wouldn't take it the wrong way when he planted a big wet one on her later.

From his seat, he could see Mia standing a few yards away downing a glass of champagne and was immediately taken by the urge to lick the stray drops of the fizzy liquor off her lips. But he'd always wanted to meet her family, and despite knowing that at least one of her brothers already had it in for him, Ford wanted to take the opportunity to get to know as much about Mia and the Sullivans as he could.

Fortunately, he had an ally in Tatiana, who found her place card at his table, as well. Unfortunately, a moment later, so did Ian, who was seated directly across from Ford.

Weddings were always full of surprises. Usually, however, those surprises came in the form of a drunk old auntie who was later found facedown in a hedge, snoring off the bottle of whiskey she'd smuggled from catering. Just think how long people would talk about this one if Mia's brothers gave him what he deserved.

"I'm a big fan of your music," the guy pulling out a chair beside Ian said to Ford as he held out a hand. "I'm Ryan Sullivan, and this is my fiancée, Vicki Bennett."

"Great to meet you both," he said before he finally realized why the guy looked so familiar. Ford had been so focused on Mia during the ceremony that he'd completely missed recognizing the best pitcher in the National Baseball League in the lineup of groomsmen. "I was blown away by your pitching last season. And," he said as he realized who Vicki was, "I'm also a fan of your sculptures."

She was obviously pleased that he knew of her work. "Thank you."

Ford was struck by how comfortable Vicki and Ryan were with each other, how they looked like two people who were clearly meant to be together. Had they ever screwed things up, or had everything in their relationship gone perfectly from day one?

"Are you two going to be the next Sullivan wedding?"

"Maybe," Vicki said with a laugh. "Unless Zach and Heather or Smith and Valentina or Brooke and Rafe beat us to it. But we're used to waiting," Vicki said with an easy smile as she leaned back into Ryan's arms and looked up at her fiancé. "Aren't we?"

"I fell for her when we were fifteen," Ryan explained to Ford, "and then she went and married some other guy. Fifteen years later, I finally convinced her we were meant to be."

"I love your story," Tatiana said. "It's so romantic."

Ford was still digesting the knowledge that Ryan and Vicki had been apart three times longer than he and Mia had, and they'd managed to make it work, when the final two open seats were taken by another couple.

"Wow," the woman said as she realized Ford was sitting there. "Hi."

When Ford grinned back at her and said, "Hello," the guy with her tugged on her long, sleek braid and quickly covered her mouth with his as if to remind her whom she belonged to. Their kiss was short, but hot, and when they finally came apart, she was both flushed and laughing.

"You're such a Neanderthal," she said in an affectionately irritated voice before turning back to Ford. "I'm Heather, and this is Zach."

He shook their hands. "Ford. Nice to meet you both."

Just as the first course was served, Mia finally took her seat beside him, a fresh glass of champagne in her hand as she shot Ian a clear warning glance. What, Ford wondered as he turned to smile at her, had she said to her brother to keep him from going for his jugular?

And was there any chance that the reason she wanted him in one piece was because she'd decided to give their relationship another go?

"Looks like Nicola and Marcus are playing matchmaker," Zach commented as he looked at Ian and Tatiana and then Mia and Ford. "Wouldn't it be something if it worked?"

Heather shoved a roll into his mouth. "Eat this so your mouth will be too full for you to say anything else that will make everyone uncomfortable."

"Okay," Zach said after he took a bite and shoved it into his cheek, "but once the meal's over, you're going to have to think of something else I can do with my mouth to keep me quiet." Heather rolled her eyes, but by the way her cheeks flushed, Ford could see that she wasn't at all averse to the suggestion.

"Actually," Mia told the group, "Ford and I already know each other. He's one of my clients."

"Since when is he one of your clients?" Ian's fork clanging hard on his plate punctuated his question.

"Since Friday."

Ian turned his glare to Ford. "You're going to buy a house in Seattle?"

Ford was six-two and worked out to stay in shape for his three-hour shows. Still, he figured Ian had to have a couple of inches and probably thirty pounds on him.

"I'm looking forward to moving out of hotels and into a house for once."

"Anyway," Mia said with another pointed glance at her brother as she speared a lettuce leaf with her fork, "I showed him a great piece of waterfront on Friday with an absolutely perfect house already built. It even has a tower room."

"A real stone tower?" Vicki was clearly intrigued.

Mia looked so pretty as she smiled at the other woman without any of her guards up. "It's really amazing," she said, "but I have a few other properties to show him, too, so he can weigh all the options."

He pushed his plate aside as he turned to her. Right now, he had an appetite for only one thing. For *her.* "You said it's the kind of house and yard that a bunch of kids would be happy playing in, right?"

"Right."

"Then I don't need to weigh any other options." Though they were surrounded by her family, right then it felt as if they were the only two people at the table. "I've already made up my mind about exactly what I want."

He could see from the look in her eyes that she knew he wasn't just talking about the house, but the moment was ruined when a loud burst of laughter from the next table over sent her back into business-only mode.

"Are you saying you want to make an offer on Alana's house?"

"Yes."

She was already reaching for her phone when he put a hand over hers. "Monday is soon enough. Today I want you to enjoy being with your family." The pulse at her wrist was racing by the time he reluctantly lifted his hand away and turned back to everyone at the table. "Where are you all from?"

"There are Sullivans here from San Francisco, Seattle, New York and Maine," Ryan replied. "We all get together periodically for family reunions and, of course, weddings."

"Got any good stories?"

"Where do you want me to start?" Zach said with a laugh. He nodded toward Mia. "Especially with Ms. Wild Child over here."

Mia raised an eyebrow in Zach's direction. "Just

remember I've got a few stories of my own about you, Speed Racer."

"I'm just saying it'd be pretty hard to forget that night at the lake when you were only six years old and didn't tell anyone where you were going." To Ford, he said, "She hid out in the woods for hours just so she could scare the hell out of us guys when we hiked past. I thought Uncle Max and Aunt Claudia were going to lose it when we brought her back home wearing a big smile on her sneaky little face." But it was clear that Zach was totally impressed with her even before he added, "To my fearless and determined cousin."

And as everyone at the table raised their glasses in a toast to Mia, Ford finally got some insight into a family who were always there for each other, no matter what. Because even now, when Ian and Mia were clearly at odds, Ford could see that it didn't diminish their bond in the least.

"Whatever happened to that guy you were with at the last wedding?" Ryan asked Mia. "Bob? Or was his name Buddy?"

Ford watched her very carefully as she replied, "He was just a friend."

"Come on, you must have someone up your sleeve. You always do."

Ford was pretty sure Vicki kicked Ryan under the table. Clearly, she'd picked up on the sparks between Mia and her client even if her fiancé hadn't.

"You know she can't answer that with her big

brother sitting here," Tatiana said before Mia could respond. Clearly, she'd appointed herself peacemaker for the table.

"True," Zach agreed. "Odds are, you'd hunt the guy down before sunset, wouldn't you, Ian? It's what I always wanted to do when I found some guy sniffing around one of my sisters. Got a few good ones in on Jake, actually, when I found out he'd knocked up Sophie. Never had a chance to slug Grayson, though, for dating Lori."

Ian's eyes were sharp as daggers and cold as ice as he stared across the table at Ford. "If I ever meet a guy and find out he's hurt my sister, I'm going to make him pay in the most painful way possible."

Mia cleared her throat and when everyone finally turned back to her, she was smiling at them over the rim of her glass as if she didn't have a care in the world. "Actually, since you've asked, Ryan, I had a date on Friday night with this *great* guy I met while I was out jogging."

"You went out with someone Friday night?" Rationally, Ford knew he had no claim on her, but just the thought of anyone else touching her, kissing her, made him crazy. "After you showed me the house?"

Mia nodded, looking extremely pleased with herself. "I did. And then on the flight here I met someone else on the plane."

"Damn it, Mia—"

Marcus's voice came through the speakers, cutting Ford off right before he broke his promise to

Mia and outed them as more than just business associates. "Thank you for being here with us today to celebrate the best day of our lives so far."

Still not able to think straight, Ford couldn't focus on what Marcus and Nicola were saying to their guests as he pulled out his phone.

DID YOU LET EITHER OF THOSE GUYS TOUCH YOU?

Her expression remained smooth as she read his message, then typed a message back and shoved her phone into her bag.

IT'S NONE OF YOUR BUSINESS IF I DID OR NOT.

He was about to respond first and think later, when Billy tapped him on the shoulder. "Your guitar is tuned and ready for you."

"Thanks, Billy." Ford knew he needed to pull it together to give Marcus and Nicola his gift before he left on his private plane to head to Los Angeles for his show.

Hopefully, Mia would understand whom he had really written the song for…

Mia had been certain she could find a way to resist Ford's sweet words, even his kisses.

But no matter how hard she worked to brace herself, she already knew she'd never be able to resist him performing one of his songs. It wasn't just how sexy it was when he was onstage that got to her...it was the fact that he loved singing and playing guitar so much that touched her so deeply.

"We're going to let all of you loose on the dance floor soon," Nicola said to her guests, "but before we do, I'm beyond excited to let you know that a friend of mine is going to give us a really special treat."

Ford was undeniably gorgeous as he wound through the tables to pick up his guitar.

"Nicola and Marcus, I'm really glad I could be here today to witness the kind of love that we're all hoping for. I wrote this song yesterday, so I apologize if it's still a little rough, but know that it comes straight from my heart. It's called 'Everything I Need.'"

Yesterday? Had he written the song after they'd seen each other again?

Mia knew firsthand that Ford didn't need to hide behind a stage or a microphone, and a shiver went through her as he began to play the acoustic guitar. Just as she had the very first time she ever heard him sing, right from the first few lines of his new song about finding forever in a kiss, a touch, a smile, Mia couldn't keep her eyes from closing as the music washed over her.

"Everything I need
You're everything I was looking for

When nothing else could have made me whole
There you were
Everything I need
When I'm holding you tight against me
I lose myself in you every single time
Because you're everything I need
Don't ever stop
Don't ever stop
Don't ever stop being everything I need."

She didn't hear the sighs of the women all around her—frankly, she wasn't aware of anything other than Ford singing a song that spoke straight to her heart. But as every new lyric hit closer and went deeper, though it would have been smarter to try to block out at least one aspect of his performance, she couldn't keep her eyes closed. She simply had to watch Ford as he poured his heart and soul into the music.

Music that almost felt written just for her.

And, my God, he wasn't just beautiful as he sang for Marcus and Nicola. He wasn't just utterly captivating, a natural-born performer.

This was who Ford was at his core.

She'd known it all along, of course, but now, as she watched him create magic with talent that very, very few other people possessed, she had to wonder how a home in Seattle could possibly fit into the life of a man who belonged onstage. And how could he even think about giving up being on the road?

Because while she knew millions of people could listen to his music through headphones or on the radio, the truth was that just being in the same room with Ford while he was singing to you—whether out in a vineyard with three hundred people or in a stadium with a hundred thousand—was a life-changing event.

When the final chord rang out, as everyone applauded and Ford kissed Nicola on the cheek and shook Marcus's hand, Mia excused herself from the table and slipped out toward the vineyards to a spot where no one in her family and none of the other wedding guests could see her.

She needed a little while out under the bright blue sky away from everyone to recover from what Ford's song, and his earlier kisses in the storeroom, had done to her.

She could accept, now, that she still wanted him, even that there was desperation and intensity to that wanting. But she didn't want to have to acknowledge anything more…certainly not all the emotions and the dreams that his song had sent pouring through her.

And yet, even though she'd told herself she wanted to be alone for a little while, she was neither surprised nor displeased when she heard footsteps in the dirt behind her. She turned to face him, knowing neither running nor pushing him away was an option anymore.

"Your new song is beautiful."

"After I saw you on Friday, the song wrote itself." He took her hands in his and lifted them to his lips for a kiss. One that moved her just as much as his music had. "I need to leave now for Los Angeles, but I'll be back in Seattle on Monday morning."

She'd miss him, she realized as she watched him start to walk away, and a pang landed deep in her belly. Five years she'd lived without him, and now, after less than twenty-four hours with him, she was already hooked again.

Hooked enough to reach for him at the exact moment that he turned to reach for her, too.

"Damn it," he said, "I keep saying I'm not going to push you, but I can't leave without kissing you goodbye."

"And I can't let you go without kissing you, either," she admitted.

Just as his song had been emotional yet edgy, so was the goodbye kiss they gave each other. His hands fisted in her hair and hers tightly gripped his shoulders. His tongue dived deep and hers met his just as violently. Her teeth nipped at his lower lip and he dragged her closer so that he could give her more of everything she so desperately craved.

And yet, even in the middle of the storm that was rising up between them in the vineyard, Mia knew their hearts weren't just thundering against each other's chests from passion…but from the deep and relentless power of the emotions swirling around them.

When they finally made themselves draw away from each other, neither of them was breathing steadily. "Have fun with your family, Mia. They're great. You don't know how much I envy what you have with them." He pulled her back against him for one more quick, breathless kiss, and then he was gone.

And as Mia sank back against a rock wall to catch her breath, she knew that wanting Ford, needing Ford, was no longer in question.

The only question left was, what was she going to do about it?

Seventeen

Mia was unlocking the front door of Sullivan Realty on Monday morning when Ford stepped out of a black car parked at the curb. His jaw was scruffy with stubble and he looked as if he hadn't had much more sleep than she'd had over the weekend. And yet, she couldn't remember him ever looking better.

Nor could she remember the last time the butterflies had started flying around in her stomach like this, even though she'd been expecting to see him this morning. They were going to put in an offer on the tower house.

"Good morning."

His dark eyes were full of appreciation as he let them run from her head to toe and then back again. "It is now."

She was extremely glad that they were the first two people in the office this morning, so that she didn't have to make introductions and pretend that everything was perfectly normal between her and her client. Not when nothing about her relationship with Ford felt remotely normal…and not when she'd made a pretty darn big decision since she'd last seen Ford at the wedding.

He followed her into her office, and as soon as the door closed behind him with a soft click, she said, "I know we have business to take care of this morning, but before we do, I want you to know that I've made a decision about us."

It had made so much sense in the middle of the night when she'd been going over and over things in her head. There was no question that they'd come to a crossroads at the wedding. The only question had been which way to turn. Last night, she'd been certain that she'd figured out the best way to deal with their ongoing attraction without making the mistake of letting herself get in too deep again.

"I think we should sleep together."

"I haven't gotten much rest since Friday," Ford said, "so I'm pretty sure I just hallucinated. You're saying that we should sleep together?"

For all the sense that her decision had made in the middle of the night, now that he was standing here in front of her, she had to silently remind herself why she was doing this. Fighting their attraction was going to be impossible. Not only that, but for a sensual woman like her, it was downright unnatural not to want the pleasure that she knew Ford could give her.

Having a sex-only affair was the only thing that made sense.

"I can't see any reason why we shouldn't have some fun, casual sex when you're in town and I'm free for a night or two."

"How many reasons do you want?" Ford asked. "Because I'm pretty sure I could fill up your entire workday with them."

Damn it, why couldn't he behave like any other guy would and just jump at the sex? "Hold on a minute," she said, letting her anger match his. "You've angled and strategized for a kiss every time we've been together, but now that I'm offering a heck of a lot more than a kiss, you're saying no, you don't want to have sex with me."

"Of course I want to have sex with you, Mia. And if I thought I could get to your heart that way, you'd better believe you would be naked and coming beneath me right now." Every inch of her skin went hot and damp at the crazy-hot picture he'd just painted, even as he growled, "How many times do I have to tell you I want more from you than your body?"

"So unless I'm ready to declare my love to you and promise you forever, you aren't going to touch me again?" she growled back instead of answering his question. "Is that what you're trying to tell me?"

"No," he said as he reached out to drag her against him, "that's not even close to what I'm trying to tell you."

Quicker than a heartbeat, his mouth beat hers to

the kiss that she'd been aching for since the wedding. At the winery in Napa his kisses had been gentle, almost reverent, as he'd roamed her skin. But nothing was soft about the way they devoured each other now, her teeth making hard nips against his lower lip, his tongue tangling with hers in a rough dance of pure lust. His hands covering every inch of her that he could reach, from breasts to hips, hers tightly gripping the dark strands of his hair to keep his mouth right where she wanted it.

Moans, gasps, pleasure, pain—Mia relished every single second of *feeling* again. Even though, as both of them continued to drag each other deeper into burning heat and desperate need, somewhere way back in her brain, a warning flag was waving, trying to tell her that this was a bad idea.

Oh, yes, she knew that what they were doing was a terrible idea, knew that she shouldn't be giving this much to Ford, shouldn't be giving him any part of her at all when he'd hurt her so badly once before. But right now, knowing better was taking a distant backseat to the sinful pleasure of arching into his large hands as they cupped her breasts through her silk shirt.

The shrill ringing of her assistant's phone only one wall away hit her like an ice-cold bucket of water.

It wasn't just a bad idea to be kissing Ford because he had the power to hurt her in a way no one else did—but also because they were in her office and her employees were going to start coming through the front door any second now.

Was she trying to be caught with him?

Her heart was scrambling as she let him go and stood on her own, her legs threatening to tremble like a bowl of Jell-O.

"We've built up sleeping together again to be too big, too important. As far as I'm concerned, the best thing we can do is get this out of our systems so that we can both move on with our lives."

"Once I have you again, Mia, I won't *ever* get you out of my system. And I won't give you up. Not to some guy you meet jogging, or on a plane, neither of whom deserve you."

Desperately fighting against the part of her that wanted to belong to Ford and believe that it was possible to have a forever with him, she said, "You say you want more than my body, but then you talk about me like I'm some toy you can be jealous and possessive over."

"Damn it, you're right." She watched him run a harsh hand through his dark hair as he paced her office like a lion trapped in a cage. "I'm saying everything wrong. Doing every goddamned thing wrong."

Was it crazy that a part of her wanted to go to him, to comfort him?

Yes, this Ford-inspired crazy was precisely why she'd suggested a casual, sex-only relationship. Because that way they could focus on their bodies and pleasure…and things like comfort and support—

and emotions that could be stripped raw and utterly destroyed—wouldn't be on the table at all.

"Five years ago, even though I was an immature punk who didn't know which way was up, I was smart enough to love you. How could I not?" Ford paused to make sure he didn't say it all wrong again. "But after we split up, I spent way too long pretending I could be a man on an island again. That I wasn't thinking of you every second we were apart."

"Ford—."

"Let me try to get at least one thing right." He moved back across her office to reach for her hands. "After seeing the way Nicola and Marcus are with each other, I think I finally figured something out. Something big that we skipped in our week together. Something between sex and love that holds everything together." He looked down at where their fingers had naturally threaded together, then back up into her beautiful eyes. "Every second since I saw you again, I've been consumed with wanting you. But sex isn't enough, Mia. It wasn't enough the first time around, and it won't be this time, either."

"But what—"

"Friends." He knew the truth of it in his bones and could see from the look on her face that it was resonating with her, too. "I need to be your friend this time. And I hope you'll eventually be able to trust me enough to be mine, too."

He'd written more than a dozen love songs, but

FREE Merchandise is 'in the Cards' for you!

Dear Reader,

We're giving away FREE MERCHANDISE!

Seriously, we'd like to reward you for reading this novel by giving you **FREE MERCHANDISE** worth over $20. And no purchase is necessary!

You see the Jack of Hearts sticker above? Paste that sticker in the box on the Free Merchandise Voucher inside. Return the Voucher promptly...and we'll send you valuable Free Merchandise!

Thanks again for reading one of our novels—and enjoy your Free Merchandise with our compliments!

Pam Powers

Pam Powers

P.S. Look inside to see what Free Merchandise is **"in the cards"** for you!

W
e'd like to send you two free books like the one you are enjoying now. Your two books have a combined price of over $10, but they are yours to keep absolutely FREE! We'll even send you 2 wonderful surprise gifts. You can't lose!

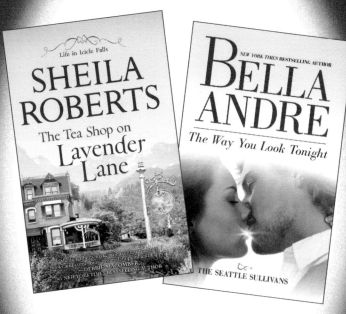

REMEMBER: Your Free Merchandise, consisting of **2 Free Books** and **2 Free Gifts**, is worth over $20.00! No purchase is necessary, so please send for your Free Merchandise today.

Get TWO FREE GIFTS!

We'll also send you two wonderful FREE GIFTS (worth about $10), in addition to your 2 Free books!

Visit us at:
www.ReaderService.com

YOUR FREE MERCHANDISE INCLUDES...

2 FREE Books **AND** 2 FREE Mystery Gifts

FREE MERCHANDISE VOUCHER

2 FREE
BOOKS
and
2 FREE
GIFTS

Please send my Free Merchandise, consisting of
2 Free Books and **2 Free Mystery Gifts**.
I understand that I am under no obligation to buy
anything, as explained on the back of this card.

194/394 MDL GGER

Please Print

FIRST NAME

LAST NAME

ADDRESS

APT.#   CITY

STATE/PROV.   ZIP/POSTAL CODE

NO PURCHASE NECESSARY!

ROM_215_FM13

he'd never truly understood until he'd fallen in love with Mia just how complicated it really was. Or how incredible it was that somehow, if two people with their own dreams and worries, hopes and fears, worked really hard and were really lucky, they might actually make it work.

At the same time, he'd continually reminded himself that *complicated* didn't have to mean *impossible*. Look at Ryan Sullivan and his fiancée, Vicki, who had made things work after fifteen years apart. And, of course, there was Marcus and Nicola, who hadn't let his winery or her music career tear them apart.

"I told you this weekend that I forgave you, Ford, and I meant it, but—"

Before she could say anything else, both of them heard two voices carry down the hall to her office.

Still, instead of her immediately dropping his hands, he felt the lightest brush of her thumbs over his knuckles before she let him go and walked over to her desk to sit down behind her computer. It gave him hope that she wasn't unaffected by what he'd just said about wanting to be her friend. The best one she'd ever have.

"Over the weekend," she told him as she slipped on thick, black-framed glasses that only served to highlight her beauty, "there was a great deal of interest in the tower house. Since I'm not at all surprised by this, and I know that Alana and her ex-husband would like to close things as quickly as possible, we should finalize the details of your offer so that we can send it over this morning." She pressed a button on her phone. "Good morning, Orlando. I'd like to introduce you to my new client. And please bring the paperwork for the tower house with you."

Though her manner was all business, he could still see the heat and desire—along with her lingering surprise over the idea of the two of them working on their friendship before hopping back into bed with each other—simmering just beneath the surface.

"My employees are used to dealing with famous and wealthy clients. But just like the guests at Marcus and Nicola's wedding, I suspect they still might be a little bowled over by you."

"I'm always happy to meet fans. They're the reason I'm where I am."

"No," he was surprised to hear her say in a fervent voice, "your talent is the reason you're where you are. Like I said," she added with a small smile, "even those of us who couldn't stand you still liked your songs."

Orlando came through the glass door carrying a large folder. "Here are the files you need, Mia. I've flagged the various—" When he realized Ford was standing next to him, the folder fell from his hands, scattering papers all around his shoes. "Oh, my God, you're Ford Vincent. I'm your biggest fan. You're a genius. I can't believe you're actually standing here in front of me."

Ford took the young man's hand to shake it. "It's great to meet you, Orlando."

Mia gently put her hand on her assistant's shoulder. "Thank you for bringing the papers in."

Orlando turned, dazed. "Papers?" A few seconds later, his pale skin turned a dark shade of red. "The papers. I'm so sorry." He was already on his knees trying to pick them up, but his hands were shaking too hard to do anything but make more of a mess.

"Actually, Orlando, I think we can take it from here," Mia interrupted. "But I'm sure Mr. Vincent would love a cup of coffee, black with extra sugar, thank you."

Loving the fact that she still remembered how he liked his coffee, Ford knelt down with Mia to help pick up the papers.

"In the year he's been working with me, I've never seen him like that." Mia looked bemused by her assistant's reaction. "Do you ever get tired of it?"

He barely restrained himself from reaching out and tucking a loose strand of hair behind her ear, knowing every one of her employees was surely watching them now through the glass. "When you're a kid dreaming, you don't know enough to think about anything but the glory. If I had understood more than that five years ago, Mia, maybe I wouldn't have screwed things up so badly."

Her gaze locked with his for a moment before she abruptly shook her head. "I know our earlier conversation was interrupted, but let's stay focused on the house for now, okay?" She quickly gathered up the rest of the paperwork, and then went back to her desk to reorganize it. "I wish I could tell you it was overpriced, but—"

"Could you live in it?"

"You already asked me what I thought of the house, and if you recall, I said it's one of my favorites in Seattle."

"I know you think it would be great for kids and a family. But what about for you?"

"You're the one buying it, Ford, not me."

She was stubborn, but so was he. And he wouldn't buy a house that she didn't love just as much as he did. Some might call him crazy for putting so much on the line for a woman.

But Ford now knew it would be crazier not to.

"If it were you looking for a house in Seattle, would you buy it?"

"I thought we were going to stick to business until we finished making your offer."

"I need to know your answer, Mia."

She sighed. "Yes. I would."

He grinned. "Good. Then let's tell Alana and her ex that I'll pay their asking price today."

She held up her hands to try to slow him down. "Even if you make a cash offer, you don't have to pay it right this second."

"I want to move in right away. Let them know I'll have the money transferred into their account by lunch. And I'll buy everything in it, too."

Mia was shaking her head at what she obviously thought was an impulsive decision, but she picked up her phone and conference called the owners. "I've got an offer for you," she told them, "and I think you're really going to like it."

Ninety minutes later, the paperwork had been signed by both parties and Ford had called his personal banker to transfer the money. Mia had done some pretty big and quick real estate transactions in the past six years, but this one blew them all away by miles. Even for a woman who had always loved speed and excitement—nearly as much as her car-racing cousin, Zach—she felt as if she'd been blown over by a hurricane. That was how strong Ford's determination was when he focused on an end goal.

And as Orlando took Ford out into the office to introduce him to the rest of her employees and she watched through the glass walls as he charmed everyone, she acknowledged, again, just how difficult it would be for anyone to resist him. Especially when he was determined and focused on having something.

Or someone.

With his deep voice and laughter carrying through to her office, knowing that the sexiest man on the planet was close by made her need a bucket load of her own determination and focus to concentrate on answering some high-priority email and phone messages.

A short while later, when she saw in her peripheral vision that he was headed back toward her office, Mia's heart rate started jumping and the words in the email she was composing about a property in escrow blurred on her computer screen.

"Your staff is great," he said with a grin as he stepped back inside her office. "And they adore you."

She clicked Send on her email and closed her laptop. "I adore them all right back." She pushed away from her desk and grabbed her bag. "Congratulations, again, on your amazing new house. How about we go pick up some champagne to celebrate?"

He looked surprised, and clearly thrilled, by her suggestion as she told Orlando that she was taking a few hours off. Still, even though Mia knew that spending even more one-on-one time with Ford was a bad—okay, it was a *terrible*—idea, she tried to justify it by telling herself that she couldn't treat him any differently than any other client who had just spent millions of dollars on a house.

But as Ford held open the passenger door of his Tesla and she slid onto the smooth leather seat, Mia couldn't deny that the lies she was telling herself about him were only getting more pathetic by the hour.

I don't like him.

He was sweet with her employees, had been great with her family at the wedding…and if she wasn't so busy grappling with not letting him hurt her again, she'd already be head over heels in love with him.

This celebration is going to be just business.

Considering that her business meetings had never

included superhot kisses before, and she was about 1,000 percent positive that this celebration would, she was either going to need to change the definition of *business*…or she was going to have to accept that spending the day with Ford was about so much more than just celebrating a real estate transaction.

Our connection is just a sexual one, no matter what Ford says to the contrary.

Oh, how she wished this were true…but there had never been a moment with Ford, either in the past or right now, when her heart hadn't been on the line.

Eighteen

"Everyone always talks about how rainy Seattle is," Ford said as Mia spread out their picnic over the thick blanket they'd brought outside his new house while he uncorked the champagne, "but every time I'm here there's bright sun and blue skies."

"Now that you're officially a local, I guess I can let you in on our secret." She leaned close and whispered, "Our weather is actually awesome nearly all the time. Don't tell anyone, okay?"

Of course, Ford took advantage of her closeness to tug her in for another kiss before he agreed, "Okay."

Their kiss was short this time, but so darned sweet that when he moved back to finish opening the champagne, a disappointed little sigh slipped out of her mouth.

She knew they still had to continue the discussion that had begun in her office, but she wanted to feel steadier before they did, so instead of digging deep again, she said, "This has always been one of my favorite areas of the city. I actually went to school not far from here." She laughed. "My poor teachers. I was a little hellion, pigtails flying, always talking during lessons."

"Something tells me you got away with it."

"I loved learning," she agreed, "but I also wanted to be outside running and playing. Looking back, my mother was amazing at getting me to do my homework by making it all seem so interesting. As soon as I'd finish with my math or science worksheets, she'd push me on the swings before we'd settle back inside with a book. One day I hope I'm that good with my kids." It wasn't until she stopped for breath that she realized she was doing it again—sharing everything with Ford while he just sat back and listened.

"I saw you playing with your nephews and nieces at the wedding. They lit up just being around you. You're going to be great with your own kids."

"I had great teachers."

"I'm sorry I didn't get a chance to meet your mother or your father at the wedding."

"My mom and dad are amazing, although sometimes I wish they were a little more clueless like my friends' parents. Because if you had met them, they probably would have guessed something was up with you and me...and then they would have asked me questions." She definitely hadn't been up to the kinds of questions her family would have asked, especially since she absolutely hated lying to her family, and her five-year omission already felt perilously close to a big fat lie.

"Speaking of questions, has my brother Ian tried to contact you?"

"He called me at midnight after the wedding."

She'd hoped Ian had taken her at her word when she said that she could take care of herself. Clearly, he needed a reminder. She reached into her bag for her phone and said, "I can't believe he thinks he can butt into my—"

Ford put his hand on hers to stop her from calling her brother and reading him the riot act. "He loves you, so I get why he's so protective. I'd never want anyone to hurt you, either. Maybe you should go a little easy on him."

She sighed as she reluctantly dropped her phone back into her bag. "At least tell me what he said to you."

"Let's put it this way…he strongly advised me to be on my very best behavior."

"Or what? He's going to hop a plane from London to Seattle just to punch you out?"

"Or he'll be calling your brothers to fill them in on what's going on with you and me so that *they* can all take care of the punching."

She blew out an irritated breath. "If I want them to know what's going on, I'll tell them myself."

"I hope you will, Mia." His gorgeous mouth quirked up at one corner as he added, "Despite how physically risky a few hours with your brothers might be for the guy you bring home."

Suddenly, she could see it so clearly, taking Ford home and introducing him as her boyfriend, even though she'd never brought a guy home before, not one single time in twenty-eight years. Her father would be protective but fair to Ford, her mother would likely fall for him at his first smile and her brothers would take a heck of a lot of convincing that anyone could ever be good enough for their little sister.

"I always envied the kids at boarding school who had siblings," he said, echoing what he'd said to her after the wedding. "I was sent to boarding school when I was five. My parents probably would have sent me away earlier, but none of the elite private schools would take a kid until he was in kindergarten."

Even though she was glad that Ford was openly sharing another piece of his past with her, the sad look on his face had her wanting to pull him down on the blanket with her to kiss him until he forgot all about it.

"That must have been hard for you, to have to leave home so young."

"It was better than staying home with the nannies. At school I had friends to play with. It was coming home at the holidays that was the worst part. My mother and father were strangers to me."

Mia *loved* the holidays with her family. The dozens of Thanksgiving, Christmas and Easter celebrations over the years had been full of laughter and fun.

Obviously, everything she was feeling showed on her face because he said, "Don't feel sorry for me. My parents might not have given a crap about me, but they never hurt me physically or verbally. No one ever said no to me, either. Not with so much money and influence behind my family name. The chip on my shoulder and I were never hungry or bruised."

Mia knew all about pride, and the lengths to which people would go to protect it. After all, when she'd badly needed support from friends and family after she and Ford had combusted five years ago, she'd shut all of them out. God forbid she should let any of them know that she had failed or made a bad decision.

"When we broke up," she suddenly needed Ford to know, "I told myself all the same things. That I didn't go hungry. That I wasn't bruised. That I had a great apartment and career. And I couldn't stand the thought of any of my friends or family feeling sorry for me. Or worse, thinking I was making a mountain out of a molehill. So I kept it all inside." She watched a lone ant head back toward a long trail of ants from which it had temporarily broken away. "But the truth was that I *did* need them. And when I finally had to spill everything to my best friends after seeing you on Friday, instead of feeling like a fool, I felt loved. But even knowing that my friends and family will always love me, no matter what, I still brought that prideful chip on my shoulder with me to my cousin's wedding and worried that people would find out about us."

He reached into her bag and handed her the phone. "Here," he said with a grin, "you can call them all now to fill them in."

She took it from him, laughing. "If it makes sense down the road for me to give my cousins news about us, I promise to block out an entire afternoon to call each and every one of them."

Maybe it had been a crazy thing to say, but suddenly the chance of a future with Ford didn't seem *completely* out of bounds. After all, he'd just bought this house in Seattle, and he was actually telling her important things about his life.

She knew that it was easier for him to focus on her than himself. But for all the anger she'd nurtured over the past five years, now that she'd spent the past few days with him, she couldn't deny that she cared again. Back then, whenever she'd had questions for him about his past, it had always been easy for him to pull her back into bed and make love to her until she'd completely forgotten all about them. And there was a big difference between begging Ford to share his life with her and his offering it up to her unprompted, wasn't there?

Or was that just her pride talking again? Because if she was really considering a relationship with Ford going forward, could she keep locking her heart in a cage like this?

She dropped the phone back into her bag and looked into his dark eyes. "I don't think we were done talking about you and your family, were we?"

Ford was silent for a few long moments before he finally said, "That week with you here in Seattle was the closest I've ever let myself get to anyone. I'd been so used to standing on my own, making my own way, everyone else be damned. And then, there you were. Not just breathtakingly beautiful, not only the sexiest woman I'd ever seen or touched, but you simply opened your arms and heart and let me in. It scared the hell out of me, Mia."

She could understand everything he'd said up until the admission that he'd been frightened. "Why would my caring about you scare you?"

"For so long, I'd told myself that I didn't need anyone else, that I didn't care if no one ever really loved the real me, that it was enough to hear the fans who screamed *I love you* from the audience to love my music instead of the man behind the guitar and microphone. But then, from the very first moment you came into my life, it was so easy, too easy, to need you...and to want you with me all the time. I felt like I couldn't breathe without you, could no longer picture living the rest of my life as a man on an island. And it was even worse, because I knew you were too independent and loved your friends and family and career too much to say yes to my ultimatum."

"Are you saying that you were already gone before you even asked me to drop everything for you?"

"I didn't know how to stay."

She needed to know. "And now you think you do?"

He let out a long breath. "I sure as hell hope so. Because if I hurt you again, it wouldn't be your brothers coming after me to tear me to pieces. I would beat them to it."

No one could ever call Ford Vincent fragile. But for the first time, Mia saw the vulnerability he'd worked so hard his entire life to hide from everyone else.

Including her, until now.

"When I saw you again out of the blue on Friday," she said carefully, "I assumed you hadn't given me a single thought in five years. But even though I now know I was wrong, you've got to understand that I really tried not to think about you at all. At least, until the past few days. I mean, I obviously can't resist you whenever we kiss, but—"

"Friends," he reminded her. "I want us to be friends first." As if to make his point, he picked up the champagne bottle and poured two glasses. Handing her one, he said, "Here's to a beautiful friendship."

He'd promised not to push her too fast again, and while a part of her was relieved that it looked as though he was going to make good on his promise, before she could clink her glass against his, another part of her couldn't resist asking, "Do you always make out with your friends?"

"Not usually," he said with a slow grin as he obviously understood where her question was coming from, "but I'm pretty big on change lately, so I say, why not throw making out into the friend bucket?"

Her lips were tingling even though it had been quite a few minutes since they'd last kissed. Heck, her entire *body* was tingling just being near him like this.

"You know, since there's a pretty big spread between kissing and having sex, maybe I should make a list of everything in between," she suggested, "and you can show me the line that you're not going to cross."

His eyes quickly darkened with desire. "Lord, the way you tempt me, Mia." But instead of reaching for her the way she wished he would, he said, "Even if you make a list that you know damn well will make me crazy, you and I are going to be friends first before I make love to you again. It's a promise I'm making to both of us, and one I'm not going to break."

Mia knew a lot of powerful, rich men. The ones she was related to were great, but the rest of them usually took whatever they wanted without worrying about what anyone else needed or wanted. Ford could have already had her back in his bed by now. But, instead, he seemed truly committed to gunning for something more than a couple of great rolls in the hay.

Who would ever have thought this was possible? Certainly not her.

Still, whether or not this whole no-sex-until-friendship plan made sense, she didn't particularly care for living by a set of rules she hadn't had any part in making. Which was why she couldn't resist messing with him a little bit more.

"I actually do think you may be right about friendship being what we were missing before, but—"

"Why do I have a feeling your *but* is going to push me right to the edge of reason?"

She lifted her lips in a smile, loving that he knew her so well already, even though they were just at the beginning of their road to friendship. "*But* I just can't see how a few orgasms here or there would be breaking your no-sex-until-we're-friends rule."

"I'll never know how to love you the right way if I don't also know how to be your friend, Mia." His dark eyes were intense as he asked, "If an orgasm will get me there, you know I'd die to give you one right now. Tell me, will making you come make us better friends?"

She swallowed hard. Every time she tried to take things to a lighter place, he made sure she knew just how serious he was about wanting to be with her.

"No," she had to be honest and tell him, "it won't."

"I didn't think so," he said softly, and then, "Do you know what will?"

It was a good question, one she hadn't really ever thought about. But even if she did, she wasn't sure that her brain was where the answers about friend-ship were going to come from. Not when her heart had always been in charge of whom she trusted, whom she loved.

So though she'd promised herself that she wouldn't let her heart lead her down the wrong road with Ford again, she simply couldn't fight the powerful urge to take his hand and pull him down on the blanket with her to stare up at the blue sky.

The two of them were silent for a long while, their hands linked together, as they watched the puffy white clouds slowly change shape above them. Birds flew back and forth between Douglas fir trees.

Finally, she said, "I think this might be a start."

And when he turned to smile at her and the last pieces of ice around her heart melted away, she knew that it really was.

Nineteen

Tuesday quickly shaped up to be one of those crazy days where Mia was on the run from house to house with so little time to spare between showings that she had neither breakfast nor lunch. Not even time, she thought with a whimper of longing, for a cup of decent coffee to jump-start her motor.

A motor that was both roaring to life whenever she thought of Ford and then sputtering as she forcefully reminded herself not to repeat her mistakes by falling so fast and hard for him again. They hadn't done more than kiss a little on the blanket in his yard, but even that had been so overwhelming to her senses that she'd ended up accepting a client's last-minute request to do an impromptu showing just to have some space to think away from Ford.

She'd tried to be rational about everything he'd done, everything he'd said since he'd reappeared in her life on Friday morning, but rational thinking had never been her forte where Ford was concerned. Plus, it was one thing when he was coming at her with straight-ahead seduction in mind. Honestly, though she wanted him like crazy, she could have discounted that.

But knowing he wanted them to be friends first? *Way to cut right through to my heart, rock star.*

Still, while he'd been on her mind nearly every second since they'd parted the day before, she wasn't at all prepared to walk through the front door of Sullivan Realty and find him sitting in the lobby, his long legs kicked out in front of him as he chatted easily with her receptionist.

"There you are." He slowly unfurled his gorgeous body from the chair and gave her a look full of so much heat that she was pretty sure her hair was in danger of catching fire. "Got a minute?"

She didn't know whether to laugh or yell at him for surprising her like this. Why hadn't he called her to say he needed to meet? Not only had she just sold him a really expensive house, but they were—

She sighed. That was just what they were trying to figure out, wasn't it? Were they ex-lovers? Budding friends?

Or more?

"Of course. Go on into my office. I'll be there in just a second and we can talk about what you need."

He studied her for a minute. "How about I make you a cup of coffee on my way there?"

She nearly groaned in anticipation of the caffeine-induced relief. "Please. The machine is in the break room. Orlando can show you the way."

As soon as he disappeared into the main part of the office as if he owned the place, Betsy said, "I'm sorry, I wanted to send you a text to let you know he was here. But he insisted we wait until you were done with your showings. I think—" Her receptionist abruptly cut herself off as though she didn't want to speak out of turn.

"I'd very much like to know what you think," Mia told the woman she liked a great deal and trusted to deal with all incoming calls and potential clients.

"I think there wasn't anywhere else he wanted to go. Because despite a few random walk-ins asking for his autograph when they realized who he was, I got the sense that he felt comfortable here."

"How long has he been waiting?"

"About an hour."

"Ford was sitting here for an hour?"

"Honestly, the time flew by. We got to talking about my kids and grandkids, and he was full of questions about local schools and Little League teams and gymnastics classes. Does he have children?"

"No," Mia said, but as she thought about what he'd said to her when they were walking through the house he'd just bought, she added, "Not yet."

Through the glass walls of her office, she could see Ford laughing with one of her extremely starstruck employees. Orlando was doing a much better job of holding it together today, but everyone else was practically trembling with excitement. Clearly, Ford was not good for her employees' productivity. But maybe that was okay, because his presence clearly made them all so happy.

Sure, she had a couple of big stars in her family, but she'd never seen someone who wasn't a blood relation deal so well with fame. Where other musicians she'd worked with to find property in Seattle had made absolutely certain that she never forgot for one second whom she was dealing with, Ford seemed to go out of his way to do exactly the opposite.

"Thank you for keeping him company, Betsy."

"It was my pleasure," the older woman said with an uncharacteristic blush. "He's not exactly hard on the eyes, is he?"

"No," Mia said with a laugh at just what an understatement that was. "He certainly isn't."

Ford had the steaming cup of espresso waiting for her when she walked into her office.

She grabbed it from him with a gasp of *"Thank God,"* then immediately took a sip.

"Damn," he said, "I never thought I'd be jealous of a cup of coffee. But I'm not sure you've ever looked at me quite like that before."

Thankfully, she could already feel the kick from the blessed triple espresso he'd made her as she pinned him with a raised eyebrow. "You didn't wait with Betsy in the front room for an hour to fish for compliments, did you?"

"No," he confirmed. "I came because seeing you is the best part of every day."

Even as his sweet words warmed her, she said, "And?"

"I mean it, you know. Seeing you makes everything a thousand times better. Even when I know I can't touch you because all of your employees are watching us." He grinned at her and she was already charmed despite herself as he admitted, "But since you mention it, there is something I'd really like you to help me with."

"Is there a problem with the house?"

"Nope, the house is great. I was filming a promo at EMP this morning for the Seattle show this Saturday, and the manager was talking about all the kids who come through the music section of the museum and don't really want to go home at the end of the day when they're locking up." Ford's eyes shuttered. "I was one of those kids, and I know if I'd had a place like that to hang out in, all that music history, all that inspiration from the original Experience Music Project building, it would have helped." When he looked back at her, his eyes were clear again. And full of excitement. "I want to open a place in Seattle for kids to come and play music with each other. A rock camp. We'll bring in musicians, local ones and some of the big-time guys, too, who owe me some favors."

"It sounds amazing, Ford." His excitement was infectious.

"It will be, but I need you to help me find the perfect space."

"I'm already two steps ahead of you." As soon as he started telling her about his idea, she'd mentally flipped through a few of the available commercial spaces near the EMP Museum. She quickly pulled them up on her computer and printed out the two top contenders. "How do these look?"

He scanned the info and nodded. "How quickly can we get into them? Any chance you're free now?"

She whistled through her teeth. "Wow, you're serious about this, aren't you?"

"I'd like to announce the project at Saturday's show if I can."

Of course she wasn't free. But somehow Ford kept convincing her to bend all of her usual rules without even trying.

"Orlando," she said when she'd buzzed her assistant, "is there any chance you could take over another couple of showings this afternoon?"

Orlando was clearly more than ready for the additional responsibility she kept giving him, and as he greeted Ford, then gleefully went off to find her clients great homes, she knew she'd need to start looking for a new assistant soon so that she could let Orlando join the ranks of her other full-time Realtors.

"I'm pretty sure rock stars like you should be

spending all their time partying in bathtubs full of champagne and groupies, not creating a musical haven for kids," she said right before they jumped into a cab outside her office. "You keep surprising me."

"I was a stupid kid before."

"We both were." Still, though she knew both of them had grown up over the past five years, and she'd forgiven him for the way he'd left her, there were still some sore spots inside.

Sitting beside him in the backseat, she felt as if there were a magnet trying to pull their hands together. Stubbornness dictated that she keep her hand on her lap even though she knew how good it would feel to slide her fingers into his.

"One thing I should probably mention," he said just as she was about to open the cab door in front of the museum, which was a block from each of the properties in either direction, "there's going to be a small film crew with us this afternoon."

"A film crew? You told the press we're going to be looking at these properties?"

"No." He looked a little uncomfortable. "There's a documentary being made about my music. Natasha was at the museum this morning filming when we came up with the idea for the camp." By the time he finished explaining, he had already pulled his phone out of his pocket. "Forget I mentioned it. I'm going to tell her it's a no-go this afternoon."

On a soft curse, she put her hand over his to

stop him from calling off the film crew. "I've never known anyone who pushes as hard as you." Mia sighed as she worked through her frustration at having cameras sprung on her. "But I'm sure she's right and you should get this on film. You're doing something big, something important." But since she'd agreed to be his Realtor that also meant that she might also be forever caught on film with Ford, regardless of what happened between them in the future. "I can deal with the film crew."

Her fingers were barely wrapped around the door handle again when he said, "There's one other thing I should probably mention."

Of course there was, she thought as she looked back over her shoulder at him. "What now?"

"Natasha already knows who you are." Before she could ask how, he explained, "While she was going through old clips, she found a couple of us from the night we met. I hadn't told her about you, hadn't told her anything at all about my personal life. But she saw you and she *knew*." The cab driver was clearly riveted by their conversation, but neither Mia nor Ford gave a damn right then. "She confronted me about how I could possibly have been stupid enough to let you go when you obviously meant everything to me."

Mia's head was spinning. "That's why you came back." Her words were barely above a whisper.

"She helped give me the final push, but I was the one who finally owned up to the fact that I'd wanted to come back every day for five years. I'm sorry it took me that long to let my pride go. More sorry than you'll ever know." He scowled. "Pride could have ruined everything if I'd let it."

He was right about pride, about the way it could ruin lives. And she knew she needed to do some heavy thinking about her own pride where Ford was concerned. Because while it was one thing to be careful about not making the same mistake a second time, it was another entirely to be stubborn simply for the sake of winning. Especially if "winning" meant not being with him.

Unfortunately, by then the cab driver was starting to look really closely at Ford, and the last thing she wanted was her very personal conversation with one of the world's biggest rock stars to end up on *TMZ* tonight. It would be too easy for the driver to grab his cell phone and record the rest of their conversation. Thinking back, she was pretty sure they hadn't said each other's names or what either of them did for a living. At this point, it would be pure speculation on the driver's part that he'd had a rock star in the back of his car.

Nodding in the driver's direction, she said, "Thanks for the ride." Turning back to Ford, she said, "Let's go, Jeffrey. We're late for that documentary they're filming about your secret acne problem."

Ford was laughing as he slammed the door shut behind them. "Jeffrey? Acne?"

She patted his perfect face. "Don't worry, you'll

grow out of it one day. If the girls are smart, they'll
wait for you."

He was still laughing when she went to say hello
to the intelligent-looking woman who was standing
beside two men with big cameras. "You must be Natasha. I'm Mia. I hear you're the one who's respon-
sible for bringing you-know-who back into my life."

"And?"

Mia looked back at Ford, and as a group of tour-
ists coming out of the EMP Museum recognized him
and surrounded him, she said, "The jury's still out."

She'd always admired how great he was with his
fans, but this time Mia wished he wasn't quite so
friendly as they vied for autographs. Some of the
women were standing just a little too close…and
when one of them asked him if he would sign her
breasts, Mia's hands actually fisted at her sides.

So far this week they'd been together only at the
tower house, her cousin's winery in Napa and her
office. How could she have forgotten that women
threw themselves at him everywhere he went? Or
that groupies would do anything to try to get Ford
into bed with them?

She'd never been an insecure woman, but who
wouldn't be threatened by that? No matter how over
the past she thought she was?

"I've been on the road with Ford for months," Natasha said, "but do you know one of the first things
that really struck me about him?"

Mia could barely drag her narrowed gaze away

from the fan who by now was practically topless. "What's that? How talented he is?"

Natasha shook her head. "That he never once went off with a groupie or brought one onto his bus."

Now Natasha had her full attention. "Never?"

"Nope. Not even once. When I realized he wasn't even the slightest bit interested in the girls who threw themselves at him, I knew for sure that he was one of the good ones. And," Natasha added after a weighted pause, "that was when I also knew that his heart must already belong to someone."

"You're not just making this documentary about him because it's your business, are you?" Mia studied the redhead with new eyes. "You're his friend, too."

Natasha nodded. "He's an easy man to like."

And to love, Mia found herself thinking before she could stop herself.

Twenty

Ford was on a total high, the kind that only the stage—and being with Mia—had ever given him. It had taken only a handful of hours for them to agree that the large warehouse half a block to the west of the EMP building was the best choice for the camp. Ford had asked Mia what a fair price for the building was, and when he promptly asked her to make a verbal offer to the seller, they accepted immediately.

Sure, everything was moving really fast, but it was all great stuff. A fantastic waterfront house in Seattle. The perfect space downtown for a camp for kids who could use music to get out of their shitty lives and into better ones.

And, he thought as he watched Mia going over the huge pile of contracts he'd just signed for the commercial property, the most beautiful woman in the world back in his life.

Since her employees had already shut down the

office for the night, instead of heading there, Mia suggested that they print out and fax in all of the contracts from her condo. They'd ordered in Chinese and eaten it out of cartons while she took him through the seemingly endless paperwork—at least twice as much for the commercial property as there had been for the home he'd bought the day before.

She was all business as they did this, and while she was busy double-checking the final details of the contracts, he got up to study the photos that covered nearly every surface in her home. The windows of her condo were big and the ceilings were high, but there was so much color, life and personality in her home that the large living room and dining room didn't feel the least bit cold or hard-edged. The house he'd just bought was great, but he knew that if Mia shared it with him, she'd be the one who would bring real warmth to it.

Five years ago, when his fans had begun to multiply outside his hotel room, they'd decided it would be easier to disappear for a night to her place. Though her previous condo had been small, he'd loved it. She obviously had a knack for creating a comfortable home and because it was the first he'd ever really known, it had been a revelation to be surrounded by so many photos of her family and friends.

Perhaps, he admitted now, it had made him feel like even more of a loner, and that was yet another reason why he'd bolted the way he had at the end of that week.

He picked up a small frame that held a picture of Mia and her brothers when they were kids. She was on her oldest brother's shoulders and only one of her pigtails was still in, as if they'd been playing hard before the picture was taken. He looked at her over the top edge of the frame. Though her hair was glossy and perfect now, he could still so easily see the happy and carefree little girl she'd been in the gorgeous, polished woman she was now.

He put down the photo and picked up another of Mia and her parents, taken at her high school graduation. They were so proud of their daughter, and instead of looking as if she wanted to bolt out of their hold, she was leaning into both of them as if there was no place she'd rather be.

It was nearly midnight by the time she announced, "All of the official paperwork is now on its way. Congratulations." She held out her hand to shake his, and he used their grip on each other to tug her against him.

But the wickedly sensual *thank you* on the tip of his tongue dried up as he realized how stiff she was against him. Clearly, he now realized, her uber-professional behavior all evening hadn't just been because she wanted to make sure she didn't miss any details of the property transaction.

He brushed his thumb across her full lower lip. "Is everything okay?"

She hesitated for a moment before saying, "I should be asking you that. After all, you're the man who just spent less time thinking over buying a major commercial property than most people take to decide what to have for dinner."

Even though it didn't escape him that she hadn't answered his question, her mouth was so tantalizingly close that he lost the thread of anything but how good it felt to hold her...and how much he wanted to kiss her.

His mouth was almost on hers when he got a really good look into her beautiful eyes—eyes that were distinctly wary. And even though the blood was pumping dangerously hot in his veins, yet again he couldn't dismiss the sense that she was much tenser now than she'd been in her office earlier in the day.

"Something's wrong." He didn't phrase it as a question this time. "I need you to tell me what you're thinking, Mia."

"You do realize you're the only man in all of history who has ever asked a woman to tell him what she's thinking, right?"

"I'm probably the only one who's ever meant it, too," he agreed. "Look," he said, trying to guess at what the problem might be, "I know I made this decision about making sure we're friends before we have sex unilaterally. And I know you don't like being given limits any more than I do. Is that what's going on?"

"You're right that I've never liked other people making decisions about what's best for me. But," she said with a shake of her head, "that's not really the problem." She turned her face away from his, as though she didn't want him to witness her vulnerability. "All the years we were apart, I was so clear, so strong, so sure I didn't want you…and that I'd never be at risk of falling for you again. But today, when I was watching you talk to Natasha and her cameras about kids who need the magic of music in their lives, I was so proud of you for putting your energy and money into a camp that's going to make such a difference." She sighed. "And that's when I realized just how full of it I was."

Elation shot through him at her admission that she was falling for him again. Sure, he could feel it in her kisses, could see it in her smiles, but this was far more than she'd yet said in words. At the same time, he hated knowing that it worried her.

"Even now," she added in a soft voice, "though I've been telling myself over and over that I should know better—and that, if you wanted to, you could be sharing a bed with any of those groupies we saw today out in front of the museum—I want a heck of a lot more than the good-night kiss I'm sure you're planning to give me so that you can stick to your friendship vow."

She was right about the good-night kiss, even though it would kill him to walk away from her again tonight, but he also needed her to know something. "I don't want them, Mia. You're the only one I want. The only one I've ever wanted."

"Then prove it to me," she said in a husky voice

that ripped through his system like a bolt of electricity.

He had her mouth crushed beneath his before she could finish her sentence, and the sweet taste of her was all it took for Ford to lose the extremely tenuous hold he had over himself. A heartbeat later he had her backed up against the wall and had lifted her so that her legs were wrapped around his hips. He needed to get as close as he could to her, and when he pressed his denim-covered erection against her and she gasped with pleasure, he immediately took advantage by sucking her tongue into his mouth.

He had been planning to give her a sweetly seductive good-night kiss…not this sinful assault on every inch of her mouth, but when he tried to pull back, he found himself doing just the opposite. He tangled his hand into her long hair and roughly pulled her head back so that he could attack the soft skin along her neck with his lips, tongue and teeth.

But he wasn't the only one losing his mind, because Mia had her hands underneath his shirt, and she was raking her nails across his pecs. When he suckled her most sensitive spot—right where her neck turned the corner to her shoulder—she had to grip his shoulders to keep herself steady as she shook with pleasure.

Ten seconds. That was how quickly he could have their clothes off and be inside of her. She'd be so hot, and so wet, and so ready for everything he could give her that every clear thought in his head turned to static, until all he could hear was the hard throb of blood in his ears.

No, damn it. He wouldn't lose their chance at forever for a few perfect minutes of rolling around on the floor naked with her.

On a forceful curse that reverberated against all the floor-to-ceiling windows in her condo, Ford made himself take his mouth from her neck and put her down on the floor.

Her breath was heaving in her chest as she stared up at him, her skin rosy and gorgeous, her eyes bright with arousal. "I didn't know a good-night kiss could be like that," she whispered.

He knew he should be taking one step away from her, and then another, but when she reached up to touch his face, he knew he'd stay if she asked him to. Every promise he'd made, every one of his good intentions, would crumble in the face of his need to be with her right now, tonight, to take that taste of pleasure they'd both just had and multiply it a thousand times over.

"*Go.*"

Her eyes were dark with need, and he knew it cost her just as much to say that one word as it did for him to obey it. Somehow, he made his feet take him one step away from her, and then another and another, until the front door was at his back.

Twenty-One

The moment Ford unexpectedly walked into Mia's office on Wednesday morning, the buzz of excitement started humming among her employees again. He was only human, but everywhere he went it seemed crackling energy followed him. It was why hiding with Ford in public was pretty much impossible. No matter how good a disguise he put on, or how deserted a location they went to, his fans could sense his presence.

Clearly, given how giddy her employees were as he greeted each and every one of them by name, none of them had gotten used to being around him yet.

Would they ever? That is, if she and Ford actually were able to make a new relationship work? It was the very question she'd spent most of the night lying awake trying to figure out...

"Good morning, beautiful."

He was holding out a to-go cup of coffee for her,

but it was his absolutely tantalizing clean male scent that hit her first. That, and the fact that he seemed to only get better looking as the days passed. Age, she knew with perfect certainty, would only make him more desirable.

"You again? You're here so often I'm going to have to start putting you on my payroll, aren't I?"

She had to tease him, all the more because it was *so* good to see him. So much better than it should have been, considering it had barely been twelve hours since he'd left her with the hottest good-night kiss in the entire world. One that had left her reeling almost as much as her growing feelings for him.

"I hope hazelnut lattes are still your favorite."

Her heart was pounding and her legs felt a little shaky as she took the cup from him. "They are, thank you." She couldn't seem to stop her voice from coming out a little breathy, not when every inch of her craved every inch of him. Knowing she'd drop the scalding hot coffee on both of them if she didn't put it down, she carefully placed it on her desk.

"I've got to head down to Oregon in a few minutes. The bus is outside blocking traffic, but I couldn't go without seeing you first."

"I'm glad you did."

And she truly was. She wasn't sure if the skies had been sunny before he arrived, but now that he was here, she felt as though she were on a Caribbean beach soaking up the strong, warm rays rather than in the cool and cloudy Pacific Northwest.

Oh, how badly she wanted to touch him, so badly that her hands were actually shaking from the urge to reach out. But she knew her employees had to be watching the two of them through the glass walls of her office…and even the slightest touch would be akin to admitting she was Ford's.

His eyes were dark and full of the same impatient longing as hers, but, amazingly, he didn't push her. Just as he'd promised, there were no ultimatums this time.

It would be easier, so much easier, if there were. Because if he just grabbed her and kissed her in front of her employees, how could she do anything but give in? And then she wouldn't have to make this incredibly difficult decision about being with him or not being with him. It would just happen because she wouldn't have the strength to make things any other way.

His lips curved up slightly as though he could read her mind. "I want to kiss you so badly, Mia, it's nearly ripping me in two."

He swallowed hard and so did she as she marveled over how gorgeous and sexy even his throat was. God, to be able to strip him naked so that she could relearn every inch of his incredible body…

"But I promised I'd wait," he reminded her in a low voice. "For both of us. For our future."

"What if I don't want us to wait any longer? You wanted us to be friends first, and we are. You know we are, even if it's only been a few days since you've been back in my life."

"I don't just want to be your friend, Mia. I want to be the best friend you've ever had. But I'm not there yet, am I?"

Yes, she'd forgiven him. And she couldn't deny that she felt closer to him with every hour they spent together. She thought about him all the time, too. But could she trust him with her deepest fears? And could she believe that he'd always be there for her, no matter what?

When she didn't give him the answer he was hoping for, the barely masked pain in his eyes made her chest squeeze tight.

She was wishing she could give him the answer he wanted, if only so that she could make that hurt go away, when he put his hand into his jacket pocket and pulled out a white envelope.

Disappointment at not being in his arms, at not having his mouth against hers, was so strong she could taste it as she took the envelope from him and opened it. A concert ticket fell out first, followed by a thickly laminated pass.

"I know you've got a lot to do today, but just in case…"

Ford had never been a tentative man, either in or out of bed. But she could feel how unsure he was as she held the concert ticket and backstage pass.

"If I could go," she said slowly, "I would, but I have a late showing and to get all the way down to

Eugene in time for the show would probably be impossible."

"It's okay," he said in a way that told her it wasn't okay at all. "I knew it was a total long shot. You can just give them to someone you think might enjoy the show."

Finally, she reached for his hand, heedless of what her employees saw or thought about the two of them, because she needed him to know. "*I* would enjoy it, Ford. So, so much. And if I could come tonight, I would."

She'd never been a liar about anything other than admitting her feelings for him. And now, as he looked into her eyes to see if she meant it, she made sure he knew that she did.

"It's been way too long since I've seen you make a stadium rock." They'd both loved that old Air Supply song, "Making Love Out of Nothing at All." "I'd really like to come to your show this Saturday in Seattle, if you can scrounge up a ticket for me."

"Do you still have the silver dress?"

She gave a wicked little smile with her reply. "If you'd asked me that last night, I could have put it on for you."

He groaned. "I need to go before I lose my mind from looking at you and knowing I can't touch." But instead of walking away, he moved so that his broad shoulders completely blocked her from the rest of her office. His large hand was warm, the tips of his fingers calloused from his guitar strings, as he stroked her cheek with his fingertips, and her chin with his thumb. "How about pizza and a movie at my house on Thursday night?"

She'd spent practically all of her free time either with him or thinking about him since he'd come back to Seattle. She should put some space between them, give herself some time to try to think clearly. But knowing she was going to miss seeing him tonight felt like too much time without him.

Until now, they'd been together because of a real estate deal, and the wedding, and a business meeting he'd wanted her to attend. And five years ago, there certainly hadn't been any dates. Just endless amounts of crazy-hot sex, which hadn't made their relationship anywhere near strong enough.

"Are you finally asking me on a date?"

"I want to do every single thing with you I didn't know how to do the first time around, Mia. So, yes, I'm asking you on a date. A real one this time, complete with pizza and a movie."

Clearly, he wanted her to see they could have a relationship away from stadiums and tour buses and his fame. If she were really still adamant about holding him at arm's length, she should say no.

Instead, she told him, "I know the perfect place to pick up a pizza on the way to your house."

His answering grin was a mile wide. "I'll come get you at seven tomorrow."

"Okay." The simple touch of his hand on her face

had heated up every inch of her until she was all but melting into him. "Have a great show, Ford."

They stood like that, staring at each other for several long moments, before he finally caressed her one last time. And as she watched him walk out to his tour bus, she knew it was just like the lyrics to the Air Supply song that she now couldn't get out of her head.

Ford had always known where to touch her...and her heart had been lost for five years looking for a rhythm that only he could play.

Six hours later, Mia finally gave up trying to focus on work. The concert ticket and pass Ford had given her had been burning a hole in the back pocket of her skinny jeans all day long...and she kept lifting her hand to her cheek, where his touch had rocked her so deeply this morning.

"I'm sorry," she told her staff just as they settled into their seats for their weekly meeting to go over new listings, "I need to go take care of something really important." *Someone* really important. "Orlando, can you please take over the meeting and my showing afterward?"

Her assistant gave her a look as though he knew exactly what—*who*—had her so distracted. "No problem, Mia."

"Thanks. See you all tomorrow."

She barely remembered to grab her bag from her office before dashing out to her car. The drive from

downtown Seattle to Eugene, Oregon, would take
four and a half hours, as long as she didn't hit any
bad rush-hour traffic. Ford's show started at eight,
but if the opener took an hour, he wouldn't come on
until closer to nine. It was four o'clock, so if all went
well, she'd get there right before he took the stage.

Things looked good at first as she made her way
out of downtown Seattle, the road emptier than it
usually was midweek an hour before quitting time.
Feeling lighter, and more hopeful than she had in a
very long time, she turned on the radio and when one
of Ford's songs came on, she rolled down her windows, opened her sunroof and blasted it for everyone
to hear. Another driver gave her a thumbs-up, and she
laughed out loud as the wind rushed through her hair.

Maybe, she found herself thinking, this was a sign
that everything was going to work out after all.

Four hours later, Mia was *this close* to standing up
and screaming obscenities at the cleanup crew on the
freeway for how slowly they were dealing with the
massive produce-truck spill just outside of Portland.

She'd been so sure she'd make his show that she'd
nearly called Ford to tell him to look for her in the
crowd. Especially since she could tell how much he'd
wanted her to come tonight, even if he'd tried to be
nonchalant about giving her the ticket and pass.

Of course, right when everything seemed as if it
was going to go right for them, she'd hit the seemingly endless wall of cars and trucks.

Why hadn't she just taken a day off work and hopped onto his tour bus with him this morning? Yes, she loved what she did for a living, and her clients were important to her...but so, she was coming to accept, was Ford.

And yet, she'd made the same choice this morning that she'd made five years ago.

Worse still, as she sat in the middle of the huge traffic jam, her doubts had plenty of time to flood back in. Particularly a flashback to that last time she'd been rushing to surprise him at one of his shows.

Miami.

She had forgiven him for his mistakes, just as she knew he'd forgiven her for hers. But that didn't mean her fears over what they were starting weren't still hovering, telling her to be careful, warning her that she couldn't be cautious enough.

Was this traffic jam the real sign? And should she heed it by turning around and driving back to Seattle? Or by the time she finally made it to Eugene, would she walk into another nasty surprise like the one in Miami?

At last, the traffic began to move, slowly at first, and then more and more quickly as all the drivers were finally let loose to head to their destinations... and Mia had a decision to make.

Only, as she pressed her foot down hard on the gas pedal and sped down the fast lane, she knew she didn't.

Because she believed he'd meant it when he told her last night that she was the only woman he wanted…and even if she only caught Ford's final song, this hellish drive would be worth it.

It was eleven-thirty by the time Mia got to the overstuffed stadium parking lot and people were already pouring out of the venue and heading to their cars. She'd called Ford's cell several times in the past thirty minutes, but when he hadn't picked up, she'd figured he was still onstage.

Damn it, she couldn't have missed him! She drove as close to the stadium entrance as she could and left her car in a red zone as she started running, not bothering to call him again. Her best chance to find him now would be on foot.

"You can't leave your car there, ma'am!"

But she didn't have time to worry about her car, not when she was guessing it would be hit or miss to even catch Ford before his bus drove away from the venue.

She ran in through the front doors, which were open now as people began to stream out. Looking around wildly, she found a woman in a security outfit. "I need to get backstage right away. Please, can you help me?"

The woman took the laminated pass Mia was holding out and saw that it said ALL ACCESS VIP, but something told her it was the desperate look in Mia's eyes that made her nod. "Sure. Follow me."

Mia and the security guard wove their way through the exiting crowd that seemed to grow bigger with every second that passed. Though she was filled with panic that she'd miss Ford, Mia was so happy for him. He must have given a truly great show given how happy everyone looked as they headed home.

Finally, they pushed through a thick metal door and Mia nearly wept when she saw his bodyguard. "Billy," she called out.

Though she assumed looking serious and menacing was part of the bodyguard code, Billy broke out in a huge smile when he saw her. He spoke into a transmitter in his left ear, and a moment later, Ford came busting out of a set of dark red double doors.

He was still dripping with sweat from being on-stage…and looked impossibly beautiful to her as he called out her name. He looked as if he couldn't believe she was there—and as if pulled together by a magnetic force field, they moved toward each other. But just when she was close enough that he could easily have reached out and pulled her against him, he stopped.

She faltered for a few horrible moments as she looked into his dark eyes. Why wasn't he touching her? Why hadn't he kissed her yet?

But then, suddenly, she realized why. Because, just like in her office this morning, he wasn't sure if she'd want everyone to know that they were together. He was waiting for her to make the decision about going public with him. Twelve hours ago, she'd made one decision.

Tonight, she made another.

The right one.

A heartbeat later, she threw herself into his arms and kissed him without holding back.

Twenty-Two

There had been a lot of great moments in Ford's life. His first sold-out show. Winning his first Grammy. Having his lyric notebooks put into the permanent displays in the Rock and Roll Hall of Fame.

But holding Mia in his arms easily surpassed them all.

Her lips were soft, but her tongue and teeth were hungry as she kissed him passionately. Her gorgeous legs were wrapped around his waist and her arms were wound around his neck as she told him without needing to say a single word just how happy she was to be here with him tonight.

Though he wished she could have been in the audience, he'd been so inspired from being with Mia during the past few days that he knew he'd given a pretty great show tonight. And maybe it was good that she hadn't made it to the stadium any sooner, because if he'd known that she'd be waiting for him backstage afterward, he might not have been able to resist cutting the show short just to have a few more minutes with her.

Though he knew he'd need to put her down soon, her soft moan of pleasure as he threaded his hands into her silky hair and took their kiss even deeper made him want to do crazy things to her...and nearly made him forget that they were making out in front of his crew.

"I drove as fast as I could," she said when he finally managed to pull his lips from hers, "but I still missed your show."

He nipped at her lower lip. "And I missed you all day."

They were so close that between his wet T-shirt and her thin silk shirt, he could feel her heart beating against his as she said, "I should have gotten on the bus with you this morning."

Of course that was what he'd wanted, but he'd been careful not to even suggest that his show might take precedence over her own busy day in the office. "You're here now." And that was all that mattered, just being with the woman he loved more than he'd known it was possible to love anyone. "I was just heading to my bus. Ride back to Seattle with me, Mia. Unless," he teased, "there's something you're dying to do in Eugene tonight first?"

"Just you. I just want you, Ford."

Slowly, he slid her to the floor. When her feet finally touched solid ground again, he threaded his fingers through hers and was heading out to his bus when she suddenly stopped.

"My car. I completely forgot about it."

So had he, in his rush to be alone with her. "Where is it?"

"I parked out front. I think it was in a red zone. All I could think about was getting to you before you left the building. For all I know, they've towed it by now."

He kissed her again, a quick press of his lips to hers, but one full of just as much possession as it was surrender to the magic that had always been between them.

"Billy," Ford called, "can you take care of getting Mia's car back to Seattle?"

"Sure thing, boss."

Mia handed him her keys. "Thank you, Billy." She described the make and model and gave him her license plate number, just in case he did need to track it down with a tow-truck company. "I really appreciate it."

"No problem at all, Miss Sullivan."

"Wow," Mia said when they stepped into his tour bus. "Your old bus was nice, but this one is over the top." She ran her hand over the shiny iron handrail by the stairs. "Please tell me these walls aren't gold-plated or that you've got diamond-studded rims on the tires."

Ford gave her a wicked grin as he pulled her inside

and closed the door behind them. "If you think this part of the bus is nice, you should see the bedroom."

Mia had never been the nervous virgin type. She didn't blush or giggle or play coy. And yet, though she and Ford already knew each other intimately, being alone in his bus while he stood beside her in a T-shirt that was damp enough to outline each incredible ridge of muscle along his chest and abdomen made her heart race and her breath come too fast.

After he buzzed his driver to let him know that they were ready to head out, Mia decided she needed to take back control. After all, she'd already abruptly left work in the middle of the day, chased Ford to Oregon, then jumped him in the middle of a crowded backstage area. Now that she was finally here and they had hours of driving ahead of them to get back to Seattle, there was no way she was going to let him hold her at arm's length again for the rest of the night.

She reached for his hand, loving the way he always tugged her against him. "Do you still have the same postshow ritual?"

She could see the combination of desire and his attempts at control as they moved across his face. "Yes."

"Good." She smiled up at him, certain now that they weren't too far at all from finally getting naked with each other again. Thank God. "Let's get into the shower, Ford."

He groaned as he moved the hand he was holding behind her back to immobilize her against his hard muscles, then slid his other hand into her hair to kiss her. All her thoughts of control, of trying to lead him where she was so desperate to go, fled as the pleasure of his tongue slicking hot and needy against hers filled her. Just being with him like this made it feel as if the ground was moving beneath them…but then when he drew back, she realized the ground was indeed already moving at a steady clip beneath the tires of the bus.

"You tempt me." He traced the swell of her lower lip with his tongue. "So much." He gently sucked it into his mouth. "Too much."

She slid her hands beneath his T-shirt to the muscles that jumped against her fingertips. "Let me tempt you tonight, Ford." She licked at his mouth just the way he had with hers, loving the way his hands tightened on her. "And," she whispered against his lips, "you can tempt me, too."

"A shower." He started to slip the small buttons along the front of her silk shirt out of their holes. "That's all we'll do tonight, Mia." Lust fought with determination in his voice as his unbuttoning revealed the lacy edge of her bra. "Soap," he said in a hollow voice, as if he was trying to remind himself what one usually used in a shower. He looked momentarily lost as to what else might be in there until he finally said, "Shampoo."

"And naked skin," she reminded him in a husky voice. "I can't wait to be naked with y—"

The rest of her sensually teasing words fell away as he reached out to brush the very tip of his finger over the exact spot on her chest where the swell of flesh met lace.

"*Beautiful.* So damned beautiful."

Mia couldn't shake the feeling that he was looking at her as if he'd never seen any other naked woman before, as if she were his first. His only. He was a rock star who could have any woman in the world and, rationally, she knew she wasn't even close to his first. He wasn't for her, either. But it had never been like this for her with any other man. And as he said again, "You are so damned beautiful," she didn't need him to tell her that it had never been like this for him with anyone else, either.

Not when she already knew the truth in every kiss he gave her, in every caress.

She was surprised to realize his hand was shaking slightly as he traced skin and lace from one side of her chest to the other, then back again. She'd assumed by now that if and when they were going to get naked together, it would happen in a race to tear off clothes and get at each other.

But yet again, Ford was surprising her with reverence where she'd expected only lust…and with sweetness where she'd worked so hard to tell herself all these years there had been only sin.

She didn't realize she was holding her breath until he finally moved to undo the final buttons that held her shirt closed. It came out in a rush as he gently pushed the fabric from her shoulders, so that it fell to the floor behind her.

Taking a fistful of her hair into his hand, he tugged her head back so that he could put his mouth, hot and needy, into the curve of her neck. Her breasts, covered only in lace now, became even more aroused as she pressed them against his cotton-covered chest. And as he began to run kisses from her neck down across her shoulders, then over the upper swell of her breasts, she had to clutch at his shirt behind his back to hold herself steady.

Breathe. She needed to remember how to breathe. In. Out. In. Out. And as his lips and the bristles on his jaw moved over her skin, she almost caught the hang of it again.

That is, until she was rocked by the unexpected slick of his warm, wet tongue beneath lace and over one nipple.

"Ford. Yes. Please. More." One pleading word after another fell from her lips as she arched into his mouth, needing him to take more, to run his perfect tongue over the rest of her. Thank God, he listened to her pleas as he found her other breast and made it just as damp and peaked as the other.

And then he was dropping to his knees, his mouth hot and desperate as he ran kisses over her stomach, dipping his tongue into her belly button before nipping at the soft skin just to the side of it.

"All night long," he said against her stomach as

she gasped with pleasure. "I could spend the entire night tasting you like this, every single inch of you."

Oh, yes, she loved that idea, of his teasing her with his mouth and hands all night long. But not tonight, not when she was going mad with the need to be skin to skin with him.

"I want to do that to you, too," she told him, but he had on far too many clothes, so she grasped his shirt in her hands and pulled it over his head.

With Ford still on his knees in front of her, she could look down on his broad shoulders, his tanned skin that had been painted with intricate tattoos. She recognized some of them, remembered well the joy of tracing them with her fingertips as they lay together in his hotel room, and her fingers were drawn to do the same thing now.

But before she could do more than skim her fingers over his warm muscles, he took her hands in both of his and kissed them. "If you keep touching me, we won't make it into the shower, Mia."

"That's okay with me," she whispered as he held her hands over his heart and she felt how hard it was beating. Nearly as fast as her own.

"No." He shook his head. "No," he said again as if repetition could somehow convince both of them that a shower could be enough. "Okay isn't good enough." His eyes were dark with desire and with emotion. "I don't want *okay* with you. I don't want *good* or *good enough* with you. I want *everything*. I want even more than that." She could see him working for his control as he suddenly said, "I don't think I ever told you that I was fourteen years old when I lost my virginity."

"That's pretty young," she murmured, wondering where he was going with this information that had seemingly come from out of the blue.

"By today's standards, not so much. But back then, yeah, it was pretty young. See, there was a girls' school across the river in Boston, and it was a badge of honor to come back to the guys and tell them you'd scored."

"And they believed you?"

"They did when you had the panties as proof in your pocket."

"Teenage boys are scum."

"In more ways than you can imagine." He shook his head. "The thing is, I didn't know anything about friendship or love back then. I wasn't trying to get anything from those girls but their panties and to hopefully be the one to pop their—"

She held up her hand. "Picture already painted, thank you." Mia knew she had no reason to be even the slightest bit jealous of any of those girls, but reason didn't always come into play where Ford was concerned.

"Every single woman I was with from fourteen on was exactly the same. None of them meant anything to me. Not until you. And when I felt like I couldn't hack it as a boyfriend instead of just a hookup, it was easier just to let the sex take over with you until it buried everything else we could have had. But the stakes are too high this time, Mia. You've given me a second chance, and I'm not going to blow it by screwing up everything we're starting to build."

She knew in that moment that he didn't just want her heart. He wanted her soul, too. And, oh, it was so tempting just to tell him that he had them both. Because then he'd stop holding back, stop keeping his vow to hold himself in check with her until they'd created something truly solid.

But she could still hear the way he'd asked her that morning in her office, *"I want to be the best friend you've ever had. But I'm not yet, am I?"*

Just as she could still hear the echo of her own silence.

She'd driven to Eugene to see him because she'd missed him all day, because she'd thought about him every single second, because she simply couldn't have made it through another night without him... and because she was still looking for answers. Answers that she knew wouldn't just come from sex alone.

"I promise I won't push you to make love to me tonight," she told him, "but I need more than just kisses."

Instead of answering her with words, he undid the button of her jeans and unzipped them. The heat of his breath over the lace of her panties made her legs tremble, especially when he quickly stripped the denim completely away. She was shaking from the force of her need and it was only the steady strength of his hands on her hips as he pressed his mouth to the top of her pelvic bone that kept her upright.

Mia had always been a strong woman, but whenever Ford touched her, even if it was just the slightest press of his mouth against her skin, she melted. Once upon a time, she'd hated herself for this weakness. But tonight, as he transformed her reality by spinning it into the sweetest fantasy she could ever have dreamed of, she finally understood that it wasn't weakness.

No, not weakness at all. Because when she and Ford came together, it was the biggest, boldest force she'd ever known. One that only a truly brave man or woman could withstand.

They hadn't been strong enough five years ago. But now?

More and more, she was beginning to wonder if they might be...

The scrape of his teeth on her lower abdomen had her releasing her breath in a gasp while he dragged her lace panties past her sex, then stopped with the fabric still at the base of her hips. She heard him take one deep breath, then another shaky one, before he groaned and pressed his lips to her bare skin.

A low sound emerged from her throat and echoed back at her from the walls of the bus as he pressed a soft kiss between her legs. It was so good that she was already nearly coming apart.

"Ford!"

His tongue was magic, even though he was just barely flicking against her. His shoulder muscles flexed beneath the tight grip of her hands and all it would take was the next slick of his tongue over her and she'd be free-falling over an edge that had never seemed quite so steep.

But the next thing she knew, instead of ripping her underwear all the way off and tasting more of her, he was back on his feet and lifting her into his arms.

"Why are you stopping?"

"Has anything changed from this morning?"

She'd never seen his eyes this dark. This intense. This hungry. This desperate for her to tell him what he needed to hear.

She knew what the right answer would get her— *all of him*—but she just couldn't lie to him. "You've become important to me, Ford. Really, really important. I know that much."

Disappointment flashed quickly through his eyes before he could bank it entirely. "We're going to get into the shower for a quick rinse and then I'm going to take you to bed so that I can put my arms around you and hear about every part of your day that I missed between this morning and now."

"I want to hear all about your day, too," she told him. And it was true. She longed for these pieces of him just as much as she longed for his body, had even longed for these secret parts of his heart *more* than another stunningly great climax when they'd been together five years ago. But now, damn it, she wanted *all* of those things! Especially when she was dangling over the edge of a release so sweet that she could practically taste it like sugar on her tongue. "But I want this, too. Your mouth, your hands on me—and mine on you—without needing to stop for any reason."

"Soon," he said, the word actually vibrating with hope. Hope that she now felt, too, and not just because she was so desperate for him to take her. "But for tonight, your naked soapy skin against my hands will have to be enough."

Twenty-Three

Rock stars weren't expected to have control. They were trained by the world to behave as recklessly and wildly as they wanted to. Ford wasn't the worst of the bunch, but he'd never been an angel, either.

How was he going to get into the shower with Mia without making love to her?

How was he going to put his hands all over her luscious curves and stop there?

And how the hell was he going to listen to the breathless little sounds she made as her arousal spiked higher and higher and not allow himself to take her all the way up to the peak?

But even though he didn't have one single answer to his desperate questions, he couldn't have stopped himself from bringing her into the shower for anything.

They were both still partly dressed when he turned on the faucet and warm water sprayed out over them. He loved having her in his arms, but he needed to put her down at least long enough to strip away her bra and panties. Yes, he knew it would be a hell of a lot wiser to keep her at least partially covered, but he was almost certain he'd die if he didn't get to see her naked inside of the next thirty seconds.

He bent to kiss her again as he reached around her back for the clasp of her bra. He was fumbling for the elusive pieces of metal when he felt her laugh against him.

"Not there, rock star." Her eyes were bright with arousal and humor as she reached around for his hands and brought them to the tiny clasp at the center front. "Here."

He could feel the tumbling beat of her heart against his hand as she held him there, and he repeated, "Here," but he wasn't talking about her bra. And by the way her eyes darkened and her smile fell away, he knew she felt it, too. A connection that neither of them had ever had—or would ever have—with anyone else.

He inhaled once, then twice, to try to get his head on straight. But it was no use, because the moment that he flicked open the clasp and Mia's incredible breasts fell into his waiting hands was one he knew he'd never recover from.

He couldn't speak, couldn't think, couldn't do anything but stare in wonder at her gorgeous pale skin, her nipples a dusky rose that made his mouth water. Palming both of her breasts, he slowly stroked both thumbs over their taut peaks. His hands were shaking, but she was trembling, too, as she stared down with what looked like wonder at his large, tanned hands on her.

"Again." Her breath was ragged, the word barely understandable as it fell from her lips. "I need y—"

But he was already giving her more with his mouth, covering one perfect nipple with his lips, laving it first with his tongue, and then using his teeth for a heady moment before licking the small bite all better. She gripped his wet hair with both hands and held him to her as she arched deeper into his mouth. He laved every inch of her breast with his tongue before he moved to take her other breast into his mouth.

They'd done this five years ago, and yet as he lifted his head to kiss her, he was amazed to realize that those memories he'd never shaken free of were suddenly receding as they discovered each other all over again.

He was still wearing his jeans, but she'd shimmied fully out of her panties, and as they kissed, the urge to back her up into the tiles and spread her thighs wide, to step between them and press his denim-covered erection against her sex, was unstoppable.

On a moan of deep pleasure, she rocked into him with her hips, once, twice, and as her body was beginning to tremble and tighten around his, the very last thing he expected her to do was tear her mouth from his.

"Just kissing you won't be enough tonight," she told him as the water streamed over her hair, then down over her curves. Her needy body arched and curved into his even as she said, "Not even close to enough, but—"

"But I made you a promise, Mia." He'd seen her with her family, with her employees. He knew that a promise was as good as gold to her, and he needed her to know that it was the same for him. "And I need to keep it, even if every second of not having all of you is ripping me apart."

She reached out and placed her hands on either side of his face. "I've never wanted anyone or anything the way I want you, but it wouldn't be fair to either of us if I made you break your promise to me." She closed her eyes for a moment and took a deep breath before saying, "Put me down and hand me the shampoo so I can wash your hair."

Lord, it was nearly impossible to step away from her, to know that she'd been less than a heartbeat away from coming twice tonight, and then not do whatever he could to take the ache away.

When he did finally move away from her, she looked down at him in surprise. "You still have your pants on."

"It's better that way," he told her.

"No, it isn't. If I can't touch you tonight, then I'm definitely going to look."

She reached for the button of his jeans, but just

the slightest brush of her fingers over his abdomen
made it clear just what a bad idea that was.

He put his hands over hers. "I need to do it myself."

He could see how reluctant she was to drop her
hands, but she finally nodded. "Okay, but be quick
about it."

He grinned at her sensual order, knowing that
only with Mia had desire and joy ever come together
this way. Wet denim was a bitch to get off at the best
of times, but with the woman he loved naked and
desperately aroused just inches from him, Ford kept
getting distracted from his purpose by the way the
drops of water rolled down over her breasts, to slide
over her nipples to her stomach, before disappear-
ing between her legs.

"The way you're looking at me…" She put her
hands on his jaw and lifted his gaze back to her
eyes. "Hurry, please, or I'm going to have to take
matters into my own hands so that I can look at you
that way, too."

Just those words from her lips had his erection
growing even harder behind the zipper he'd pulled
only halfway down. Moving fast now, he undid his
boots and kicked them off, then shoved down his
jeans and boxers, leaving them in a heap on the tiled
shower floor.

"Oh, Ford." There was awed lust in Mia's voice,
and it was a long time before she lifted her gaze

back to his. "Have you grown bigger in the past five years?"

"Yes," he teased her, his laughter reverberating from the tiled walls as he bent down to kiss her. "Especially after five days of endless foreplay."

"Haven't you taken care of yourself?"

"No." He kissed her again. "A hundred times I thought about it, a hundred times I was halfway there…and a hundred times I knew it wouldn't help. Because even if I got myself off, it wouldn't be your hands on me. It wouldn't be your mouth on me. And it wouldn't be you hot and wet around me."

"Stop." She pressed her face against his chest. "Please stop saying things like that to me. Especially now that you're naked."

He knew she was right, that he wasn't helping either of them hold to the promise, but first he needed to know, "Have you touched yourself?"

Her frame shuddered against him as she admitted, *"Yes."*

"Good." He tilted her face up to his and kissed her to let her know he meant it. "When was the last time?"

Her pupils had dilated so much by now that they had nearly pushed all the blue from her eyes. "This morning."

Hell, she might as well have dropped to her knees and put her hands and mouth on him by this point, he was that close to the edge. "Before or after I came by your office?"

He'd never seen her skin flush so deeply as it did when she said, "Both."

Oh, Lord, he could all too easily picture her with her hand between her legs twice today with that look of sweet ecstasy on her beautiful face as she climaxed. "I need to know one more thing." He paused, knowing he shouldn't even be going there, but unable to help himself. "What were you thinking about as you made yourself come?"

When she looked up at him he already knew the answer, even before she said, "You. It's always been you."

He crushed her mouth beneath his, gripping her hair tightly in his hands so that he could keep her exactly where he wanted her.

Exactly where he needed her.

"I love the way you kiss me." Her voice was husky with desire and pleasure. "Like you'll never get enough."

"I never will."

Her eyes, already clouded with passion, went soft with emotion. "Come and sit down here," she said as she gently tugged him down onto the tiled ledge. She moved between his legs and squirted some shampoo from the wall dispenser into her hands. "Close your eyes and tilt your head up a little bit."

With his eyes closed, he was even more aware of her scent, the light rose of her perfume mixed with female arousal. He couldn't keep his hands to himself, had to reach out to circle her hips with his hands, and he heard her suck in a breath at the contact just as she began to massage the shampoo into his hair.

No one had ever touched him like this before. Yes, anytime her hands were on him their sensual connection couldn't be denied, but the feel of her fingers lightly moving along his scalp and her palms pressing against his cheeks and neck were incredibly comforting. Even as a young child he couldn't remember anyone being this gentle with him, this caring.

"Tilt your chin up higher," she said softly, and then she was washing him clean with handfuls of the warm water.

And as she poured one handful of water after another over him, Ford couldn't help but feel that it wasn't just his hair she was washing clean…but that she was washing away his mistakes one at a time, too.

"There," she said as she ran her hands over his skull, brushing his wet hair back from his face. "Perfect."

He didn't want to open his eyes yet, wanted nothing more than to pull her closer and lay his head against her chest and hear her heart beat. And when he did, her arms came around his shoulders so that she was holding him.

Ford didn't know how long they stayed like that, but it was long enough that the water started to cool.

"Looks like shower time is over." He could hear the same regret in her voice that he felt. "Fortunately, your shampoo was sudsy enough to get both of us plenty clean all over."

"That's what I missed while my eyes were closed?" Ongoing—and ever-increasing—need had his hands instinctively tightening on her hips. "Soap bubbles running over your naked body?"

"Just a few hundred or so," she teased, but before he could grab a bar of soap to create a few hundred more, she gave a little yelp and jumped away from the stream of water. "It's freezing!" By the time she turned off the faucet, he had already opened the door to grab a thick towel.

It was his turn now to give her the comfort of wrapping the plush cotton around her and rubbing his hands over her curves to dry her off.

She closed her eyes and leaned into his touch. "Mmm, that feels good."

Did it ever.

Now that he had her wrapped up in the towel and fighting his reaction to her nakedness wasn't taking every ounce of his concentration, he could see the dark smudges beneath her eyes. She was tired, and he knew he was the reason. Not just because of her long drive to Eugene today, but because he doubted she was getting much more sleep than he was. At least, she was relieving a little bit of the pressure by touching herself—

No, that was exactly the wrong road to go down. Later, when she wasn't right here tempting him, he'd let himself fantasize about how she might have touched herself. Although, hopefully, soon she'd trust him enough with her heart that he wouldn't have to fantasize…because he'd be right there with her in the bed.

He picked her up, grabbing a towel for himself as he headed from the shower into his private bedroom at the back of the bus. Without opening her eyes, she reached out to wrap her arms around his neck and nuzzle his still-wet skin.

"Time for bed."

Her heavy eyelids fluttered open. "Not yet."

Of course, he also wanted to spend more time talking, teasing, laughing with her, but he was trying to think of what was best for her as he said, "You must be tired after your long day and drive."

"No," she swore as he gently laid her down on the bed, "I'm not the least bit tired." He'd barely wrapped up in a towel and come behind her to draw her against him, her back to his front, when she said, "I want to hear all about your show."

"It was good." He stroked her wet hair as it lay spread across his pillow. Her skin smelled like his shampoo, but her hair still held her signature rose scent. "I played the new song I wrote for you."

She ran her hand down the arm draped across her waist until she could cover his hand with hers. She lifted it to tuck it between her breasts as she said, "They must have loved it."

Her head fit perfectly beneath his chin, and he

barely stifled a groan as she wiggled her bottom more tightly against his hips. "They did."

"How does it feel to be up there in front of so many people who all love what you do so much?"

"Lucky." She shifted slightly to look at him over her shoulder as he thought about how to answer a little better. "There are millions of kids with guitars. A million more who are trying to get away from their current lives into a better one. I think about that every time I get up onstage, how everyone in the audience is willing to part with time and money they don't have any extra of to spend a night with me. I'd be nothing without them."

"Yes, you would." She gripped his hand tighter against her heart. "Even if you'd never hit it big, even if your songs had never been on the radio, even if you were playing dive bars instead of stadiums, you'd still be amazing, Ford." She spread his hand flat against her heart so that he could feel it beating against his palm. "Amazing inside and out."

If he'd thought it was difficult not to make love to her, he suddenly found it was a thousand times more difficult not to scare her off by telling her exactly how much he loved her…and to keep from begging her to love him back just as much.

"How many houses did you sell today?"

He couldn't see her smile, but he swore he could feel it as she said, "Just one, before I decided to high-tail it to Oregon. It was for a family that is going to be really happy with the neighborhood and the nearby beach. Even better, we were able to close the deal without breaking the bank. I hate to see people overextended."

He would have expected most Realtors to celebrate the higher-priced sales, because those sales meant an automatic rise in their salary. Mia had gone from being fairly new in the business to having her own thriving brokerage since they'd first met. But he could easily guess that the reason she had been able to build it so quickly was because she matched people up with the properties that were right for them, regardless of how much they cost or how small her percentage might end up amounting to.

"Having a home is important." It was something he'd only just learned.

And yet, as she slipped into sleep in his arms, even though they were in his tour bus rather than his new house, just holding her made him feel as though he was finally home.

Twenty-Four

Mia had always been a big sleeper. She loved waking up on cool mornings warm and cozy beneath a thick duvet, and would often linger long past the first ring of her alarm clock. But this morning she felt so good, so warm and safe that she didn't want to wake up all the way.

No matter how hard she tried to fight the truth, everything was better with Ford.

Especially this.

After a shower that had teased them both nearly senseless with naked skin neither of them could touch, she'd loved the way he'd curled up with her on the bed. At some point, she must have fallen asleep and he'd tucked them both beneath the covers.

Just enough light was coming into the bedroom of his tour bus through the edges of the blinds that, as she slowly turned in his arms to rest her head in the crook of his shoulder, she asked herself yet again, what did being Ford's friend mean? *A bond of mutual affection* is how the dictionary defined friendship, but that wasn't even close to describing the enormity of what she was beginning to feel for Ford. Affection was there, of course, but so were intimacy and attachment and empathy and comfort.

But even if she couldn't pinpoint every element that went into being Ford's friend, last night had changed everything. When they'd been talking she could hear the sensual desperation in his voice. But, for as much as they wanted each other, she'd been absolutely certain that their need to *know* each other was even greater.

This morning, however, she was more than willing to let their physical attraction come back to the forefront for a little while. With the best-looking man who had ever graced the earth this close—and naked beneath the bedcovers with her—how could she resist pressing her lips to his chest, where his heart was beating slow and steady beneath her ear?

And how could she resist lightly running her hands down over his warm skin?

And why on earth would she be stupid enough to give up the chance to keep raining more kisses all across his chest, his arms, and then down over his taut abdominal muscles as he continued to sleep?

She knew how much energy he put into his shows and how deeply he slept afterward. And it was a very good thing that he was so exhausted. Because there were so many other places she wanted to touch, to kiss, before he woke up and tried to stop her in the name of growing their friendship first. Ever since he'd stripped off his jeans and boxers in the shower last night, she'd been utterly distracted by the need not only to look, but also to touch.

And to taste.

She hadn't been flirting with him when she'd asked if he was bigger now than before. Because... *wow*. She licked her lips in anticipation as pure female instinct claimed her so that she simply *had* to lean down to press a soft kiss to the hard ridge of his erection.

Ford's groan came first, quickly followed by her name on his lips and his hands in her hair. "Mia—"

She'd promised to stick to the rules last night. But this was a new day, and while she still agreed that they should keep working on their friendship before they had full-on sex, she couldn't see the point of being puritanical about things, either.

For Mia, falling in love with someone wasn't only a cerebral experience and it wasn't just something she felt inside her heart. It was also deeply physical. So, before he could say or do anything more to try to stop her, she slicked her tongue over him in one long, delicious stroke.

He automatically bucked up into her waiting mouth, and she was just shifting to take him deeper when he used his hands in her hair to lift her gaze away from his groin. The slight pinch of his grip on her scalp sent her arousal ratcheting up even higher.

"Last night," he ground out, "we agreed not to do this. Not yet."

"I didn't break our promise last night, and I'm not going to break it today, either. We won't have sex. Just this."

She knew she was pleading, but she was desperate for him not to stop her. Because coming this close to such pleasure and having to pull back was a bad thing. *Very bad.* And wasn't it true that the definition of sex had many different interpretations?

"Ever since last night in the shower, when you told me why you haven't taken care of yourself, I've needed to put my hands and mouth on you, Ford. Not just for you…but for me, too."

Finally—*thank God*—he curled his hand over hers so that she was gripping his erection even harder beneath his hold. Together they stroked him, and she couldn't tell her moans from his as they sounded off the bedroom walls of his tour bus.

Being like this with him again was so perfect and beautiful and sexy. She felt so close to him and knew if he tried to stop her now she would die…because she *needed* this, needed some sort of completion after all the days of stopping after superhot kisses.

Mia shifted up onto her knees on the bed, her long hair falling over him as she took him into her mouth. Ford's hands moved back into her hair, and together they found a perfect rhythm, one that was so natural, one that felt so much a part of her, that she wondered how she'd managed not having him in her life for so long.

Using her lips and tongue, she took him up, up, up, then reveled in sending him all the way over. Ford was always strong, always in control, so those few moments when he gave himself completely over to her were incredibly precious. She couldn't remember ever being so aroused before, yet she honestly believed she didn't need anything more than what they'd just done—simply because it felt so good to give him pleasure.

When she could finally catch her breath, she looked up his chiseled body and asked, "Feel better now?"

"No."

Before she knew it, Ford had hauled her up his body, then shifted them so that she was lying in his place on the bed and he was levered over her. He nipped hard at her lower lip as he slid his hands through hers and held her immobile, each arm pulled up on either side of her head.

"Not even close to better." His teeth found one of her earlobes next, right before he growled, "Not until I get my mouth on you, too."

She nearly came apart right then and there with her hands held firmly in his and his tongue tracing the tendon from her lobe to her collarbone. And when his mouth closed over her nipple, all she could do was arch up into him and beg for more.

"Please," she said, even though she'd never been a

woman who begged anyone for anything. Only Ford had ever reduced her to this. And when he gave her exactly what she needed by scraping his stubble from one breast to the other, her pleas gave way to just his name, which fell from her lips over and over again.

She would have wrapped her legs around him to pull him closer, but he didn't just have her hands pinned, he had her legs trapped beneath his, too. Ford had been the most dominant lover she'd ever had, and for once in her life she'd loved letting someone else lead. For five years she'd never allowed another man to lead in bed, and now it felt amazing to let go.

Ford had her exactly where he wanted her and she couldn't deny that it was right where she wanted to be, even though just minutes earlier when she'd been touching and tasting him, she'd been the one in control of their pleasure.

Maybe, she found herself thinking with the few brain cells that were still operational, this time around neither of them would need to be in charge. And if this morning was any indication, this new balance between them—both as lovers and as real friends—would make things even hotter than they'd been before.

He kept her hands in his as he rained kisses along the undersides of both breasts, then down over her stomach. "You smell so good," he said between kisses. "I can't wait to taste you again."

But instead of rushing down over the rest of her curves the way she so badly wanted him to, he took his time to trace the lower edge of her ribs with his tongue, to taste the hollow just beneath her hip bone and then to breathe her in when he finally made it down to the V between her legs.

"Oh, baby," he said as he stared down at her, "you're so wet for me. So ready."

"Please, Ford," she begged again. "I can't wait any longer for you."

"I can't wait, either," he said, and then his tongue was there, slicking through her wetness, once, then twice, then three times, before he decided to stay put over her clitoris.

He was holding her hands at the sides of her hips now, and as Mia felt the earth begin to slide out from beneath her, she gripped his fingers tightly with hers.

"Come for me, Mia," he said, and between his urgent words and the sweet feathered touch of his lips over her core, it was all it took for her to come shuddering apart into a million little pieces.

He'd brought her quickly to release, but he stayed right there with her as she came down slowly, his lips gentle on her oversensitive skin as he pressed kisses to the insides of her thighs and then to the soft flesh at the sides of her hips. She was trying to catch her breath and her eyes were still closed when he moved back over her to pull her into his arms.

Just as she had when she'd awakened, she felt safe and warm.

And loved.

Yet again, thoughts of *love* were what brought her

back to reality. It was one thing to become Ford's friend who shared his bed. It was another entirely to fall in love with him…and to trust that it would be forever this time.

He brushed the hair back from her forehead and said, "I'm glad you came to Oregon and spent the night with me. Really glad. I asked Robert to take us to your place so you'd be able to leave when you needed to."

"We're in front of my building?" She slid out of his arms to lift up the shade an inch. "We must have been here for hours." No doubt everyone in her building was wondering which superstar was blocking traffic outside. And judging by how high the sun was already, Mia knew she needed to leave to get ready for her appointments. "I should go."

He got out of bed, gloriously naked, and pulled her back against him. "One more kiss first."

Despite the fact that Mia knew she still had plenty to think about, their kiss was more unrestrained than ever. Because how could they possibly go back to the hellish control they'd been maintaining when they'd just given each other heaven?

"I'll pick you up at seven."

His kiss had her brain still mushy as she echoed, "Seven?"

"For our date tonight."

Finally, she remembered. "Pizza and a movie." From a stadium and a blinged-out tour bus to an evening on the couch watching a B-grade film—it shouldn't have made any sense.

But, somehow, it did.

Twenty-Five

Ford had never thought much about what he wore until he became famous. Over the years, he'd learned how to blend in when he needed to. Tonight he made sure his baseball cap came down low and his long-sleeved shirt covered up his tattoos. A couple of people did double takes as he walked into Mia's building, but he just kept moving. At least, until she stepped out of the elevator and made his brain and body grind to an abrupt halt.

Because it was a warm night, she was wearing a cream-colored halter dress that hugged her curves and left her gorgeous shoulders bare. Regardless of how good the pizza or movie was, he wasn't sure he'd be able to do anything but stare at her all night long.

As she walked toward him in strappy heels that made her legs look as if they went on forever, she said, "I think you look great, too." And then she gave him a soft, sweet kiss that rocked his world all over again.

Last night it had been a big deal when she'd kissed him backstage in Oregon, even though he knew that no one among his crew would talk publicly about the two of them. But this was the first time she'd ever kissed or touched him intimately in a truly public space.

"I called in our order fifteen minutes ago, so the pizza should be ready for us to pick up." She studied him in his ball cap and nondescript dark jeans and shirt. "Do you want to hide out at my place while I go get it so you don't create mass hysteria on the street?"

It was probably a good idea, but he badly wanted to see if she'd hold his hand in public. He knew he was being greedy, that the kiss should be enough. But it wasn't. Not even close.

He wanted all of her, heart and soul.

And he wanted it as soon as possible.

"I'm willing to risk it if you are."

"Now that you own a house here, I suppose people are going to have to get used to seeing you around town," she said with a shrug. "Why not start tonight?"

She didn't take his hand as they walked outside, but she also didn't avoid being seen with him in public. Ford reminded himself about what an improvement that was compared to where they'd been even a few days ago.

"Looks like you've been busy today," she said as she pointed to a newspaper stand with his face on the cover.

Just then, a large man jostled her as he rushed by and when she stumbled in her heels, Ford was glad for the excuse to put his arms around her.

"I've got you."

In the middle of the crowded sidewalk she didn't immediately pull away, but stood there with her hands pressed flat on his chest. "You really mean that, don't you?"

"Yes."

But words weren't enough. He needed to kiss her, even if it wasn't fair to push her into a public declaration like this. Ford had reached his limit of self-control this morning at exactly the same time she had, and now it seemed there was no way of getting that control back.

He could nearly taste the hint of mint on her lips when a crisp—and very familiar—voice said, "Rutherford, what a coincidence this is."

Despite the fact that Mia's hands were still on him, he couldn't stop himself from stiffening. She looked up at him in confusion, then to the well-dressed couple standing in the entry to an expensive-looking restaurant.

"My parents are here."

She looked back and forth between the three of them. "Those are your parents?" she asked in an incredulous voice.

As he nodded he wondered what the odds were that these two people couldn't have just ruined his childhood, but that they could also find a way to screw up his future, too? With Mia still on the fence about being with him, meeting his parents right now certainly wasn't going to help his case any. Not when she'd actually see the genes that would pass through to the kids he wanted to have with her. He'd described his childhood to her, but it was much worse for her to actually see it for herself.

He was bracing himself when Mia slid her hand into his and smiled up at him. "I've got you, too."

They were just four simple words. But they instantly changed everything.

Mia knew there had to be a family resemblance between Ford and his parents, but she honestly couldn't see it. They were so starched-up and pinched looking, whereas he was so relaxed and comfortable in his skin.

"Catherine. Lance. This is Mia Sullivan." He didn't say he was glad to see them, and neither did they to him.

"Hello." She reached out to shake their hands, even though they hadn't yet offered their own.

They didn't leave her hanging, but they didn't look particularly impressed with her, either, in her cute little dress with her hair up in a ponytail and artsy cut-glass earrings on instead of pearls or diamonds. She was sure they still had dreams of seeing their son with a perfectly bred girl from the Junior League, not a woman like her who had grown up in a middle-class family…and who had begged their son just hours ago to let her have at his glorious erection.

His mother turned cool eyes back to him. "How are you, Rutherford?"

God, Mia thought, it was like watching distant acquaintances meet on the street then struggle to exchange pleasantries. She squeezed Ford's hand to remind him that he wasn't in this alone.

He smiled down at her, and she was glad to see the spark leap in his dark eyes before he turned back to his mother. "Everything is great, thanks. What about you guys?"

His father's brows came down over his eyes at the casual way Ford spoke to them. Clearly, Lance Vincent had been bred and trained for another kind of response entirely. "We are well, thank you. Seattle has become quite the art scene, and we're here to solidify a few acquisitions for your mother's gallery." He looked slightly uncomfortable as he added, "This meeting is extremely fortuitous, as one of our main local investors has informed us that he enjoys your music. I'm sure he would like to meet you, if you would come inside with us."

"We've got a pizza waiting for us. But tell your friend I'm glad he's digging my music."

Ford's mother finally reached out to touch her son on the arm. There was nothing motherly about it, especially since the way her nails sank into his skin showed that she was feeling more irritated with him than anything else. "You are here now and we leave tomorrow evening. Surely your pizza can wait a few minutes."

Before Mia could think better of it, she asked, "You're here in Seattle to meet with investors, but you're not even staying a little longer to see the final show of your son's latest world tour?"

"We have obligations. Besides, we're not fans of his kind of music," his mother said, as if that explained everything.

"No?" Mia's voice was deceptively gentle. "What music do you like?"

"Rutherford's father and I are on the board of the Boston Lyric Opera and the Boston Symphony Orchestra."

"Surely, despite that, your *obligations* can wait another day so that you can see his show."

His mother made a sour face, at least as much as she could, given how badly her Botox injections had frozen her expression to one of almost perfect blankness. "Lance and I find it so difficult to listen to all that screeching and hammering. Rutherford had such talent when he was young. He could have been a classical musician. He could have been a respected composer if only he had put his mind to it instead of fooling around with that electric guitar."

"Fooling around? He could have been respected? Screeching and hammering?"

Rage was nearly knocking Mia flat on the sidewalk. Only Ford's hand on hers kept her from toppling over. Maybe Ford would be happier not to engage with his parents, but she'd been raised to say what she thought. And if this was going to be her only chance to lay into them, by God, she was going to take it.

Because she thought his parents *sucked*.

"Your son is one of the most incredible people I've ever met. He not only has more talent in his little finger than any of the *proper* musicians that you obviously revere but, far more important than that, he's also one of the kindest, funniest, most wonderful men I've ever known. Which is even more impressive, now that I've met both of you." She sneered at them, not caring what they thought about her attacking them, because their opinions didn't count. "I used to think it was sad that you weren't bragging about him to your friends, but now I'm glad you don't, because neither of you deserve to call him *son*. And," she needed to add before they could completely edge away from her and into the restaurant, "His name isn't Rutherford. It's *Ford*."

His parents gaped at her in outrage, but she was done with them. Ford was staring at her, too, his expression unreadable as she tugged him away from two people she was *this close* to slugging.

Mia was so furious that she had no idea a crowd had formed about them as she'd told Ford's parents exactly what she thought of them. He'd seen recognition in at least a dozen strangers' eyes as they headed down the sidewalk and into the hole-in-the-wall pizza joint, but Mia was so obviously driven to keep them moving that no one tried to intercept them.

He could still feel her bristling as he paid for their pizza, then hailed a cab to take them to his place. She was uncharacteristically silent as she stewed over the unexpected meeting, but she never once let go of his hand. And even while he paid the driver, she waited on the seat beside him so that they could both get out of the cab without needing to let go of each other.

Once they were inside, he put the pizza box down on the kitchen counter and pulled her against him. "Have I mentioned recently that you blow my mind?"

Normally, he knew, she would have come back with a joke about having "blown" another part of him that morning. But tonight she simply looked up at him and said, "I heard everything you said about them, but I guess I didn't really want to believe it. I wanted to think that maybe one day I could bring you back together to become a real, loving family." She blew out a hard breath. "Instead, when I realized how far off base I really was, I yelled at them in the middle of the sidewalk." Her expression hardened again. "Which they totally deserved. But still. I didn't check with you first. I just let loose. I'm sorry, Ford, for not being able to help mys—"

He cut off her apology by brushing a fingertip down her nose and was glad to see the corners of her mouth reflexively curve up just the littlest bit at his purposely ticklish caress.

"No one has ever stood up for me like that. Even my teachers, who had to know how fractured my relationship with my parents was and how much I dreaded going home, didn't step in. I'm sure because they didn't see bruises, they didn't think it could be that bad. And, honestly, when I was away from home, which was most of the time, I pretty much blocked them out, so it didn't seem that bad."

"So you're not mad at me for making a total scene and ripping them to shreds?"

A million people could call out his name from an audience and he would never feel as loved, as appreciated as he had when she'd given his parents hell in the middle of the sidewalk.

"I love you, Mia."

The fire, the worry, immediately went out of her eyes, only to have that wariness about their future together take their place. "Ford—"

"And I love knowing that you're going to protect our kids just as passionately, without reserve, without 'thinking,' if anyone ever tries to get away with not treating them well."

She narrowed her eyes at him. "I know what you're doing. You think that because I'm all riled up over your parents, it must mean that we're besties now and you can start talking about marriage and kids again." She whirled out of his arms. "I'll have you know that I'm still making up my mind about us, and no amount of sweet talk about how great our kids and life will be together is going to get me to decide sooner. So you can just stop being so gorgeous and awesome and smelling so damn good and saying such beautiful things about how much you love me, because I'm telling you right now that I'll make up my mind when I'm good and ready and not a moment before!"

Maybe he shouldn't have laughed at her soliloquy, but she looked so cute as she told him off that he couldn't help it. A snarl left her beautiful lips, and as she launched herself at him, he caught her in his arms and lifted her up.

"It's a warm night for Seattle, don't you think?"

He was big enough to easily pin her arms and legs against him as he carried her out through the kitchen to the back patio. The cool water would be the perfect way to jolt away the bitterness that had lingered from seeing his parents. He was used to them and knew exactly what to expect in the rare instances when they ran into each other, but she had been completely blindsided.

"What the hell are you doing, rock star?"

"Cooling off my hotheaded girl."

Twenty-Six

Mia's eyes went wide as she realized he was taking her straight toward the pool. "Oh, no. You'd better n—"

He held on to her until the very last second, then tossed her a few feet away from him so that their arms and legs wouldn't collide when they went under the water together.

She came splashing up to the surface. "You're in for it now."

He was more than happy to let her launch herself at him, and as she shoved him down under the water, he pulled her down with him. When they came up this time, her arms and legs were around him and he was kissing her.

Though the water had made her skin cool to the touch, her lips remained full of heat. He'd already told her just how much it meant to him that she'd taken his side earlier... Now he wanted to show her with his kiss.

But where his nip at her lower lip started out playfully, the way she responded so passionately with a low groan of pure, sweet desire made it impossible to do anything but devour every inch of her mouth while his hands cupped and stroked her body, eliciting even more moans of pleasure out of her. And as his greedy need for her took over, he couldn't get enough of her mouth or her tongue against his. He wanted nothing more than to strip her dress away and have her wet curves totally bared to him as she'd been in the shower on his tour bus the previous night. Only, tonight, he knew that if they stripped away their clothes, there would be no chance of stopping.

Each time he made himself pull away from her, it sent him closer to the edge of madness. There was no one else he'd willingly lose his mind for. Only Mia. And a chance at a future with her was easily worth every painfully hard erection he'd had to deal with this past week.

"Look at you," she said as she brushed his wet hair back from his forehead with a slightly shaky hand, "so smug, thinking you've just kissed me out of being mad at you."

Despite his raging libido, it was easy to grin at her, considering he felt a hell of a lot more than smug with the most beautiful woman in the world in his arms. "Well, are you still mad?"

Her lips twitched before she finally admitted, "No, damn you."

"Actually," he said as he nuzzled the wet skin where her neck met the curve of her shoulder, "it's pretty hot when you get riled up. Maybe sometime I'll let you have at me in the bedroom during a fight."

He could see by the sparkle in her eyes that she liked the thought of it, too, but she said, "We weren't fighting."

He nuzzled the other side of her neck. "No?"

"No. I was merely informing you that you were acting like a Neanderthal."

She tried to swat his kisses away, but she ruined it with a giggle. Not to mention the fact that her halter top wasn't exactly meant to get soaking wet, and when she pulled back a few inches in mock irritation, he got a *fantastic* eyeful of her lush breasts and hard nipples.

"Damn," he said as he took a long, hot look, "you're pretty."

She ogled his shoulders and chest in his wet T-shirt just as he'd been drooling over her. "Right back at you, rock star."

Their eyes met and both of them instantly understood that they were teetering on the edge of a precipice. Either they both had to agree to jump over it together tonight…or they had to back away completely.

A week ago, he wouldn't have thought twice about taking advantage of the softness in her eyes or the hot press of her body against him. But now he knew he'd never forgive himself if he pushed her a step further than she was ready to go on her own.

Fortunately, both of their stomachs grumbled at the same time. "How about we go dry off and finally get to that pizza?"

She put her hands on either side of his face and kissed him before saying, "You should probably prepare yourself, because I think my dress has gone completely see-through." She leaned in to whisper in his ear. "And I'm not wearing anything under it."

She kicked out of his arms and swam to the edge, the wet, translucent fabric clinging to every inch of her perfect body as she got out and headed inside the house. By the time he'd worked to get his erection to go down at least a little bit—to no avail—and followed her wet path upstairs, she was standing in his bedroom wearing one of his T-shirts and a pair of his jeans.

She'd knotted the gray cotton T-shirt at her waist and had his jeans folded over at least two times at the waist and at the hems. She looked like a little girl playing dress-up, and though his T-shirt and jeans hid nearly all of her curves, Ford knew he'd never seen anything more beautiful in all his life.

All he'd been thinking about was winning her back.

He hadn't realized that she'd help him heal his past, too, by making it stop hurting.

She tossed him a towel, but she wasn't looking at him, she was staring in dismay at the growing puddle at his feet. "As a seller of fine homes," she said with a little grimace, "I just can't stand leaving the floors wet like this. It drives my parents and brothers crazy, but I can't help it." She skidded along the floor with a towel beneath each foot and wiped it clean as he dried off and changed out of his wet clothes.

A short while later, he found her sitting on the couch with the TV remote in one hand and a slice of pizza in the other. "The pizza's cold," she informed him right before shoving the huge slice into her mouth. Around pepperoni and black olives, she said, "Good thing I've always liked it better that way."

And as he settled next to her and they began a spirited debate over which movie they should watch, Ford knew with absolute certainty that playing stadiums and flying around the world in private jets to meet royalty had absolutely nothing on hanging out on his couch with his girl to watch the positively terrible movie he was going to let her insist they see.

Full from the large pizza and the bottles of beer that had been, rather predictably, the only thing in Ford's enormous state-of-the-art fridge, Mia easily settled into his arms. They were both suffering their way through a movie she'd known was going to be a total joke. She had wanted to see it anyway because she couldn't deal with anything emotional or thought-provoking right now. Fart jokes and characters falling down for no reason whatsoever were her limit tonight.

Ford had obviously thrown the two of them into the pool to try to erase their confrontation with his parents. Then he made her laugh with his ongoing commentary that was way funnier than anything in the movie. Having been slippery and wet against him in the pool had made her *want* him, just like always—but all the while her heart ached for him.

A week ago she thought she'd hated him. But tonight, what she felt for Ford was so far from hate that all she could focus on, as the movie on the large TV screen blurred before her, was what she could possibly do to help heal his wounds.

She was so lost in her thoughts that she was surprised when Ford pressed a kiss to her forehead and said, "I never knew a blank screen could be so riveting." Startled that she'd missed not only the end of the movie, but also the fact that he'd turned off the TV, she shook her head.

"Sorry. I—"

God, she couldn't tell him what she'd actually been thinking. She had four brothers and knew exactly how sensitive their pride could be. The last thing she wanted Ford to think was that she pitied him in any way. On the contrary, she could see just how strong he was now.

Everything she'd achieved had been with the full support of her parents and family.

Everything he'd achieved had been despite his parents' disappointment.

The ache intensified as she shifted in his arms so

that she could put hers around his neck and snuggle closer. "I'm just tired. And your couch is really comfortable."

It would be so easy to convince Ford to make love with her tonight, to help heal both of them by taking away everything that hurt and replacing it with pleasure. But even though she was close to grasping at any reason at all to be with him, after waiting this long she knew she wanted their first time together again to be full of love.

And only love.

"I know you have your big show on Saturday night," she said slowly as he stroked her hair and she let herself sink even more fully into his strength and warmth, "and I know you're probably going to be really busy until then, but once a month my parents put on a Friday night dinner, and—"

"Yes." He tugged her tighter, so tight her breath caught in her compressed chest. "I'd love to come to dinner at your parents' house."

The ache for him was still there inside her heart, but suddenly, so was joy. She smiled as she said, "A couple of my brothers will probably be there, too. They're both fans of yours. At least, they were. Because after they find out you're dating their sister..."

He grinned back at her, but she was pretty sure she could see that same ache behind his beautiful smile. "Whatever it takes to win them and your parents over, I'll do it."

"No." Her response was fierce. "You can't change

who you are for anyone. Promise me you'll just be yourself, egomaniac rock star and all."

His promise came as the sweetest kiss he'd ever given her, one that spiraled out and out and out into more and more pleasure with every breath they took from one another. She wanted to surrender all of herself to him, and she wanted to demand every part of him. She wanted to completely lose herself in him, in the wild pleasure of naked skin against naked skin, in whispered promises of never-ending pleasure that came true over and over again.

Soon, she knew deep within herself. Soon, they'd make love. Not just because their bodies would demand it, but because their hearts wouldn't let them hold back another moment.

Which, amazingly, made the sweetness before the sinning even sweeter.

So even though she knew she'd be aching and desperate for Ford by the time he dropped her off at her condo, she relished every single second of making out on the couch with the friend whom she was falling head over heels for...

Twenty-Seven

Walking up the brick path that led to her parents' front door on Friday night, Mia slipped her hand into Ford's. He was holding a huge bouquet of roses in his other hand, flowers she knew her mother was going to go nuts over.

"I've never brought anyone home to meet my family before," she told him, her throat tight with emotion.

Just then, her father opened the front door and said, "Pumpkin, you're here." He drew her in for a long hug, as though it had been far longer than one week since she'd seen him at the wedding. By the time Mia squeaked, "Daddy," her mother was wrapping her into a hug, too. As always, she was comforted by the familiar smell of the lemon-scented shampoo her mother had used for as long as she could remember. Mia had always considered herself an independent woman, but the truth was that when she went more than a handful of weeks without seeing her parents and brothers, she started to feel a little lost.

"I'd like to introduce you to my friend Ford." Upon hearing the word *friend*, Ford squeezed her hand. "Actually," she said, needing them to know, "he's my friend *and* my boyfriend."

She almost felt like a teenager again. Somehow, despite everything she and Ford had done already in bed years ago, all their long kisses good-night this week had given a surprising innocence to their current relationship.

Ford shook her mother's and father's hands. "It's great to finally meet you, Mr. and Mrs. Sullivan. You raised an amazing daughter."

Just as she'd expected, Mia could see that her father was going to take a while to make up his mind about the rock star who was trying to claim his daughter's heart, but her mother was immediately charmed. "It's lovely to meet you, too, Ford. And Mia is the best daughter I could ever have hoped for."

"Right back at you, Mom."

Her mother went to put the flowers in a vase and her father was heading into the kitchen to grab a beer out of the fridge when her brother Adam walked in the front door.

"Hey, Mia." He kissed her on the top of her head, but he was looking out the front window to the curb. "Looks like some high roller moved into the neighborhood with his fancy c—"

He cut the word short when he finally realized Ford was standing beside her. Mia nearly giggled at the look of utter surprise as her brother came unexpectedly face-to-face with his musical hero...standing in his parents' house...holding his sister's hand.

"Adam," Mia said, "I don't believe you met Ford at Marcus and Nicola's wedding. Ford, this is my second oldest brother."

"It's great to finally meet you," Ford said in an easy voice.

But instead of reaching out to shake Ford's hand, Mia could see the wheels in her brother's head turning as he looked between them, once, then twice. "You two met at the wedding last weekend?"

"Nope," Mia said with a cheerful smile as she slid her arm around Ford and leaned into him. "We met five years ago. You know the story, young foolish love and all that. But we didn't see each other again until a couple of days before the wedding, when Ford hired me to find him a house in Seattle."

Given how freaked out she'd been by being with Ford at the wedding, introducing him to her family tonight was surprisingly fun. It was amazing what a difference a week could make.

Then again, wasn't a week with Ford all it had taken to change everything inside her heart five years ago, too?

"Five years ago? Young love?" Poor Adam looked as if he was going to pop a vein. "What the hell, Mia?

We've heard his songs on the radio a thousand times and you never once mentioned that you knew him."

"I'm sorry that I didn't. But the past doesn't matter," Mia told her brother. And she meant it. "All you need to know is that we're together now."

Given the heated—and borderline deadly—glare Adam gave Ford at that point, Mia realized that her brother had completely put aside his appreciation of Ford's music in favor of protecting her.

Right then the side door into the kitchen slammed, and she knew Dylan had arrived. He skidded to a halt in the doorway between the kitchen and the living room when he saw Ford standing there. Looking as if he'd just come off the water, Dylan looked back and forth between Mia and Ford with a frown that deepened more with every pass.

"Ford, this is my brother Dylan. Dylan, this is my—"

"Boyfriend," Adam growled from behind her.

Her big, tough sailor brother looked as if he was going to swallow his tongue. "*He* is *your* boyfriend?"

"Wow," she said with a laugh, "glad to know you think I'm such a prize."

"Jesus, Mia, that's not it. You're great. But he's—"

"A goddamned rock star," Adam filled in again.

"If either of you want to take a few swings at me to get them out of your system," Ford offered, "I'm game."

"Don't be ridiculous," she told Ford before turning her glare on her brothers. "I'm sure my over-protective brothers can find it in themselves to trust their sister to have *some* taste—and to wait to bring home a man until she found one who was worth it. Right, boys?"

Dylan folded first. "I gotta get a beer." But before he could escape, her father came in with enough cold bottles for everyone.

As Adam downed his first one in a long, clearly irritated gulp, Mia said to Ford, "Let's go see if my mom needs some help."

"Mrs. Sullivan," Ford said as they walked into the kitchen, "everything smells great."

"Call me Claudia, please."

Mia couldn't resist reaching into the salad bowl to pull out a candied walnut. "Here, taste this. She roasts them herself."

Ford made a sound that told both Mia and her mother just how good he thought the small sugared nut tasted. "Claudia, what can I help with?"

"Why don't you and Mia finish setting the table?"

One week ago Mia had called Ford a self-centered egomaniac. Now she knew there wasn't one inch of Ford that was a rock star prima donna who expected to sit back and be served. On the contrary, Mia got the sense that he really enjoyed putting the colorful plates and pretty blown-glass tumblers on the table.

Adam scowled as he wandered past, and Mia decided she'd better deal with him before he pushed her so far that she'd have to leap across the dinner table to slug some sense back into him.

"I've got that thing in the car for you, Adam."

"Thing? What thing?" But he followed her out the front door.

"This thing." She hit his upper arm hard enough that he winced. "That's for being a jerk to my guest. Up until fifteen minutes ago, you were Ford's biggest fan."

"That was before I knew he was screwing around with my sister."

"Really? You think I'm such a victim that I let guys screw around with me?"

"You know that's not what I'm saying."

"Maybe you should try saying it a different way, then."

He ran a hand through his hair, clearly frustrated with the whole unexpected situation. "That guy has the whole world on a silver plate if he wants it."

"It's the same for Smith," she pointed out. "And you don't treat him like he's the scum of the earth simply for daring to breathe in your presence."

Clearly irritated with her logic, he scowled in the direction of the living room. "I grew up with Smith. I don't know Ford. I don't know how he treats women."

She knew she shouldn't be angry with her brother. Sure, he was totally overbearing in the same way Ian had been at the wedding, but his heart was in the right place. "Give him a chance tonight, Adam. For me. Because I care about him."

He studied her carefully. "How much do you care, Mia?"

"A lot." She hadn't even needed to think about it, hadn't hesitated. But instead of Adam looking happier, strangely, his frown deepened. "Adam?"

"When you were born I couldn't believe how little you were. We had always played rough, but with you—"

"You made sure I didn't get hurt, and I love you for that. But we're not on the playground anymore, and I don't think you can control whether or not I get hurt this time." She pressed a kiss to his cheek. "Sorry I had to slug you. Probably makes you wish you hadn't taught me such a solid jab, doesn't it? Because I'm pretty sure that's going to bruise."

She was glad to hear him laughing as he followed her back inside.

"How long have you known Nicola, Ford?"

Mia knew she could count on her mother to break the ice as they all dug into their full plates.

"I caught one of her shows a couple of years ago and was really impressed. As she started to play her guitar I could immediately imagine the first chords and lyrics of the song we would write together in my head." He laughed at himself. "She ended up taking those chords and lyrics and making them a thousand times better, of course. I was honored to be at her wedding."

"I remember Mary calling me after a family lunch they had in Palo Alto, where Marcus declared his love for Nicola in front of all of them," Claudia said. "It sounded so sweet."

Mia could feel Ford's eyes on her, and because she could read his mind, she shot him a look that said, *Don't you dare, rock star.* The answering grin he gave her did nothing whatsoever to make her believe that he wouldn't pull a Marcus on her. Stuff like that sounded so romantic, but even though she and Adam had had their little chat out front, she wasn't sure how well he'd deal with Ford making a grand declaration of his feelings in front of them all tonight.

"Your family is great. Even after Mia told me how close you all are, seeing it for myself at the wedding was amazing." With an easy grin, he turned to her brothers and said, "Adam, Mia told me you work with historic houses. And, Dylan, you design sailboats, don't you?"

Just that quickly, Mia knew there would always be a seat for him at her mother's table. And as he got Dylan and Adam to start talking despite their rocky start, she was struck by just how well Ford fit into her family…and how much he seemed to thrive on being with them.

Twenty-Eight

"I'm really glad you brought Ford home to spend some time with us tonight," Mia's mother said to her as they walked into the kitchen to heat up the apple pie Claudia had made for dessert. "I like him very much, honey. He seems like a good man."

Mia loved that her mother didn't refer to Ford's talent or his fame. She hadn't said something like, *"Considering how rich and successful he is, he's a nice man."* Instead, Claudia was looking only at the man he was at his core, and at the way he treated her daughter. There were very few people for whom Ford's career and bank account wouldn't matter, but Mia's mother was one of them.

"Thanks for being so nice to him tonight, Mom. Especially given what a tough crowd Dad and the boys were at first. Ford has never had much of a family, and I think it means a lot to him to be here with all of us tonight."

"He's the first man you've ever brought home. Even if that didn't tell me how special he is to you, I would have known from watching the two of you together at the wedding."

Mia stopped halfway to reaching for a stack of clean forks. "You could tell there was something between us last weekend?"

"You've always looked at the men you've dated playfully, flirtatiously. They can't take their eyes off you, but you've never had a problem looking away. Ford is the only man I've ever seen you with where you couldn't stop staring right back at him, too. But it's not just his good looks that draws you to him, is it?"

"No. Although when a guy looks like he does, it's hard to remember why I should even try to resist him."

"What do you think will make you happier, honey? Finding a way to keep resisting how you feel about him?" Her mother's eyes were warm with understanding. "Or giving in to what you feel whenever he's near?"

It was both a blessing and a curse that her mother seemed to have emotional X-ray vision with her children. On the one hand, it meant she was always there for them, even before they accepted that they needed her support. On the other, it made hiding from the truth downright impossible.

Which, Mia suddenly realized, was why she hadn't brought Ford home five years ago. Not just because she didn't want to give up even a few precious hours in his arms, but because even though she'd been head over heels for him, she must have known that neither of them was ready yet to truly love each other. Her father and brothers would have been just as protective as they had been tonight…but her mother would have seen all the rest.

Still, Mia's mother had never tried to push her one way or another, whether in love or career. Claudia simply supported all her children in whatever direction they chose to go. Even if that direction sometimes ended up being a mistake.

"When he came back into my life a week ago, I thought I knew exactly who he was. But he keeps surprising me in really good ways. I'm happy with him, Mom, so much happier than I can ever remember being. But—" She broke off, not knowing how to put what she was feeling into words. "Why is it that the happier I feel when I'm with him, the more and more scared I get about losing myself in that happiness?"

"I was just as frightened with your father," her mother said as she stroked Mia's hair. "I was afraid to let myself love him all the way *just in case* something went wrong and tore us apart. The truth is, honey, things go wrong all the time, but they go right, too. Finally, I realized that there was no one I'd rather share all those right and wrong times with."

Claudia's arms had come around her, and Mia was glad to let herself be held. "I don't know why

I didn't talk to you about this before now. I should have told you what happened between us five years ago, but I worked so hard to keep it from everyone."

"If you ask me, it's perfectly natural that when we feel so much, when our entire world begins to revolve around someone else, that's when we're sure that no one else can possibly understand what it's like to love so deeply, aren't we?"

Over the past few days, Mia had been coming closer and closer to accepting that what she was feeling for Ford was real. And that it could last.

Tonight, she decided, she would finally tell him everything that was in her heart. And she wouldn't let herself be afraid anymore of the rights and the wrongs, the good and the bad, as long as she had her best friend beside her.

"He needs a family." Mia's heart broke all over again when she thought about the man and woman she'd met the day before who were too stupid to know what an amazing son they had in Ford. "He hasn't been as lucky as I am to have all of you. I so want that for him." She reached for her mother, needing her to know how much she appreciated the support, the encouragement and the unconditional love that Claudia had given her since the day she was born. "I love you, Mom."

"I love you, too, honey. And while Ford might not have had a great family to grow up with, he is still a very lucky man."

"You mean because of his success?"

"No." Her mother's eyes were soft with emotion for her youngest. "Because he has not only your friendship, but your love, too. All that's left is to give him your trust."

Yes, Mia thought as her mother's words rang true. Watching him with her family felt like putting the final puzzle piece into place. One that had been an obvious fit all along, but had eluded her until tonight.

Because if she could trust him with her secrets, with her body and with her family, then she knew she could now trust him with her heart, too.

Even after the wedding in Napa the previous weekend, when Ford had seen how close the Sullivans were, this family dinner with Mia's parents and two of her brothers was a revelation. It was all so normal, so easy—from the colorful plates, to the table and chairs Max had built himself, to the gray-muzzled dog snoring on the cushion in the corner. He could see where Mia came by her decorating prowess, particularly when it came to color and family photos on every table and wall. Ford especially loved the pictures of Mia growing up, from a beautiful baby to a cute little girl with pigtails and missing teeth to a knockout teen all dressed up for the prom. He'd already been on the road by the time his own prom had rolled around, and he hadn't given it a single thought. Now he wondered, what would it have been like to go with a girl like Mia Sullivan on his arm?

But he already knew how great it would have been to be the luckiest guy on the planet…because it was exactly how he felt now, every single second they were together.

Most of all, it struck him just how comfortable the Sullivans were with each other. All throughout dinner there had been so much laughter, friendly debate and support. In many ways it reminded Ford of the way his crew and band were together while they were touring for months on end.

Struck by the thought, he paused. All this time, he'd thought he didn't have a family. But had he made one for himself out of other musicians? Only, while he'd shared plenty of beers and nights around the poker table backstage, he'd never truly trusted any of them the way Mia had taught him this week that you trusted a friend.

"You spend a lot of time on the road, don't you?" Adam asked, the second the door closed behind Mia and her mother.

Ford turned his focus back to Mia's brother. Nodding, he said, "I've spent most of the past decade on the road."

"How long until you head back out?" Adam had thawed a little during dinner, but he was clearly still prepared to go to the mat for his sister.

"I've got plenty to do for the kids' music camp I'm starting up here in town. I'm not planning to tour again anytime soon." But he knew what Adam thought, that Ford was just toying with Mia while he was in town. There was only one way to prove to her brothers that he was serious about her. "But the biggest reason I'm not going back out on the road is because I'm hoping to convince your sister to marry me."

"Marry you?" Adam shot his father and brother a look. Max didn't look particularly surprised, but Ford wasn't sure he looked wholly pleased, either. "How well did the two of you know each other five years ago?"

Mia had said again and again that the past didn't matter anymore, but Ford still planned to spend the rest of his life making it up to her, and to everyone who loved her. "I loved Mia from the first moment I saw her, but I was young and stupid."

This time Dylan was the one growling, "You cheated on her with some groupie?"

"No. But just because I didn't cheat on her, doesn't mean I deserved her."

Finally, Mia's father spoke. "What makes you think you deserve to be with my daughter now?"

Ford had assumed Max Sullivan was a great father simply because of how much Mia adored him, and he'd immediately liked the man, but during dinner his respect for Max had only continued to grow. Not only had he raised five great kids, he had also managed to keep the love alive with his wife for nearly four decades.

Ford's parents had been a terrible example of how to parent and love well. He hoped he'd have many more chances to watch and learn from Max and Claudia.

"I know you think no one will ever be good enough for your daughter. And you're right—she deserves a better man than me. But I can promise you that no one will ever work harder to make her smile. No other man will ever support her dreams the way I will. And I will love her more and more every day for the rest of my life."

Again, a look passed between the brothers and their father, before Adam said, "You expect us to believe you'd give up everything for her?"

Ford had held his temper all night long with Mia's brother. Now he let it fly as he leaned forward and growled, "Your sister is beautiful. She's intelligent. She's fiercely loyal to her friends and employees and family. And I wouldn't hesitate for even one second to give up everything I have if it meant getting to be with her for the rest of my life."

The three men were silent for several long beats as they studied him to feel out his sincerity. Finally, her father said, "The day Mia was born, even though I'd already had four kids, I knew I was in for it. I could see not only the spunk and intelligence in her eyes, but also just what a beauty she was, and I knew how easy it would be to live in fear of her being taken advantage of, getting hurt by men who only saw her beauty and wanted to claim it as a prize."

Five years ago, Ford had been at least partly guilty

of that, but he'd already confessed his idiocy to her family, so he remained silent as her father continued.

"I promised myself that day that I would trust Mia to make the right decisions, and to teach her by example to always insist on the best and the most powerful love." Max Sullivan raised his glass across the table. "I'm not saying it will be easy to let my little girl go, and to know that I'm no longer the first man she'll turn to, but if anyone is going to take my place, I'm glad it's you, Ford."

Before Ford could begin to express how much Max's faith in him meant beyond clinking their glasses together in a quick toast, Mia and her mother came back in carrying a huge, warm apple pie and six forks. And as everyone dug straight in, Ford knew that even if Mia's father hadn't just said he approved of their relationship, he would have known it by the way her family assumed he'd fight for his pieces of apple from the center of the pie just like the rest of them…and then by the way Mia leaned over, midbite, and kissed him in front of the people she loved most in the world.

Ford caught a glimpse of Max and Claudia Sullivan smiling at each other right before he closed his eyes and kissed Mia back.

Twenty-Nine

Mia wasn't normally in such a rush to get out of her parents' house after a Friday night dinner but tonight, as soon as the final apple had been scraped out of the pie pan, she jumped out of her seat and yanked Ford up with her.

"Thanks for dinner. It was amazing. I promise to do all the washing up next time!" She let go of Ford's hand just long enough to kiss her mother and father and hug her brothers goodbye. She barely gave Ford a chance to say his own thank-yous before she dragged him out of the dining room and through the living room to the foyer. "Love you guys, and we'll see all of you tomorrow night at the show."

Before anyone in her family could do or say anything to delay their departure, she opened the front door and pushed Ford out of it, slamming it shut behind them.

"Hurry!" she urged Ford as she moved as fast as

she ever had in her heels to throw herself into the passenger seat of his car. He was barely behind the wheel when she grabbed the front of his shirt and planted a crazy-hot kiss on him. He tasted like apples and beer and *Ford*. "Even though I know my entire family is standing at the front window watching us right now, if you don't start the car in the next couple of seconds, I'm going to jump you anyway."

His grin was at once brilliantly happy and darkly sensual as he started the engine. By the time he pulled out onto the road, she had half the buttons on his shirt undone.

He put one hand over both of hers and held them firm against his chest. "Tell me where there's a dark place to park. And make it quick or we're both going to get arrested for public indecency."

Every inch of her thrilled at the sensual threat in his voice and the hard-rock beat of his heart against her hands. "Turn right here. Left there. Now right again." With every turn he made, there were fewer houses and streetlights, until they reached the end of the neighborhood and the trees grew thicker as they entered a forest. "Now go straight until we come to the end of the road."

They were completely shrouded in darkness when Ford turned off the engine. She leaped across the stick shift onto his lap, and though it was a tight fit between the steering wheel and his seat, she relished the hard press of his muscles against her curves.

She loved how hard he was between her thighs,

how hungry his hands were as they roved from her breasts to her hips and then back again in a rough and restless pattern of lust. Though it was already pitch-black in the car, she closed her eyes as she rocked her pelvis against his to focus every ounce of her concentration on the pleasure that was coming over her in waves.

Her hands were in his hair, her cheek pressed to the side of his as her skirt bunched up beneath his hands—when he stopped cold and gripped her hips hard to hold her still.

"Mia."

Beyond pleased that he'd just discovered her bare skin, she informed him, "I took my panties off right before dessert."

"You," he said as he slowly moved his hands beneath her skirt to caress her naked hips, "are a very bad girl."

The sinful feel of his fingertips grazing the sensitive skin at her inner thighs made her laugh husky as she urged him, "Be bad with me, Ford."

"It's gotten to the point," he replied in a voice made raw with both emotion and lust, "where I'm coming up with a new fantasy about you every goddamned minute of every day. How I'm going to strip off your clothes. How you're going to beg me to kiss you, to touch you. But—"

"All week long you've teased me," she growled against his mouth before nipping hard at his lower lip. "I'm done, Ford."

"Done with what?"

There wasn't enough light from the moon above them for her to see his eyes, but she could hear the tension—and the hope—in his question.

"Done with doubting you." She held his face in her hands and turned it slightly so that she could press a kiss to one cheek. "I'm done with being scared of what I feel for you." She kissed his other cheek. "And I'm done falling in love with my best friend."

"Tell me what you're saying." His words were rough, instead of gentle. "Tell me *exactly* what you're saying, Mia."

"I know we can't erase our past, but there was enough good about what we had during that first week before it all imploded that I don't think I'd want to erase it even if we could. And this week has shown me what a future with you could look like." God, yes, she was desperate for more of him—all of him—but she wanted all the little things, too. "Falling asleep in your arms, feeling safe and loved. Waking up with you beside me in the morning, knowing I've finally found my other half. Spending our free time during the day laughing, and loving you more with every second, even when you're pushing all of my hot buttons." Threading her fingers through his, she said, "And you should know you have my mother's stamp of approval, too."

Mia hadn't realized how much she'd needed that support and approval until her mother had gently pushed her to have faith in what she was feeling for

Ford…and to know that it was natural to second-guess a love this powerful, even for a woman as amazing as her mother.

"You're the person I want to laugh with. You're the person I want to cry with. You're the person I want to tell all of my secrets to. You're the first one I want to call when I close a big new deal and also to make up new curse words with when one goes bad. You're my best friend, Ford, and I know you always will be. I'm saying that I want to be yours in *exactly* every possible way."

All week, when things had gotten heated and desperate between them, Ford had always been the one to stop them from going too far. But tonight, after telling him he was her new best friend, he immediately pulled the lever that lowered the seat back and flipped them over so that she was lying beneath him.

"Do you remember our first night together?" he asked.

The memory sent thrill bumps racing across her skin, even though she was burning up from the inside out at his nearness. *"God, yes."*

When they'd left the venue, the limo door had barely closed and the privacy screen hadn't quite rolled all the way up to the ceiling when they'd attacked each other. She could remember everything about making love with Ford for the first time in the back of his limo, except whose clothes had come off first. They'd been that desperate for each other.

"You ruined limos for me," he told her.

In the dark, all she knew was how deliciously heavy Ford was as he pressed her into the seat, his clean, masculine scent taking over her senses one shaky breath at a time.

"Next limo we're in," she whispered into his ear, "I promise I'll make it up to you." Her teeth closed over his earlobe as she yanked his shirt all the way open. "Want a preview tonight?"

"I want *everything* tonight," he said a beat before his mouth covered hers in a kiss that was shockingly possessive, thrillingly dominant...and utterly loving.

Mia was hot and needy and so damned ready everywhere he touched, but even as he greedily ran kisses over her face, her shoulders, the swell of her breasts, and then up her thighs to her hips, he knew he'd never be able to get enough of her in the cramped seat. He wanted to see her skin flush. He needed to watch her eyes spark, then cloud, as he took her closer and closer to pleasure, then sent her rushing all the way past.

"Home." But even as he made the nearly impossible decision to wait a few more minutes to have her, he had to press his mouth to the spot on her neck where her pulse was racing and she smelled like hothouse flowers. "I'm taking you home, and then I'm going to make love to you until neither of us can move."

"No." Her arms tightened around his back as she

turned her face so that her lips brushed against his. "I can't make it that far feeling like this."

She moved, limber and insistent against him, and when his hand that was beneath her skirt slid against her slick heat, he silently agreed that he couldn't let her suffer for the short ride back to his house.

He didn't give her so much as a word of warning before he thrust two fingers hard and deep inside her. She rewarded him with a low moan of pleasure that resonated all the way down to his soul. Shifting on the seat just enough that she could push her hips against his hand, he urged, "Show me what a bad girl you are by coming for me, Mia. Just like this, in the car, with my fingers inside you."

Oh, yes, he thought as her climax approached like a runaway train, she still loved dirty talk. For five years he'd remembered every naughty moment with her in the week they'd spent together. He'd need at least fifty more years of loving her to make it through the new list of naughty fantasies he'd come up with this week.

Cupping her left breast with his free hand, he teased her erect nipple mercilessly as he increased the pace and force of his fingers inside. And even though he should have been prepared for her climax, he wasn't even close to ready for it.

Because she wasn't just coming for him, she was shattering completely, and totally, against and beneath him. Surrendering not just her body...but all of her doubts and fears, too.

Despite being harder than he'd ever been in his life, he gathered her close and simply held her until her breathing evened out. Somehow, he managed to let her go for long enough to gently lift her back into her seat and slip the buckle over her, and to corral his focus so that he could drive safely out through the neighborhood and onto the freeway that would take them to his house.

He'd heard her come, he'd felt her come, but, damn it, he needed to *see* her come. And that wouldn't happen in his car on a dark, deserted road. He needed to get them back to his house in one piece so that he could take her inside, turn on every goddamned light in the place and strip off her clothes to appreciate every inch of her.

In the faint glow of the streetlights, Mia was so beautiful that he could barely trust himself to look at her without crashing the car. But though he made sure to drive carefully, he simply didn't have the control not to take a glimpse of her for a brief moment whenever it was safe to look away from the road.

Her high heels had come off as they'd tangled together on his seat and her legs were curled up beneath her, her face turned to him as she relaxed against her headrest. Her eyes were closed and he might have thought she was sleeping off the after-effects of her powerful orgasm, were it not for the way her hand was creeping steadily but surely across his thigh.

"Are we almost there?" she murmured in a heavy voice without bothering to open her eyes.

"Keep doing that with your hand, and I sure as hell will be," he warned her.

Of course, instead of moving her hand away, her beautiful lips curved up into a smile and she shifted in her seat so that she could feel him up even more.

Sweet Lord, if her fingers came one inch closer to his erection they were going to be in danger of his crashing the car into a utility pole. Thankfully, he pulled onto his street and through his security gate moments later.

Seconds later, he was scooping her up into his arms and making a dash for the tower. She wrapped her arms around his neck and nuzzled him, soft and trusting for whatever he had planned for them now that they were home.

Home. At the base of the tower stairs, he faltered, and she finally opened her eyes to look at him. "Ford?"

Her beauty, and her goodness, humbled him. "I love you."

"I love you, too."

Though she'd told him how she felt about him in the car, it was the first time she'd said those three words, simple and pure, in five years.

His hands tightened around her. "Say it again."

"I love you."

Knowing she could keep saying the words in an

infinite loop and he'd never get tired of hearing them, he said, "Again."

"Oh, Ford." She slid her hands from his neck to frame his face. "I love you so much. More than I even know how to tell you. More than I'll ever be able to show you."

The kiss she gave him was so sweet he actually felt an ache from the sensation of his heart expanding inside his ribs.

"You already have," he swore to her, and it was touch and go for a moment as to whether or not he would simply lower her to the floor and take her. But then, he barely, just barely, managed to corral the absolute last bit of his self-control to make himself move up the stairs with her in his arms.

From the first moment he'd seen the house, he'd wanted to make love to Mia in the tower. Upon moving in on Monday night, he'd found a cupboard hidden in the stone walls that was filled with soft blankets and pillows.

He could hardly bear to let her go long enough to make a bed, but as soon as he opened the door to the linens, she made a happy sound. Pulling out a colorful quilt, she spread it out on the tiled floor so he could drop the blankets and pillows over it.

Barefoot, Mia stood in the middle of the soft makeshift bed and held out her hands to him. "Come here, rock star, and let me love you."

He went to her, and she threaded her fingers through his before lifting her mouth to his. It could have been minutes, or maybe it was hours, that they stood like that, kissing with the bright moonlight streaming in over them through the tower windows.

"I need you naked," she said in a breathless voice, when their lips finally drew apart.

"Anything for you," he told her as he grabbed a condom out of his back pocket to drop onto the blankets, then worked on his belt buckle and the zipper of his jeans while she pushed his shirt off his shoulders. By the time he shoved his pants down, she was on her knees undoing the laces on his boots.

When she finished slipping them off, she looked up at him with a *very* wicked gleam in her beautiful eyes. Before he could stop her, she had one hand wrapped around his shaft and her mouth on him.

Ford was too close to the edge to let her love him like this for too much longer, but, Lord, the way she licked and sucked at him as if she'd never tasted anything so good—

He barely shifted away in time, and when he saw how flushed with pleasure her cheeks were, and how darkly dilated her eyes had become as she'd gone down on him, it almost didn't make any difference that she wasn't touching him anymore. He was that far gone.

With a growl, he kicked his jeans and boxers away. He bent down and gripped her dress in a hard fist to bring her back to her feet right before he ripped it off her. But she'd always known how to up the ante as she plucked the condom from his other hand and, seconds later, slid it over him.

"Now, Ford," she demanded. "I can't wait another second for you."

They'd made a bed of pillows and blankets, but as she leaped up into his arms and wrapped her arms and legs around him the same way she had backstage at the stadium Wednesday night in Oregon, they didn't need a bed yet. Thank God this time there were no clothes in the way as Ford instinctively moved them against the wall.

Their tongues slipped and slid together as he entered her, her slick flesh stretching, then tightening around him. Unable to remember a pleasure more intense, Ford had to give in to the urge to thrust into her to the hilt.

And all the while, *I love you* was the chorus not only to the most beautiful song Ford had ever heard…but also the most inspired one he'd ever been fortunate enough to play. Over and over the melody played on repeat with their bodies, with gasps of pleasure, with roving hands and, finally, with exquisite release that spiraled, hard and desperate, through them both.

Thirty

Mia lay sprawled across Ford's chest on the bed they'd made in the tower room, his heart beating strong and fast beneath her ear. Their legs hadn't been steady after they'd made love against the wall, and she loved recovering her strength with him like this.

There were no secrets between them anymore, no anger, no bitterness. Only love…and endless pleasures to be shared.

The evening was cool and clear and from where they were lying, they could easily have seen the sparkling lights and the moon over the water through the large windows. That is, if either of them cared to look at anything but each other.

"Your parents are great," Ford said suddenly, and she propped herself up on his chest so that she could see his face more clearly. "Your brothers aren't so bad, either. Especially after you got Adam to stop giving me those death glares."

She loved that they'd been having frantic sex just minutes ago and now it was just as natural to speak of family. Especially since five years ago, that hadn't been the case at all.

Finally, she knew for sure that their sex life would be as hot as their friendship was sweet.

"He couldn't help but like you when you started talking about the historic houses you've seen all over the world. And offering to leave tickets waiting at the box office for them tomorrow night so that they could come with me to your show wasn't a bad touch, either."

"Who knew dinner with my girl's family would be such an aphrodisiac?" he said with a sexy grin as he pulled her higher up his body so that he could kiss her.

His kisses made her weak. His hands roaming over her curves made her ache. But though Ford now knew just how much she loved him, there were other things she wanted him to know, too. Important things.

Forever things.

"I've been thinking a lot this week about why people fall in love."

"So have I," he said as he gently brushed the hair away from her forehead. "Chemistry is definitely part of it." He slid one fingertip down the side of her ribs to her waist and made her shiver with the best kind of goose bumps to further make his point.

"Yes. And respect," she said, knowing she could stare into his dark eyes forever and never need to look anywhere else.

"And trust." The five-letter word from his lips was pure emotion.

She laid her hand flat over his heart as she added, "And a real, solid friendship."

One that she prayed would grow stronger through all the *right* times, and withstand all the *wrong* ones, too…especially since she was barely able to silence the voice in her head that told her a friend would never hold back another friend from what he was born to do.

"I have an idea," Mia murmured as she stretched to enjoy the scratch of the hair on Ford's chest across her breasts. They'd just made the most incredible love, but instead of sating her, she hadn't even begun to get enough of him. "Want to hear it?"

His erection instantly grew another couple of inches, and his heart rate sped up beneath her. She knew better now than to let sex overtake everything else, but she couldn't bear to ruin their perfect night with her concerns that Ford was making the wrong decision about giving up touring to settle down in Seattle. Besides, tomorrow night at his show, she'd finally be able to see if he was giving up the stage for her, or if he was actually ready to retire from performing anyway.

Until then, she wouldn't allow herself to feel guilty about drowning in the decadent, all-consuming pleasure that only Ford had ever been able to give her.

"Hell, yes," he confirmed, "I want to hear your idea."

"Well...you know that list of fantasies you've come up with this week?" He was already shifting them on the blankets, so that she was on her back beneath his deliciously hard muscles by the time she said, "I want you to pick one for us to bring to life tonight."

He'd threaded one hand through her hair and his hand tightened down in the sexiest way as he asked, "Just one?"

She lifted her head to whisper against his lips, "At least one."

He crushed her mouth against his, and she met his tongue stroke for stroke, his teeth bite for bite, his throat growl for growl. Finally, he said, "Ever since you told me that you touched yourself this week and made yourself come, I've hardly been able to think of anything else. Show me how you were touching yourself. I need to see it. I need to see *you*."

She would give him anything he wanted, but she'd waited so long to have his hands on her again that even as she nodded her assent she was saying, "Help me show you, Ford. Help me come again for you."

He kissed her again, hard and fast. "Where do you want me?"

"Behind me, with my back to your chest and your legs on either side of mine."

Moving quickly, he propped himself up against the pillows, then pulled her against him. His erection was huge and throbbing against the small of her back as she relaxed into him.

"Now what?" His two words were barely more than a whisper of need.

"Now put your hands on my thighs and open them wide."

He swallowed loudly as he slowly ran his finger-tips down from her waist to her thighs. She loved how big his hands looked on her, and warmth and wetness pooled between her legs as he gently gripped the soft skin of her inner thighs and drew her legs apart.

"Mmm," she encouraged him, "that's perfect."

"So damned perfect," he agreed in his deep, reso-nant voice that had captured her from the very first moment she'd seen him onstage. "Tell me what you need now, Mia."

"You," she said before turning her face to his for a kiss. "And for you to know, to see, to *feel* just how much I want you. Just how much I need you, Ford."

She put her hands over his and took them both on a slow slide over her skin, from thighs to hips, from hips to stomach, until they were cupping the under-sides of her breasts together.

"God, I love that you're a guitar player," she told him in a shaky voice as his calloused fingertips scratched and scraped over both of her nipples at the same time.

She arched into their combined touch, letting him know with her own hands that she wanted more, that she wanted everything he needed to give her.

Where whispered endearments had once fallen from his lips, all he needed to say to her now was, "I love you, baby. So damned much. And I need you to show me how you want me to make you come. *Now.*"

Her hips were already lifted for his touch by the time she drew his right hand back down from her breasts to the damp and needy flesh between her thighs. And when he touched her exactly where she needed to be touched—his calloused fingertips sliding in the most deliciously dirty way over, and then inside, of her—Mia instantly shattered.

His fingers played in a perfect rhythm of pleasure over her damp flesh until she stopped trembling. And though the force of her climax should have drained every last ounce of energy from her, she'd never felt more powerful as she quickly shifted on the blankets so that she was straddling his hips.

She had no idea where he'd gotten this second condom from, but was beyond thankful that he already had one on as she lowered herself down over him, one glorious inch at a time.

"How'd you know this was going to be the next fantasy on my list?"

She loved the way he teased her even as they passionately loved each other. Five years ago, there had been no laughter during sex. Yes, they'd had incredible heat, but back then, they were quickly kindled flames rather than a slow and steady burn that could be trusted not to go out.

"Something tells me pretty much *everything* is on your fantasy list," she teased back.

"Only one way to find out," he said as he flipped them back around so that he was levered over her. "We'll have to bring every one of my fantasies to life at least once."

"Well," she said as she lifted her hips to take him even deeper, "if you *absolutely* insist…"

Thirty-One

In the middle of the night, when the tower had grown too cold for their pile of blankets to keep them warm enough, Ford carried a sleeping Mia down to the master bedroom.

"My prince," she'd murmured against his chest. "Just like I always knew you were."

His heart had been so full, he'd nearly had to wake her to tell her, again, just how much he loved her. But he'd kept her up late enough as it was, and considering his last show was in less than twenty-four hours, he'd known it was a good idea for him to get some sleep, too.

Now, as he lay with Mia soft and warm against him in his bed, he was glad they'd slept, and not just because they'd both needed the rest. Having her breathing softly and steadily in his arms was nearly as good as the way he was planning on waking her up.

Letting the fingers of one hand play through her

soft hair over the pillow, he slowly splayed the fingers of his other hand across her stomach. Even if he hadn't felt her breathing change pace immediately, he would have known she was awake from the little wiggle of her bottom into his erection.

He'd loved everything about their fast, fierce lovemaking so far, but now he wanted sleepy and slow. Pressing his lips to the curve of her shoulder, he slid his hand up from her stomach to cup the soft underside of one breast.

The little sound of pleasure she made shot right through him, making him even harder than he already was.

"Good morning," she murmured as she put her hand on his hip, scoring his skin lightly with her fingernails.

From the first moment she'd ever touched him backstage in Seattle all those years ago, he'd been rocked by the intensity of their connection. To have gone without her for so long—and then to come back together in a full week of endless, erotic foreplay—had built up an unquenchable hunger in Ford. Yet making love with Mia last night hadn't doused the madness, the obsession…

No, the more he had of her, the more he *needed* to have.

"Every day, Mia," he growled between the kisses he ran up the side of her neck. His fingertips found her nipples hard and waiting for his touch. "I want to wake up with you like this every single day."

"Yes," she said as he squeezed the taut tip of her breast. "God, yes. Just like this. Every day."

He'd never been a morning person, and his years on the road had only solidified his nocturnal habits. But with Mia naked and warm against him beneath the thick bedcovers, he could suddenly see the beauty of the early-sunrise hours. He loved the way her skin heated up even further with every kiss, every caress over her curves. There were so many fantasies he wanted to live out with her, and he was impatient to experience every one of them.

"Last night, you showed me how you played with yourself, how you made yourself come. And I loved it." He shifted his hand to her other breast and the achingly hard nipple that was begging for his touch, and as she shuddered against him, he asked, "But do you know what I want this morning, baby?"

Lord, she was responsive, her hips moving even closer to his erection and her thighs opening as if to take him inside even before he told her what he was planning to do. "Please," she said in a voice still husky with sleep, but also drenched with desire, "just take me, Ford."

He'd never been more tempted by a woman, but after the way he'd taken her the previous night, he needed to savor. To linger. To adore.

And, he thought with a slow grin, to tease.

"Soon," he promised her. But not until he'd given her another taste of the wicked and naughty future they were going to have together.

"Tell me what you want," she urged him as she moved her hand from his hip to surround his erection. "Tell me and I'll give it to you."

"I know you will," he said on a low, dark chuckle against her soft hair. Just as he would always give her anything she wanted. He moved his hand away from her breast, and she made a soft sound of protest, one he intended to quickly turn into a gasp of pleasure. "Roll over onto your back."

Moving with innate sensuality, she slowly shifted her weight on the bed so that she was lying flat on her back, her hands gripping the sheets at her sides, her eyes big and full of anticipation as she waited for him to say what he wanted next.

But instead of speaking, he simply took her hands in his and lifted them up above her body, so that she could reach the headboard. He curled her fingers over the cool iron bars.

"No matter what I do to you, I want you to keep holding on."

He loved the way her eyes dilated even further and her chest rose and fell in faster and faster beats. Her skin flushed a deeper rose as he let his gaze slowly roam over her perfect breasts to her waist and then back out to the gorgeous flare of her hips. He pushed the covers completely out of the way so that he could admire the damp, already aroused flesh between her thighs.

"What are you going to do to me?"

Her breathless question had him nearly giving in

to the urge to kiss her full lips, shiny and wet where she was licking them in heady anticipation. But he knew what that one kiss would lead to…way the hell faster than he wanted it to.

"I'm going to make you feel good."

"How good?" He loved the challenge in her eyes just as much as he knew he was going to enjoy rising to meet it.

"Better than you've ever felt before."

She shivered at his promise, her fingers tightening on the iron bars as if to show him just how closely she was planning on following instructions.

"Close your eyes, baby."

This time she didn't hesitate, didn't question him. She simply *trusted* him…and it meant the entire goddamned world to him that she did. Every minute of every day that they'd been together this past week, his goal had been to earn her trust. Now that he had it, he vowed never, ever to break it. No matter what he had to do to prove himself worthy of her.

Every last inch of her body was so beautiful that he could hardly decide where to start. As if in answer to his silent question, she shimmied her upper body, and watching her full, natural breasts move made his mouth water. And yet, while he wanted nothing more than to cup the oh-so-soft flesh in his hands and lave her nipples with his tongue, he knew it would be even better for her if he took his time to get there.

Leaning forward, he slowly licked between her

two lowest ribs, first on one side of her chest and then the other. "You taste so good," he told her before he moved up her rib cage. He wanted to savor every inch of her, but he was enough of a realist to know he wouldn't last nearly that long this morning. Not when being this close to her naked, gorgeous body already had him hovering on the verge of madness.

At least, he thought as he pressed a kiss to the sweet patch of skin directly below her left breast, he wasn't the only one having a hard time restraining his need. Because from nothing more than a few wet swipes of his tongue, Mia was already gripping the iron bedpost so hard her knuckles were turning white.

Especially, he noted a moment later, when instead of moving all the way up over her breasts to take the taut peaks into his mouth, he shifted his attention down from her rib cage to her hip bones. He came closer and closer with each flick of his tongue and brush of his lips to the parts of her that were begging for his attention…but he deliberately never quite made it all the way there. But though she continued to hold on to the bed frame, that didn't stop her from shifting her torso and lower body to try to get his mouth to go where she wanted it.

Another time, he'd take the game to the next level by making her stay still, too, but this morning he knew that wouldn't be fair to either of them. Not when they'd both waited so long to be together again like this. In fact, Ford suddenly decided, it was long past time to reward them both.

Without giving her any warning, he slid his hands up and over her breasts at the exact moment that he covered her sex with his mouth. His name erupted from her lips on a scream of pleasure as he opened her wide for his tongue and slid inside her clenching heat. Her skin was damp beneath his palms, her nipples hard beneath his fingertips, her arousal sweet against his tongue.

No doubt about it, lifting his mouth and hands from her a moment later was one of the hardest things he'd ever done. Even harder than it had been for him to stop at good-night kisses all week.

"Ford?" His name was more gasp than word. "Why did you stop?"

"Shh," he whispered as he moved up over her to press a soft kiss against her neck. Her mouth was still a no-go zone if he wanted to have even the slightest prayer of prolonging their pleasure. "We're almost there."

With her eyes still closed, she didn't see that his hands were shaking as he sat up to slip on a condom. Or that it took every last ounce of his self-control to position himself between her legs without thrusting into her.

"Open for me, baby." She was so turned on, so ready for him to love her, that his heart nearly stopped as she did what he asked. "Wider," he urged, barely above a whisper, needing more even as he knew that he'd never get enough of her.

As she shifted her thighs apart even farther, a little moan fell from her lips, and he had to reach up to rub his thumb across them as if to soothe her. Her tongue sneaked out to lick at him. She sucked his thumb all the way into her mouth, scraping her teeth over it in a way that made him pulse inside the condom without his erection even touching her yet.

Taking his hand away from her mouth, he put it on her hip to hold her still. Seeing that her eyes were about to flicker open, he said, "Remember, hands on the bars and eyes shut."

He could see her warring with herself for a few moments, but then, she obviously decided it was in her best interests to keep following his sensual orders. And he damn well planned to make sure that she didn't regret it as he curved his hands around to cup her hips and lift her slightly off the bed so that she was even more open to him. He used his other hand to prop himself up on the bed beside her…and then he slid the full length of his erection against her sex.

Her gasp of surprised pleasure tore at him, making him want to give up the sexy game and slam all the way into her in the next breath. Only, knowing he could make Mia feel this good, and that she trusted him to take her to exactly the place she needed to go, gave him the strength to hold on to his original intention.

To make her feel better than she ever had before.

Again and again, he slid back, then forward, and she moved with him, lifting her hips from the bed so that they were as close as two people could be without actually making love.

"I have to look," she pleaded. "Please let me look."

She was right, it wasn't fair that only he had the pleasure of watching their bodies slip and slide against each other like this. "Open your eyes."

On a deeply relieved exhale, she lifted her lids and immediately locked her gaze on his erection as he slid once again up against the slickly aroused V between her legs. "Oh, God, Ford. You're so beautiful."

"So are you," he told her. "The most beautiful woman in the world."

He held out for as long as he could, teasing both of them just like that until her abdominal muscles began to tighten and he knew she was right on the edge of release. Ford wrapped his hands around Mia's and together they held on to each other and the bed frame as he finally slid hard and deep inside her.

With both of them racing together toward ecstasy, just as her body began to pulse and pull at his, he lowered his mouth to hers to tell her how much he loved her in every possible way he could.

A little while later, Mia sat on a stool at Ford's kitchen island sipping the coffee she'd made and wearing one of his long-sleeved shirts with nothing on underneath it. He'd pulled on a pair of boxers, which rode low across his hips. With nearly every last inch of skin and muscle and tattoo on display, she was definitely hungry. Only, not nearly as hungry for the yummy smelling breakfast he was making her as she was for *him*.

"Wow," she said as he quickly mixed the batter together and poured it onto the sizzling waffle maker, then began to beat the six eggs he'd pulled out of the fridge, "I didn't know you could cook."

"Living on a tour bus for as long as I have, you get pretty good at figuring out a few things you can make without having to go into another greasy spoon or eat out of another takeaway box. Turns out that waffles and eggs work for breakfast, lunch and dinner if you need them to."

On the one hand, she could see that life on the road hadn't always been glamorous, regardless of how fancy his bus had been or how much money he had to pave his way from city to city. But on the other, even as he talked about being tired of greasy spoons and too many takeout boxes, it was obvious that he hadn't really minded the downsides of his career all that much. And, after all, didn't every job have a few difficult aspects? Being a Realtor, for instance, meant that her weekends were usually busy with showings, whereas most people took Saturdays and Sundays to relax with friends and family. But she enjoyed what she did enough that taking Mondays off instead of Saturdays never bothered her.

After liberally covering the waffles with butter

and syrup, he carried one big plate of food over to the table.

"You planning on sharing any of that?"

He sat down and patted his lap. "Come here and you'll find out exactly what I've got planned."

Despite the fact that he'd just blown her mind in a half-dozen different ways in bed, her body instantly revved up for another round. His cotton shirt scratched against her sensitive breasts in the sexiest possible way as she slowly walked over to him, then lifted one leg over both of his so that she could straddle him on the chair.

Their mouths came together at the same instant, his erection growing bigger and hotter against the V of her legs as she rocked closer to him.

"Jesus, Mia," he said as he finally drew back, "I swear I was planning on feeding you breakfast."

Unfortunately, just as she was about to tell him breakfast could wait a little while longer, her stomach let loose a loud growl of hunger. Clearly determined now to get some food into her, he carved off a large piece of waffle with his fork and popped it into her mouth.

"Mmm." She closed her eyes to appreciate his culinary skills…and the feel of his deliciously hard body beneath hers. "So good."

He pushed another piece against her lips and she opened to take it in and then, a few seconds later, the next one he offered her. Soon, they settled into the sexiest breakfast in history, with both of them eating off the same fork, half of each piece of waffle going into her mouth and half into his. And yet, beneath the endless desire she had for him, was something even sweeter than the syrup he'd been so liberal with. She felt his love not only in the way he touched her, in the way he wanted so badly to give her pleasure, but also in how he wanted to make sure she was well fed and happy.

She wanted all the same things for him...wanted more than anything to know that he was happy.

"I can't wait to see your show tonight."

He popped another bite of waffle into her mouth. "The last time you were in the audience, I gave the best show of my life." He grinned as he bent forward to lick a drop of syrup from her chin. "You'll never know how happy I am that you'll be there for my last big show. I'm planning on blowing the doors off for you tonight."

Last night, this morning, had been fairy-tale perfect. Not just the amazing sex, but knowing that Ford loved her as much as she loved him. But now, as he spoke about giving up his touring for her, all of the worries she'd told herself it was okay to push away for a little while longer rose up inside of her. "Ford—"

But before she could express her concerns, he was saying, "I've wished you were in the audience a thousand times, Mia. Hell, for months after we split up, I kept thinking I saw you in the crowd. But I knew better, knew you would never be out there."

"Actually," she said as she decided it was long past time to come completely clean with him, "while you're right that I wasn't in the audience at any of your live shows, I might have watched a couple of your performances that were streamed over the web."

She could still remember how much it had hurt to see him again, how impossible it had been for her to stop looking at her computer screen. Despite how badly he'd hurt her, she'd been helplessly spellbound by his performance.

At his look of surprise, she said, "You're amazing onstage. I've never seen anyone sing a song the way you do, with your heart and soul in every note, every line. Even when I told myself I couldn't stand the sight of you, I couldn't look away…and I couldn't stop falling even more in love with you."

He kissed her once, twice, then again and again until all the other things she'd been planning to say to him about not feeling right that he was giving up his passion for her spun right out of her head. Only the sounds of their simultaneously ringing phones could have brought them up for air.

"Speaking of shows," she gasped as she worked to get her breath back, "I'll bet that's Carol wondering where you are."

"And Orlando reminding you of all the people who need you to find them the perfect home today. Which means I should probably let you go, shouldn't I?"

"I guess so." She wrapped her arms even tighter around his neck, even though he was right that she

had a handful of very important showings scheduled that day. "Although now that I'm done with
breakfast, I do need to take a shower. You know, a
little soap," she teased as she thought back to their
supersexy shower on his tour bus in Oregon, "a little shampoo."

Less than a heartbeat later, he was pushing back
from the table and carrying her out of the kitchen
and into the large and luxurious master bathroom.
"I almost can't believe I'm going to finally get to
watch those bubbles roll down over your naked skin."

"Those waffles you made us for breakfast were
so good," she said as she looked up at him with a
grin that promised to match his wickedness from
their lovemaking earlier that morning, "I may let
you watch even more than that."

His groan—and then his kiss—told her exactly
how much he liked that plan.

By that afternoon, when Billy let him know that
Mia had arrived at the back entrance to the stadium,
Ford felt as if he'd been waiting forever for her to
show up. He was surrounded by his crew and Natasha and her cameramen, but when Mia walked in
wearing that little silver dress, everyone but her instantly ceased to exist.

"Mia."

He had to kiss her once, twice, and then again a
third time before he could even begin to pull himself
together. He was so proud of being able to finally call

her his girlfriend as he introduced her to everyone...
but at the same time, it nearly killed him to have to
wait any longer to be alone with her again after the
endless hours he'd endured without her since this
morning.

Natasha's grin was that of a triumphant matchmaker, and all the guys in his band and crew were
giving him a way-to-go-man look. But the second
she shook the hand of his last crew member, he made
the world's crappiest excuse for dragging her into his
dressing room, and didn't give a damn that everyone
knew exactly what the two of them were about to do.

He was a rock star, wasn't he? Might as well live
up to the hype for once in his life and do something
dirty in his dressing room...especially when he had
the prettiest, sexiest woman in the world to do it with.

As soon as they stepped into the small dressing
room and Ford locked the door behind them, Mia
made a beeline for his guitar. She ran her hand over
it, admiring its curves and hollows, then picked it up
from the stand and lifted it over her head.

"I've always wondered what this feels like." She
stroked the dark and shiny mahogany reverently before looking up at him with a naughty grin. "No wonder you like holding it so much. It feels good. And
sexy, too." She ran a nail over a string and seemed
surprised when sound rang out from the large amp
beside her.

He had a sudden vision of Mia lying on his bed
naked with the guitar draped over her gorgeous

curves. With the guitar still strapped across one of her shoulders, he lifted her up to sit on the amp it was plugged into and stepped between her legs. Their mouths met, hungry after their hours apart. Her hands tangled in his hair; he pulled her hips in closer to his, and though his guitar should have been in the way, he didn't feel any rush to take it off her.

On the contrary, having the woman he loved holding on to one of his most prized possessions was a total rush.

His hands automatically roved up from her bottom to her waist and breasts. He wanted to pull down the slim strap holding up her dress, but while last night, and this morning, he'd given up all control, now he tried to find it again so that he didn't overwhelm her.

"I know it's too much," he said as he buried his face in her sweet-smelling hair and tried to get a grip. "Even after I've had you a half-dozen times since last night, I still need you too much."

"It's *not* too much. It could never be enough." Where his hands had stilled on the bodice of her dress, she moved hers to help him pull the fabric down. "I want you just as badly, Ford."

She punctuated her words by giving a little wiggle from where she was sitting on the amp. When her breasts popped out of her bodice and lay soft and perfect along the top edge of his guitar, all Ford could do was stare. Especially when Mia slowly began to slide her body and the guitar in opposite directions so that cool wood teased her nipples the way his hands and mouth had just hours earlier.

"Wanna play me, rock star?"

"Hell, yes. But you need to be naked first."

Her eyes went wide for a split second before they darkened with the unquenchable lust he knew had to be mirrored in his own eyes. "I've been waiting hours and hours to get naked with you again."

If it had been any other dress, he would have ripped it off her. But this one represented too much of their history—past, present and hopefully future—to ruin it in the heat of the moment.

His hands were shaking with need for her so she had to help him slide the dress down and over her hips. Wearing only little red lace panties, sitting on top of his amp with his guitar on her lap, she was every teenage boy's fantasy—hell, every man on the planet's fantasy—come to life.

Kneeling in front of her as he reached behind his guitar for the lace, he pressed soft kisses to her calves, her knees, her thighs. "Lift your hips again, baby," he urged her, and quickly he had her panties off and balled up in his hand.

He tucked the lace into his pocket, then took a step back to look at and drool over her again. She was already more than he could handle—the beauty of her flushed skin, the way she trusted him to strip her clothes off with dozens of his crew roaming around just outside the dressing room door—when, in one slow, seductive movement, she lifted one leg up onto the amp. With the guitar barely covering her, Ford knew he didn't have a prayer of lasting much longer. Jesus, at this rate, he was going to explode without ever unzipping his jeans or touching her.

She licked her lips, then said, "I'm ready to be played now."

On a groan, he quickly moved behind her. He grabbed a condom from his back pocket before shoving his pants down to his hips. He quickly slid the condom on before lifting her by the waist so that he was the one sitting on the amp...and she was sitting on him.

As he brought her down over him one hot inch at a time and she leaned her head back against him, her eyes fluttered closed.

"Watch us, baby," he urged her. "Look how beautiful you are."

He could feel how much effort it took for her to open her eyes, but the moment she caught sight of the two of them in the mirrors told him his request was exactly the right one.

"Oh, God, Ford. This is so hot." Her words rasped out of her throat. "I love it." She held his gaze in the mirror. "I love you."

"Hold on tight to the guitar," he told her in a low voice, and as soon as she obeyed his heated instructions, he began to thrust his hips up against her, going deep, then deeper still as he used his hands at her waist to guide her body nearly off, then back down over his erection again and again.

Her fingers slipped and slid over the strings, and the accidental music she made as he took them both closer and closer to the edge joined their moans and gasps of pleasure.

"Yes. Please. Harder." Her eyes had closed again, but he knew she didn't need to watch anymore, because both of them already had this perfect, sexy moment backstage burned into their memories forever. *"Now!"*

Burying his face against the nape of her neck, he thrust into her one last time, then held her tightly against him as she climaxed…while the one surprisingly perfect chord she played rang out as the soundtrack to their lovemaking.

Thirty-Two

Mia loved being in Ford's audience with her parents and brothers. Considering how much Ford meant to her, it was strange to realize she'd only ever seen him play one show—the night they met. He hadn't had any more tour dates that week they'd holed up in the hotel, and then after they'd broken up, she couldn't bear the thought of watching him play. As excited as the capacity crowd was for him to take the stage now that the opening act was over, Mia knew no one's anticipation could match her own.

Her parents had arrived not long after she'd emerged from his dressing room. Her mother gave Ford a hug and her father's handshake was warm and totally welcoming. Dylan had arrived next, looking as if he'd come straight from one of his boats. But where, Mia wondered, was Adam?

Reading her mind, her mother put a reassuring

arm around Mia's shoulders. "He'll be here. Don't worry."

As though those were the magic words, Adam suddenly appeared. He was trying to act cool about their special boxed-off seats right at the front of the stage, but Mia knew it was his rock-and-roll dream come true.

Tempted to punch him again for making her worry that he was still upset about her dating Ford, Mia handed him her Slushie instead. If their positions had been reversed and her brother was falling for a woman whom she wasn't sure would stick around through thick and thin, Mia knew she wouldn't be able to keep her mouth shut, either. They loved each other too much to stand by quietly while someone hurt them.

Adam took the peacemaking drink from her and after a long sip where he demolished half of it, the lights onstage and throughout the stadium went completely black. The hooting and hollering began in earnest alongside the chanting of Ford's name.

And then there he was, her beautiful rock star, standing in the middle of the spotlight, effortlessly commanding the attention of the massive crowd.

From the first note he played on the same electric guitar that she'd held in his dressing room while he made love to her, Mia was utterly spellbound. His songs, his musicianship, his humor, his intensity— every single aspect of Ford's show was simply mind-blowing. Add in the fact that he singled her out in the huge crowd and sang all of his love songs straight to her, and Mia ended up so lost in the music that ninety minutes later she was more than a little surprised when the lights suddenly went up for intermission.

After her parents and Dylan told her how great they thought Ford was, then left to go pick up some T-shirts for everyone before he came out to play his second set, she knew Adam had stayed behind because he wanted to say something to her.

"You were right," he grudgingly admitted. "Ford's a good guy."

She grinned, thanking God that her brother didn't have the faintest clue what Ford had done to her in his backstage dressing room two hours earlier. "I know. And I also want you to know that you shouldn't feel too bad about the way you behaved through most of Friday night's dinner, because I'm planning on being just as tough when you finally fall in love."

Clearly intent on ignoring her sisterly threat, Adam gestured toward the massive crowd behind them. "I don't know many people who would give all this up the way Ford said he's going to. He really does love you, Mia."

She knew her brother was only trying to finally say the right thing and let her know that he approved of her relationship, but instead of relaxing her, the reminder that Ford intended to give up shows like this for her made her chest clench tight.

Adam was leaving their box just as Natasha stepped into it. "I've never seen Ford perform like this. Honestly, it's one of the best rock concerts I've seen in my entire life. I knew you'd be good for him, Mia, but I had no idea that the change would be *this* big. He was amazing before, but now..." The filmmaker grinned. "Well, I don't need to tell you. You were here. You saw it for yourself."

And she had. She'd seen how happy he made people. How deeply he inspired them.

She'd told herself that she needed to see for herself whether he was truly giving up touring because of her, or if he was ready to retire from shows anyway. Now she knew the truth.

Ford should be *nowhere* close to retiring.

Right when she had finally admitted to both herself and Ford that she loved him with every last piece of her heart, Mia had to face the painful truth: he didn't belong stuck in a waterfront house in Seattle with her trying to keep himself busy with projects while she ran her real estate business.

He belonged to *this*.

Natasha pressed her finger to her earpiece and listened carefully for a moment before nodding her head and saying, "Sure, I'll let her know." She looked at Mia. "Ford would like you to come backstage before he goes back on." Natasha laughed and rolled her eyes. "Typical rock star stuff, right?"

Mia made herself laugh along with the other woman, even though she could no longer ignore the twisting of her gut. And the snippets of conversation she heard from Ford's fans as she walked past them to get to the side of the stage only reinforced what she now knew she'd need to do.

"I've been sober for five years—ever since I saw Ford play live and I told myself all I needed to do was make it from one show to the next."

"I never would have picked up a guitar if I hadn't wanted to play along to his songs, and now I teach music in schools."

"I was having the worst day before I got here to-night, and now it's one of my all-time best."

Natasha disappeared to join her film crew as soon as they found Ford. He was talking with his drummer, but when he saw Mia, he quickly closed the distance between them and picked her up to swing her in a circle.

"I love having you here tonight."

Her throat felt tight as she said, "Your show is amazing, Ford. I didn't forget how good you were, but seeing you onstage again is just mind-blowing."

He kissed her then, and she poured all of her love for him into it.

"I love you, too," he whispered against her lips. "Stay backstage for the rest of the show. Right here where I can see you, where I can come and kiss you anytime I need to. Like now." He traced her lips with his tongue. "And now." The gentle bite of his teeth against her lower lip made her knees even weaker than they already were.

His band had already launched into the opening

bars of the first song of his second set when she whispered, "I would do anything for you."

And a few minutes later, as she listened to Ford thank the crowd for all the great years they'd given him on the road, knowing it was his way of saying goodbye to them even if the audience members didn't understand that yet, Mia knew that she would truly do anything for the man she loved.

Even if it meant letting him go…instead of letting him give up everything for her.

The rain was pouring down hard by the time they got back to his house and ran toward the tower. There was no shower in the tower room, but the heavy downpour had taken care of washing him clean.

Through their linked hands, Ford could feel how hard Mia was shivering when they reached the top of the tower stairs. He'd purposely gotten her wet the other night when he'd thrown her into his pool, but tonight, though her silver dress stuck to her every curve like a sexy second skin, he only wanted her dry and warm and in his arms. Maybe it would have made sense to stop in the master bedroom and bathe first to warm up and dry off, but without even needing to discuss it, it had been clear that they would bypass the house for their special room, high up in the Seattle sky.

Seconds after closing the tower door behind them and turning on the lights, he had her dress off and was wrapping her in a thick blanket. Again and again he ran his hands over her until she stopped shaking quite so hard.

"I promise I'm going to warm you up all over in a minute."

Stripping himself down as quickly as he'd stripped her, he picked up another blanket to wrap around his damp body, then pulled her down onto his lap. Tonight, knowing they were going to begin their new life together, he'd stashed a little blue box under one of the pillows.

"I need you closer," she whispered as she shifted on his lap to burrow beneath his blanket so that they were skin to skin, her chest pressed to his, her arms around his back, her legs wrapped around his waist. "I never want to let you go, Ford."

For once, he didn't have any protection on him, but he knew how much she loved family, and he couldn't wait to start making one with her as soon as possible. Little girls and boys who would fill up their home with laughter and love.

"I never want to let you go, either," he said as he lifted her slightly over him so that she could wrap her legs fully around him and sink down over his erection on a sigh of pleasure that shook through both of them. It was the first time he'd ever been inside of her bare, with nothing between them but damp skin and heat, and he knew nothing in the world would ever feel this good. Except making love with Mia.

"You're still shaking," he murmured against the crook of her neck. He was no longer sure if it was because she was chilled from the rain. Just in case she still had any doubts, he desperately needed to put them to rest. "Don't you know I'd do anything for you? Don't you know that I'll always put you first?"

"I love you so much," she said in a raw voice that shook just as much as her body still was, even as their lovemaking heated up more and more with every stroke of his body inside her. "More than I ever knew it was possible to love."

And as they took each other over the edge of pleasure that was both sweet and sinful, Ford knew it was finally time to ask her to be his.

Forever.

Ford was stroking his hands over her back and Mia was trying to get her synapses to start firing logically again when he said, "The first time I saw you here in the tower, I wanted to ask you to marry me."

Drawing back from the crook of his neck where she'd been resting her head, Mia watched Ford reach beside them to pull a little blue box out from beneath a cushion.

Oh, God, he couldn't do this now. He couldn't ask her to marry him when she'd finally accepted just how much she loved him...and that loving him meant setting him free. She opened her mouth to try to stop him before her heart broke any more than it already had, but the sheer force of emotion in his dark eyes stole her words away.

"I look around this house, I walk through this

city, and you're everywhere. You haven't just made music matter again for me, you've made *everything* matter." When he opened his hand, there was a ring in it with a large sparkling yellow diamond in the center. "Marry me, Mia, and make me the happiest man on the planet."

She hadn't cried over him since that night in Miami when she'd believed nothing they'd felt for each other was real. Now that she knew just how real their love was, her tears finally fell again.

"You can't stay in Seattle."

He stared at her as if he couldn't have heard her correctly. But disbelief quickly gave way to confusion. "Everything I want is here, Mia. Especially you."

"That's not true." When she saw the hurt rise up in his eyes, she went down on her knees before him and took his face in her hands. "I know you love me and you want to be with me. But you also belong onstage, Ford. Not just at an occasional fund-raiser, but playing stadiums in front of hundreds of thousands of people."

"Maybe I needed that before, but I'm not a kid dreaming of glory anymore."

"You keep talking about glory, but when you're onstage, it's so much more than that. When you sing to people, magic happens, Ford. You make people happy. You inspire them. You touch their hearts and their souls with what you do and who you are. I know my brothers weren't exactly acting like your biggest

fans that night at my parents' house, but you should
have heard the way they talk about your shows. And
it's not just because you're so talented and your songs
are so great. It's because *you* are so happy and inspired up there that there's no way it can't rub off on
absolutely everyone in the audience."

He covered her hands with his, closing his eyes
as he moved his face so that she was stroking his
stubble-covered cheeks. She could feel the ring between them, the ring that she wanted so badly to let
him slide onto her finger.

But she could never forgive herself for stealing
him away from the place where he truly belonged.

"I love being onstage," he finally said when he
opened his eyes again so that she could see everything he was feeling. "I would never lie to you and
say that I didn't. But I want to be here for you. I
wasn't willing to give up the road before, didn't even
consider it, though I expected you to give up your
life for me. But I need you to know how much I love
you, Mia, enough to give up absolutely *everything*
for you, without regret, without ever looking back."

"Oh, Ford." She leaned her forehead against his.
"I used to think love was all about the grand gesture,
red roses and sunset serenades. But now I know love
is wanting you to be everything you're meant to be
and never wanting you to push away a part of yourself for any reason. Not even for me. I don't need
you to run through a burning building for me or to

write me a love song to know that your love is real. All I need is for you to tell me what you *really* want."

"You, Mia. I just told you, you're what I really want. Why won't you believe me?"

It should have been exactly what she wanted to hear, but just as she had with Colbie and Brooke in the bar, she knew in her heart when one of her best friends was simply telling her what they thought she wanted to hear rather than the truth. She would never want her girlfriends to feel that they had to hold back what was in their hearts because they were worried about how she'd react…and she wouldn't let the man she loved do it, either.

"Of course I believe that you want me, just as much as I want you. But I can handle hearing the rest of it, Ford, hearing what else it is you really want. We're best friends, remember? And that's what friends do—they talk to each other and say things they really mean, even if they think it might hurt the other person to hear them."

He hesitated for a long moment before saying, "I won't lose you again."

She knew where his fear of losing her came from. When his parents had wanted him to be someone he wasn't, and he couldn't do it, they'd turned their backs on him forever. Obviously, it was what he thought she was going to do to him now.

A lightning bolt jumped in the sky just then, and Mia felt as if it had struck her. Because what if loving Ford didn't mean setting him free?

What if loving Ford meant never, ever letting him go?

She put her arms back around him and hugged him tightly, the sweet press of their still-connected bodies as sensual as it was comforting. "No matter what you say you want, you're not going to lose me. I love you just the way you are. You don't ever need to change for me because you think I won't love you if you're not following my rules for how life is supposed to go." She pressed a kiss to his lips. "Now tell me what you really want, and no matter what it is, I promise I'm not going to go storming off or take my love away."

"You," he said again. "I want you." But then he finally pulled out of her arms. As he stood to pace the tower, the blanket pulled away from his body so that he was gloriously naked when he finally admitted, "I want music." It sounded as if the words were being wrenched straight from his gut. He took a deep breath. "I want family." Finally, he turned back to face her. "*Everything. I want everything, Mia.*"

Even though he was finally telling her the truth, she could see the fear in his eyes as he said, "But I could never ask you to leave your work, your family, behind for me. Not when I know how much both of those things will hurt you. I don't want you to change for me, either."

Another lightning bolt shot through the sky as she moved to stand in front of him and take his hands in hers. "I already have changed, Ford."

She hadn't fully realized this truth an hour ago, had believed there was only one way for both of them to stay true to themselves—by leading separate lives. But now she finally understood something that she'd been too young, too frightened, too overwhelmed, to understand before. Even though her mother had tried to help her see it at dinner on Friday night.

"I know who I am now, Ford, in a way I didn't know before. When I was twenty-three, I was so scared of how quickly I lost myself in you and your life. That fear of not knowing how to hold on to my own identity made me believe that I was better off without you. But now I've finally learned that loving you, supporting you, isn't going to make me any less. It doesn't mean I'm going to be nothing more than an extension of you, or a footnote in your documentary, unless you pack up all your touring gear in a storage locker in Seattle so that you can be home every night to celebrate one of my deals."

"So," he said slowly as his thumbs rubbed gentle circles into the backs of her hands, "if you don't want me to give up touring and I don't want you to give up your career in Seattle, but neither of us wants to be apart—"

"Then I suppose we're just going to have to figure it out one thing at a time, even if it means I have to give up a few big deals along the way—"

"And I skip playing some stadiums—"

"And we miss a few family dinners if we have to."

"No, I don't want to miss too many family dinners," he told her, his eyes warm and loving.

"I agree," she said with a smile as she brought their hands up to hold them over her heart. "We definitely shouldn't miss too many of those. And if things start to feel out of balance, we'll work together to fix it. I'm not young or foolish enough anymore to think it will be easy, but—"

"You're worth it."

"So are you, rock star."

The next thing she knew, he had her on her back on the blankets, and he was levered over her, her breasts pressed hard to his chest, her thighs trapped between his.

"Now that we've got all that settled, how about an answer to that question I asked you earlier?"

Of course he had to know what her answer would be, and the *yes* was right on the tip of her tongue. But just as the anticipation of waiting to make love again during the past week had ended up being more fun than she could ever have imagined, she had to wonder just how fun it would be to add a little anticipation to his marriage proposal.

"You promised no ultimatums this time around," she reminded him in a sassy voice, one she knew always got him going in a big way, especially judging by the feel of his erection against her thigh as he began to kiss his way down her body.

His stubble scraped in the most deliciously sinful

way over the swell of her breasts as he said, "True, but I never promised not to seduce a *yes* out of you."

"You wouldn't make love to me until you knew for sure that I loved you, but now that you know I do, you're planning on using sex to get your way with everything from here on out?"

He lifted his head from her breasts to grin at her. "Sure am."

"But—"

How could she finish her sentence when he was licking one nipple while he played with her other breast? Just as she was figuring out how to catch her breath again, he switched his hands and mouth to the other side.

"Mmm?"

The vibration from his throat to her skin made her shiver. And when he began to lick and nip his way down the undersides of both breasts, it would have been so much easier just to give in to his seduction and forget what she needed to say. But somehow she found the will to get out her next words.

"—that's not—"

She gasped as he slipped his fingers between her thighs and into her. Clearly, it had been smart to keep sex out of their relationship until they'd built a strong foundation first, because she could barely hold a thought in her head when he was touching her like this.

But even more than she loved his touch, she loved *him*.

"Oh, hell," she finally said, "go ahead and do your worst."

"Already there, baby," he murmured against her stomach, before kissing his way lower, and then lower still. "Only you're about to get my very *best*."

And he wasn't kidding, because just then his mouth covered her and his tongue and hands were slipping and sliding over and into her in the most wonderful way. She was so close, so damned close, and she was going crazy right there on the edge... until he suddenly homed in like a laser with his lips and tongue and fingers and gave her exactly what she needed.

"Yes! Yes! Yes!"

Her orgasm was still rocking and rolling through her when he slid the ring onto her left hand. His grin was a mile wide as he moved back over her so that she could wrap her arms and legs around him.

While admiring her new engagement ring over his shoulder, of course.

"Think you're pretty sneaky, don't you, doing whatever it takes to make me say yes?"

"If you think that was sneaky," he rasped in a husky voice against her mouth as his hands roamed possessively over her, "you should see what I'm going to do next."

"Let me guess—it's on that list of yours, isn't it?"

"It is," he confirmed as he thrust deep inside her in one hard stroke to stake his claim on her body as well as her heart.

"Have I mentioned," she managed to inform him with her own saucy grin, even though it was really, really difficult to string coherent words together when he was moving inside her like this, "that I've got a list of my own? One that starts with blocking out all of tomorrow to call each and every one of my family members with the news of our engagement, just like I promised you I would."

And as he told her just how much he liked that plan by crushing her mouth and body even closer to his, her last clear thought before her climax stole her every functioning brain cell was that life would always be an adventure with the man who was not only her best friend and her lover…but also the other half of her heart and soul.

Epilogue

"I'm so, so happy," Mia said to Ian. "But I'd be even happier if you were here with all of us tonight."

Through their Skype connection on his tablet, Ian could see that Mia was glowing. Everyone was at their parents' house to celebrate her engagement, but since he hadn't been able to get from London to Seattle in time for the party, his sister was now sitting in front of their father's laptop in the den to try to include him in the party.

"I wish I was there, too." He was still bitter about the meetings he hadn't been able to shift today without potentially losing millions of his investors' money. "Next month, when I'm back in Seattle for good, you'll have to save me a night so I can take you out to celebrate."

"Me *and* Ford," she reminded him in her usual sassy way. Just then, her fiancé moved beside her and slipped his arm around her waist.

Glad she couldn't see his hands tighten beneath his desk, Ian nodded. "Right. Both of you." Knowing it would upset his sister if he didn't try a little harder than that, he nodded at the rock star. "Congratulations, Ford."

The other man grinned at him, looking ridiculously pleased with the way things had turned out. "Thanks, Ian. I'm the luckiest guy in the world."

To drive his point home, Ford kissed his sister in full view of the camera. As if to keep his blood pressure from shooting up too high, Ian's cousin, Smith, and his fiancée, Valentina—who had walked into Ian's office right after he and Mia started talking— both chimed in with their own congratulations.

"Wow, you're having your own Sullivan party in London, aren't you?" Mia said, grinning at all of them.

"Just for a little while longer, while we wrap up production on our latest film," Smith said. "Valentina and I will be settling into Seattle soon for the new movie."

Mia asked Valentina, "Won't Tatiana be in the area, too?"

Valentina nodded happily. "She just confirmed that she'll be based in Seattle for a while, starting next month. I'm so glad we'll be in the same city again."

"We're all going to have a lot of fun together," Mia said, looking specifically at her brother as she added, "won't we, Ian?"

He could see by her mischievous expression that she hadn't forgotten his reaction to Tatiana at Marcus and Nicola's Napa Valley wedding. Fortunately, however, Valentina didn't seem to have any idea that he'd spent some time with her younger sister…or that there had been bigger sparks between Ian and Tatiana during those fifteen minutes in the vineyards than he'd ever experienced with another woman in years.

A few minutes later, after Mia and Ford had signed off to rejoin their party, Ian got up from his leather office chair to pour himself and his guests some stiff drinks. "I'm still trying to get used to the idea of Mia with—" it was still hard to even say the guy's name without growling it "—Ford."

But it wasn't just the fact that she was marrying a guy with a lifestyle like Ford's that bothered him. Personal experience had taught Ian how hard it was to keep a marriage together. Still, he forced himself to acknowledge that just because he would never make the mistake of getting married again—or falling in love—that didn't mean it wasn't the right path for his sister.

"She obviously knows you're happy for her," Valentina said with a gentle smile. "And that some changes take a little time to get used to."

After handing them each a glass, he took a long drink from his own. "How did you deal with your sisters' relationships, Smith?"

"Honestly," his cousin said, "it wasn't easy. Sophie and Lori both kept things quiet at first, although once Sophie ended up in the hospital and I found out Jake had gotten her pregnant with twins, I pretty much lost it. But then, I saw how she looked at him, and how Lori looked at Grayson, and that changed everything. All I've ever wanted is for my sisters to be happy, and when I realized the men they've married would give anything and everything to do that, it got a little easier to deal with."

"I just know I'm going to be a total basket case when my sister falls in love," Valentina said. "The whole world sees Tatiana as this beautiful, confident movie star, which she is, but I know the real person down deep inside…and how innocent she really is." Valentina sighed. "All I can hope is that when she does finally fall, it will be for a guy who's worth it—who realizes just how special she is."

"Otherwise," Smith said in an ominous tone, "I'll have to kill the guy for hurting my new little sister."

Ian drank the rest of his Scotch in one long gulp.

He hadn't been able to stop thinking about Tatiana since the wedding. Before both of them moved to Seattle, he was going to have to force himself to forget how badly he'd wanted to touch her.

He'd have to do whatever it took to stop thinking about what it would be like to kiss her.

And, no matter what, he'd have to find a way to completely push away the insane urge to make her his own.

* * * * *

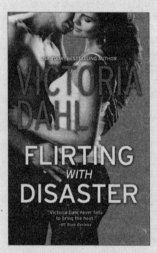

REQUEST YOUR FREE BOOKS!

2 FREE NOVELS
FROM THE ROMANCE COLLECTION
PLUS 2 FREE GIFTS!

YES! Please send me 2 FREE novels from the Romance Collection and my 2 FREE gifts (gifts are worth about $10). After receiving them, if I don't wish to receive any more books, I can return the shipping statement marked "cancel." If I don't cancel, I will receive 4 brand-new novels every month and be billed just $6.24 per book in the U.S. or $6.74 per book in Canada. That's a savings of at least 22% off the cover price. It's quite a bargain! Shipping and handling is just 50¢ per book in the U.S. and 75¢ per book in Canada.* I understand that accepting the 2 free books and gifts places me under no obligation to buy anything. I can always return a shipment and cancel at any time. Even if I never buy another book, the two free books and gifts are mine to keep forever.

194/394 MDN F4XY

Name _____ (PLEASE PRINT) _____

Address _____ Apt. # _____

City _____ State/Prov. _____ Zip/Postal Code _____

Signature (if under 18, a parent or guardian must sign)

Mail to the Harlequin® Reader Service:
IN U.S.A.: P.O. Box 1867, Buffalo, NY 14240-1867
IN CANADA: P.O. Box 609, Fort Erie, Ontario L2A 5X3

Want to try two free books from another line?
Call 1-800-873-8635 or visit www.ReaderService.com.

* Terms and prices subject to change without notice. Prices do not include applicable taxes. Sales tax applicable in N.Y. Canadian residents will be charged applicable taxes. Offer not valid in Quebec. This offer is limited to one order per household. Not valid for current subscribers to the Romance Collection or the Romance/Suspense Collection. All orders subject to credit approval. Credit or debit balances in a customer's account(s) may be offset by any other outstanding balance owed by or to the customer. Please allow 4 to 6 weeks for delivery. Offer available while quantities last.

Your Privacy—The Harlequin® Reader Service is committed to protecting your privacy. Our Privacy Policy is available online at www.ReaderService.com or upon request from the Harlequin Reader Service.

We make a portion of our mailing list available to reputable third parties that offer products we believe may interest you. If you prefer that we not exchange your name with third parties, or if you wish to clarify or modify your communication preferences, please visit us at www.ReaderService.com/consumerschoice or write to us at Harlequin Reader Service Preference Service, P.O. Box 9062, Buffalo, NY 14269. Include your complete name and address.

ROM13R

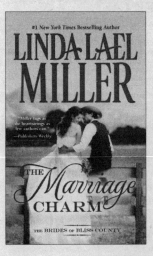

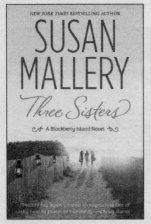

BELLA

31730 THE WAY YOU LOOK TO
31701 KISSING UNDER THE MI
31617 ALWAYS ON MY MIND
31608 COME A LITTLE BIT CLOS
31600 LET ME BE THE ONE
31560 IF YOU WERE MINE
31559 I ONLY HAVE EYES FOR
31558 CAN'T HELP FALLING IN LOVE ___ $7.99 U.S. ___ $8.99 CAN.
31557 FROM THIS MOMENT ON ___ $7.99 U.S. ___ $9.99 CAN.
31556 THE LOOK OF LOVE ___ $5.99 U.S. ___ $5.99 CAN.

(limited quantities available)

TOTAL AMOUNT	$ _____
POSTAGE & HANDLING	$ _____
($1.00 for 1 book, 50¢ for each additional)	
APPLICABLE TAXES*	$ _____
TOTAL PAYABLE	$ _____

(check or money order—please do not send cash)

To order, complete this form and send it, along with a check or money order for the total amount, payable to MIRA Books, to: **In the U.S.:** 3010 Walden Avenue, P.O. Box 9077, Buffalo, NY 1426-9077; **In Canada:** P.O. Box 636, Fort Erie, Ontario, L2A 5X3.

Name: _____
Address: _____ City: _____
State/Prov.: _____ Zip/Postal Code: _____
Account Number (if applicable): _____
075 CSAS

*New York residents remit applicable sales taxes.
*Canadian residents remit applicable GST and provincial taxes.

MIRA®

www.MIRABooks.com

MBA0215BL

3 1901 05713 5479